"Hurry up, Marshal, get some cuffs on her. How else you gonna get her home?"

A quick scan of the woman indicated she didn't have a weapon strapped to her side or in her hands. His gaze moved from the unusual shoes she wore, up indecently clad legs encased in denim pants. How else could he describe it? When his eyes reached her torso, his body jerked in response. Beautiful breasts were fully outlined by a skintight blouse. There was nothing left to the imagination. All her attributes showed through the thin, pink fabric. His face burned with anger. It was down right scandalous. No decent woman would dress so provocatively. Then he noticed the flame-colored curls. Hans eased his hold, and her head jerked upward. His eyes met hers, and his heart stopped. God, she's beautiful. He looked at her face again and thought he'd faint from sheer joy. His bliss quickly turned to rage.

With a growl, he bit out, "Get your hands off my wife."

“Linda LaRoque weaves a wonderful story of compassion, loss and triumph. You won’t be disappointed with this story. It will grip your heart and emotions and take you for a ride that will stay with you forever. I laughed, cried, despaired and cheered at everything Texanna and Royce went through in their quest for love. It’s a keeper on my bookshelf.”

Carrie Destler, Author, *Ride a Cowboy, Love Me, Love My Rafferty*

“Linda LaRoque’s *My Heart Will Find Yours* is a wonderful Western time travel. Her characters are extremely likeable and faith-filled. The way LaRoque plays the past and the present using one to change the other makes this story truly unique. I loved the characters and unexpected plot twists. *My Heart Will Find Yours* is fast paced and compelling. I read it in one sitting.”

Laurel Bradley, Author, *A Wish in Time, Crème Brûlée Upset*

“This tale swept me away. I immediately fell in love with Texanna and Royce and hated that their story ended. A+ for Linda LaRoque.”

TJ Killian

My Heart Will Find Yours

The Turquoise Legacy
Book 1

by

Linda LaRoque

This is a work of fiction. Names, characters, places, and incidents are either the product of the author's imagination or are used fictitiously, and any resemblance to actual persons living or dead, business establishments, events, or locales, is entirely coincidental.

My Heart Will Find Yours

Contact Information: info@thewildrosepress.com

Cover Art by *Kim Mendoza*

The Wild Rose Press
PO Box 708
Adams Basin, NY 14410-0706
Visit us at www.thewildrosepress.com

Publishing History
First Cactus Rose Edition, 2008
Print ISBN: 1-60154-490-1

Published in the United States of America

Dedication

To all those who helped me put this story to paper—T.J., Laura, Sandy, Dawn, Zaynah, Judith, Erika, and J.L., who introduced me to ley lines, energy and spin torsion fields.

Acknowledgements

Waco, Texas, located south of the Dallas/Fort Worth area and North of Austin and San Antonio has a rich, intriguing history. The author strived to keep the flavor of the early town as authentic as possible; however, a few alterations were made so that history would fit the story line.

Though Jim Bass did visit Waco and consider robbing a bank, the year was 1778 and as legend goes, he was impressed with the amount of law enforcement personnel or the quality and decided to move on.

While the railroad did serve Waco in 1876, at the time this story begins, it did not reach south to the San Antonio area until around 1877.

The author acknowledges the following:

T-bird, Ford Motor Company

Gunsmoke, Created by Jim Meston, CBS Paramount Television

Gone with the Wind, Margaret Mitchell, McMillan Publishers

Winchester, Winchester Rifles and Shotguns

Colt Peacemaker, Colt's Manufacturing Company, LLC

Mr. Coffee, Sunbeam Products, Inc.

My Prayer, Written by George Boulanger and Jimmy Kennedy

Cinderella, Jacob and Wilhelm Grimm

Chapter One

June 15, 2008, San Antonio, Texas

Texanna Keith settled into the plush upholstered seat of the passenger car on the train bound for Waco. She shook her head in consternation and muttered to the wall in front of her, "I can't believe I'm doing this."

Pearl was barmy, had gone around the bend. Doing the older woman's bidding made her doubt her own sanity. But, she loved her dearly, so here she sat, wearing Pearl's antique locket, an old wedding ring, and carrying a packet of letters to some lawyer in Waco. And to top it all, Pearl insisted she carry the documents, along with some old clothes and a photograph, in an ancient moth-eaten carpetbag. She plopped the bag in her lap and sighed. Why she couldn't have driven her classic T-bird, she'd like to know? Or mailed the documents? Pearl wanted her on this train for one purpose—to travel back in time.

She looked down at the gold wedding band on her finger and removed it to read the inscription. *Love until the end of time, Royce 1872.* That's the kind of love she wanted—one that would transcend eternity. She snorted. Three broken engagements left her with the conclusion love wasn't in the cards for her.

****

Just yesterday, she'd visited Pearl. For the first time in several months, her portrait business had slowed, and she looked forward to vacation time. But, she couldn't deny Pearl's urgent request.

Grasping her hand, Pearl settled back against the sofa cushions. "I need to tell you the conclusion of the story I've been sharing with you for years—the one about the woman in the locket with the turquoise stone."

"You mean there's more?"

A glint of tears shone in her eyes. "I'm the woman in the photograph of the locket. In 1876, I traveled forward in time to 1936 leaving behind my husband, Marshal Royce Dyson, and our son, Garrett."

She patted the hand she held. "My dear, I need you to take a journey for me, back to 1880 and deliver a message."

Shock stole Texanna's breath. She tried to speak, but no words came from her mouth. All she could do was sit, gape, and try to listen without interrupting.

Agitated, Pearl spouted theories about ley lines and spin torsion fields. Texanna didn't like the flush and the look of anguish on the older woman's face, or the tears leaving a trail on her powdered cheeks. She feared for her friend's sanity, as well as her health. Her heart wasn't strong, and she'd had several spells in the past two years.

Time-travel wasn't possible. Otherwise, people would be flitting back and forth from one century to another. It would totally wreck the idea of time as seen today, and history would be a mess.

"Pearl, now you don't really believe in time-travel, do you? This is all a good story, but…"

"Young lady, would I lie to you?"

"No, ma'am. I..." *Lord, I'm going nuts.* She sighed.

"If this theory is true, why don't other people on the train disappear and move forward or back in time?" *Aha, got you.* Texanna couldn't wait to hear her answer.

Pearl didn't bat an eyelash. "Because of the ancient stone in the locket—it's the key. I told you it's magical. The stone must accept the wearer. I knew you were the one the day its energy alarmed you. Remember? You dropped it in my lap."

Yes, she did remember that day. With a sinking sensation in her stomach, Texanna decided she might as well give up, give in, and get it over with. It wouldn't cause any harm to humor her. Of course, Pearl would be terribly disappointed when her ruse didn't work, but... "Okay, I'll do whatever you want."

"I love you, child. I'm ninety-four-years-old. Too old to make the trip myself, and I didn't realize the locket was the key until ten years ago, too late for me. You're my only chance to see Royce is warned about the robbery and history is changed. God keep you safe and happy all the days of your life." Tears ran down her wrinkled cheeks, and she drew Texanna to her.

Still in shock at her request, Texanna could do nothing but clasp the weeping woman's frail shoulders and pat her back. "Don't cry, Pearl. I'll do this for you. Everything will be fine. I'll see you tomorrow or the next day. Okay?"

Pearl smiled through her tears and patted Texanna's cheek. "Okay, sugar."

****

Texanna fingered the locket she wore around her neck, feeling the smooth piece of turquoise embedded in the gold face and the heat it generated. Inside was a picture of a two-year-old Garrett Dyson, supposedly Pearl's child and on the other side, Pearl herself. The back was engraved with the initials PBD in script, Pearlina Baines Dyson. In the carpetbag was a tintype photo of Royce and Pearlina on their wedding day. Texanna couldn't deny she looked a lot like the young woman in the picture. From earlier pictures of Pearl, those studio portraits they took in black and white and then touched up with paint, she knew their hair possessed the same strawberry blond hue, and their eyes were sky blue. But their faces varied in shape, and Texanna's eyes were darker.

Remembering Pearl's verbal instructions, she opened the carpetbag and pulled out an envelope addressed to her. Inside she found a note and an old newspaper clipping.

Waco News Sentinel, June 15, 1880. The City Council met today to finalize plans for the July 4th celebration. The Ladies Aid Society as well as local church groups will sell baked goods to raise money for our local charities. As usual, Mrs. Edna Murphy will head the committee for the baking contest. The First National Bank of Waco has graciously consented to donate the silver cup for this year's horse race. Entry fee will be $5.00. First Community Bank will add the additional funds to raise the prize to $500.00. See Huck Smith for entry forms. Judge Stone has ordered fancy rockets from China and promises a fantastic fireworks display this year. Anyone interested in volunteering see...

Texanna finished reading the article, folded the paper, and put it back in the bag. Smiling, she leaned her head against the seat and imagined herself sitting on the banks of the Brazos watching fireworks and dancing on the courthouse square. Of course, she'd be wearing Pearl's old clothes. The older woman wanted her to wear one of the Victorian dresses in the carpetbag today. That's where Texanna drew the line, especially the god-awful underwear. *If* she landed back in 1880, her jeans and tank top would have to do. No way would it happen anyway, so it wasn't an issue. She wiggled her toes in her running shoes and giggled at the sheer outlandishness of the whole situation.

Texanna closed her eyes. What was life like in

1880? It probably wasn't a fun period, especially for women if the clothing bore any indication. She absently rubbed the locket with her thumb. It had been hard for Pearl to part with it. She'd held it in her fist as tears squeezed from beneath her closed lids. The older woman's last words tore at her heart.

"Tell Royce I loved him so, and my son, Garrett."

A bright burst of white light exploded penetrating her closed lids. The train rocked and came to a stop, throwing her forward against the wall in front of her seat. Her head bounced against the hard surface, and everything went black.

****

June 15, 1880, Waco, Texas

Marshal Royce Dyson closed the desk drawer with a bang.

He shoved aside the pile of "Wanted" posters and arrest warrants, propped his feet on his desk, and leaned back in his chair to think.

It was time to accept the inevitable. He'd done everything in his power to find his missing wife. Along with his brothers and Pearl's, he'd spent six months combing the countryside for a hundred-mile radius between San Antonio and Waco. No one remembered seeing her get off the train at any of the stops between the two cities. It appeared she'd vanished into thin air. He shook his head in regret. Pearl was dead, and he and their son, Garrett, would never know where her body rested, never be able to put flowers on her grave. He didn't know the particulars, but would talk to Judge Stone and find out if he needed to have her declared legally dead. The nicker of horses and rumble of wagon wheels rolling over the hard dirt street drifted in through the open window of his office. The light breeze was welcome as it washed over his skin, ruffling papers as it passed. Through the open door, Pete's off-tune whistling was muted by the clang of metal as the deputy locked the steel door after checking on the prisoners. His boot heels thudded across the room to the desk in the front office where he plopped down in the hide-bottomed chair. It creaked as the leather bore his weight. These familiar sounds should have been comforting, but they weren't. It wasn't everyday a man laid his wife to rest.

His feet hit the floor. Dammit, he needed to get some fresh air. Shoving his chair back, he stood and strapped on the pistol that lay on the corner of his desk. He grabbed his shotgun and hat and strode through his office door to the outer area.

Pete sat with feet propped on the desk. He dropped them to the floor when Royce entered, the wood planks vibrating from the force.

Royce stopped in front of the deputy. "Who's working with you tonight?"

"Jason and Ross."

Royce nodded. "Keep an eye on Ross, and send for me if you need me." Ross was his newest deputy and had yet to prove himself.

"Yessir, Marshal."

Stepping outside, his gaze scanned the street. Hopefully, things would remain quiet tonight. No cattle drives were due through until tomorrow night, and his jail cells were empty but for one drunk who'd leave when he sobered up.

Royce started walking down Austin Avenue. He tipped his hat at ladies as they passed, nodded at the men. The hot breeze dried the beaded sweat on his forehead, cooling him for a short time. He turned on Third and walked toward Mary Street.

For the first time in the nine years he'd been marshal, Royce stepped into the Brazos Saloon as a paying customer instead of as a lawman. Today would be a turning point in his existence, he'd put Pearl behind him, move forward, and build a life for him and Garrett. Men cleared a path, and those at the bar located a table. Hans, the big Swede serving drinks scowled at him.

Royce sat down on one of the stools and laid his shotgun on the bar. "Whiskey, Hans." In the reflection of the big mirror behind the bar, he saw all eyes were on him and his shotgun.

Hans sat a glass on the bar and poured Royce a drink, then started to turn back, but Royce reached out and caught the big man's arm. "Leave the bottle."

"Sure thing, Marshal." Hans studied him closely. "You all right?" He leaned over the bar and whispered. "You're not exactly good for business, you know."

Royce nodded. He tossed down the whiskey. For a moment, his heart stopped. The burning liquid took his mind off the ache lodged there. He poured another glass, and with one hand on his shotgun, he turned and raised the glass to the quiet group of men. "Relax, gentlemen. Cheers."

"Cheers," echoed around the room in sporadic bursts, but they lacked sincerity. The men started talking again, but with subdued enthusiasm. In the mirror, Royce watched the whirl of the wind-up ceiling fans. It reminded him of his life—a merry-go-round ride that never ended—today he intended to jump off and get his life settled.

Royce studied the amber liquid in his glass. Pearl had been missing for four years today. Tonight, for the first time since she disappeared, he'd visit the Reservation, Waco's red-light district, and pay for the company of a woman. Before today, touching another woman would have felt like cheating. His Ma and Pa, God rest their souls, raised him and his brothers to be honorable men, men who were faithful to their women. But his wife was dead, and his body screamed for release. There were a number of women in town who'd expressed their sympathy when his wife went missing, and several made obvious their eagerness to give him comfort. He'd do his own picking and choosing when the time came. Until then, one of the girls for hire at Josephine's would do.

Royce studied his face in the mirror, ran his hand over his jaw, feeling the scratch of whiskers. Shaving everyday was a pain, but he couldn't stand the dandified mustaches and beards so many men favored these days. If he started courting, he'd have to shave twice a day. He glanced over in time to see Judge Stokes in the big double window as he passed by the saloon. The judge's daughter, Danielle, was still single. At twenty-eight-years-old, she was well into spinsterhood.

Just last week she'd made a point to speak to him and Garrett after the monthly Saturday social. She'd blushed prettily when she invited them to dinner. Before Pearl, he'd escorted Danielle to a number of social functions and considered marrying her. But he'd made that trip to San Antonio, met Pearl, and then no other woman would do. Odd Danielle had never married. She was a beautiful woman and well thought of in the community. He might just invite her to the upcoming July Fourth dance.

Hell, he'd ask her as soon as possible. It couldn't be tonight though as he'd never approach a woman with the smell of Josephine's clinging to his clothes. He grinned at the thought and shook his head. Tomorrow night he'd go home, clean up, and he and Garrett would ride out to the judge's place. Maybe take her a handful of those gardenias she liked.

He finished his drink and laid money on the bar. "Thanks, Hans."

"Anytime, Marshal."

The heat, fueled by the high humidity of summer, hit him as he stepped outside. He tilted his hat forward a notch to keep the sun out of his eyes, yet allow him to see clearly. A man couldn't be too careful on the streets, especially a lawman in a town nicknamed Six-Shooter Junction. Trouble could come from any direction. His eyes studied a stranger in the alley leaning against the wall of the hardware store, and then flicked to the angry cowboy riding by, whom last week Hans had tossed from his saloon into the street. Probably most dangerous was the cocky kid, spoiling for a fight and out to make a name for himself, ambling toward him now. He stayed alert as he passed the boy and walked toward the banks of the river.

The suspension bridge looked odd stretched out across the Brazos. Though completed ten years ago, it looked foreign and disrupted the stark beauty of the river with its grass and tree-covered banks. But industry was changing towns, and folks had to accept modern inventions or be left behind in the rush for prosperity.

He found a big oak, sat down, and leaned against its large trunk—a barrier for bullets, stray or otherwise. Its rough bark was uncomfortable against his sweat-soaked back, but he didn't care. It would be dark before too long, then he'd go to Josephine's. Prostitution was legal, but it went against the grain to be seen going in a whorehouse in broad daylight. He removed his hat, let his head rest against the tree, and closed his eyes.

Goodbye Pearlina, my lovely Pearl. Rest in peace.

Chapter Two

Texanna woke to see a mustached man wearing a three-piece, old-fashioned suit bending over her; a gaggle of curious faces were looking over his shoulder. Her eyes flicked from his to the watch chain hanging from the small pocket on his vest, and then back.

Mouth agape, he sputtered. "My God, she's not dressed." He shucked out of his jacket and laid it across her chest.

She shoved it away and tried to rise. The man took her arm and helped her to stand. She swayed as the floor beneath her feet rocked to a different beat—a clack-it-tee-clack unlike the sound of the train she'd boarded. If she wasn't mistaken, burning coal generated the black smoke rushing past the window. *What was going on here?*

Voices and expressions of shock echoed around her.

"Well, I never...dressed like a harlot."

"Never seen a camisole like that, especially one that color. Why that's the pinkest pink I ever saw."

"Cover yourself, young woman." Mr. Mustache held the coat, trying to block her from view. Too shocked to do otherwise, she took it and held it across her chest.

A harlot? What was wrong with her clothes? Her pink tank top and jeans were nothing unusual. She turned ready to send them a rude gesture when, with a hand to her aching head, she saw the other people in the car. They were dressed in nineteenth-century clothing and looked like an old tintype photograph, not a smile among them. Too shocked to speak, she sat down on the hard, low-backed seat and pulled the carpetbag close. Gone were the plush seats and air-conditioning. Hot wind blew in from the open window, bringing black soot with it. Panic rose in her chest. Before she could assimilate what was happening, brakes screaming, the train slowed, pulled into the depot, and lurched to a stop.

Texanna's breath rushed from her lungs at the scene outside the train car window. Traffic filled the dirt roads paralleling the wooden depot. The ripe scent of horse manure reached her nostrils making her nose twitch. She covered her nose and mouth with her hand. *Oh dear Lord, please tell me I'm dreaming.*

A voice at her side made her jump. "Ma'am, my coat if you please." Numbly Texanna handed it to the mustached man feeling naked with nothing but the carpetbag to hide behind. He took it and left. The other passengers filed out behind him, each casting her a scathing glance as they passed.

Knees shaking, Texanna stepped off the train onto a wooden platform. Horse and mule-drawn wagons lined the street as people milled back and forth collecting luggage or stacking theirs to be loaded. Swirling dust caught on a breeze and blew in her face. She tried to brush dirt from her face and sneezed. Her chin quivered, and she bit her lip to still it as people gave her ample space and formed a wide circle around her.

She started across the street. The crowd parted but followed at a distance. Body tense, she fought the rising hysteria. *This isn't real. It's a dream. There's no such thing as time-travel.*

Their words reached her ears.

"Oh my Lord, it's, Pearlina Dyson."

"My God. I can't believe it. Look how she's

dressed."

"Somebody get the marshal."

A tall thin cowboy with a star on his shirt advanced toward her. When he touched her arm, she snapped. Remembering her Kung-Fu instructor's teachings, she moved, and in a flash had his arm in a joint lock hyperextending it. He shrieked in pain.

****

A woman's scream and the grunts of men fighting woke Royce. Maybe he'd been dreaming. But no, there it was again. This time a man's yowl split the air.

As Royce hurried up the riverbank to town, Pete rushed toward him, agitation evident in his every move.

"Marshal, you gotta come quick."

Royce quickened his step and wondered, what now?

A large crowd gathered in front of Hans' Saloon.

"Shoot her in the foot." He recognized the baritone immediately. It was Hans. "If you don't, she's going to hurt someone else. I think she's already broke Jason's arm."

She? Royce broke into a run. *What the hell was going on? They'd never had a woman cause trouble before.*

A female resounded, "Don't come any closer, leave me alone." She attempted to sound controlled, but her voice became shriller with each word. But still not at all like what he'd expect of a woman gone wild.

Jason's voice, filled with pain, broke through the mumbling of the crowd. "Stop...stay back...she's scared. Royce will...be here...in a minute." Jason's statement ended with a groan.

"Yeah, well I'm not going to let the Missus' hurt anyone else," said Hans.

Royce shoved his way through the crowd. He

glanced quickly at Jason to see if he was breathing, then turned to the woman the crowd had backed up against the boardwalk in front of the saloon. Hans eased behind her and quickly caught her under the arms and locked his hands behind her head. Head pushed forward, the woman fought to break Hans' hold. She kicked backwards, but Hans lifted her off the ground and swung her from side to side so her feet couldn't make contact.

"Hurry up, Marshal, get some cuffs on her. How else you gonna get her home?"

A quick scan of the woman indicated she didn't have a weapon strapped to her side or in her hands. His gaze moved from the unusual shoes she wore, up indecently clad legs encased in denim pants. How else could he describe it? When his eyes reached her torso, his body jerked in response. Beautiful breasts were fully outlined by a skintight blouse. Her pebbled nipples showed through the thin, pink fabric. His face burned with anger. It was downright scandalous. No decent woman would dress so provocatively. Then he noticed the flame-colored curls. Hans eased his hold, and her head jerked up toward him. His eyes met hers, and his heart stopped. *God, she's beautiful.* He looked at her face again and thought he'd faint from sheer joy. His bliss quickly turned to rage.

With a growl, he bit out, "Get your hands off my wife." At least, he thought it was his wife. The hair was the same, but her eyes were bluer, her nose thinner, and damned if she didn't have kohl on her eyebrows and lashes.

Hans looked around for support. "Are you sure, Marshal?"

No one spoke. Hans shrugged. "All right, Marshal, but look out."

Royce's eyes never left Pearl's. "Jason, are you all right?"

"Yes, I'm fine. She's scared to death, Royce. She didn't recognize me. And be careful. Her feet and hands can move faster than anything I've ever seen."

Royce handed his shotgun to Pete then held out his hand to her. "Pearl?"

Her eyes flicked from his hand to his face. "I'm not Pearl. I'm Texanna." She backed up a step. "And I'm sure as hell not your wife."

The crowd gasped at her language, and Royce felt his face heat. His wife didn't talk like this woman. He frowned, tamping down his anger. Regardless of who she was, it was his responsibility to see she got help, and put on some decent clothes.

"Watch your mouth, young woman." Royce took off his jacket. "Here." He tossed it to her. "Put it on. You're not dressed proper."

Damned if her chin didn't shoot out an inch, but she caught his jacket. He stretched out a hand to her. "Come on now—let's go somewhere and talk."

Royce watched her. *She's scared but doing a darn good job of hiding it. Something's definitely wrong. Of course there is or she wouldn't be dressed so, or have been gone for four years.* Had she been held in captivity and those were the only clothes she owned? His throat clogged with emotion. God, what if it wasn't Pearl, just someone who looked like her playing a cruel joke on him? Or it was Pearl, and she'd lost her mind.

He started toward her. Before he took a step, she threw his jacket at his head and took off running. She was fast. Shock filled him, as did a sense of pride. Wherever she'd been, she'd not let them beat her down.

"Somebody give me their horse."

In less than a minute, he was riding after her. When she heard the horse pounding close behind her, she turned back to look and tripped. Royce caught her by the waist of her pants before she fell and sat her sideways in front of him on the saddle.

She screamed and fought, but Royce pinned her arms and pulled her body against his. "Stop it, it's all right. I won't hurt you. You're safe now."

Her screams turned into sobbing mumbles. Something about time-travel, Pearlina, and going crazy. She stopped shrieking and fighting but remained stiff in his arms. Taking a chance, he loosened his hold on her arms. She pulled free and grabbed his shirtfront in her fist. "You'll never believe me. I can't believe it myself." She dropped her head to his chest and moaned. "Oh God, I want to go home."

He eased an arm around her waist. "It's okay, Pearl, we'll straighten everything out." Tears gathered in his eyes as he held her close and patted her back. He so wanted this woman to be his wife, but he just wasn't sure.

Royce turned the horse and walked it back toward the jail. He needed to know if she was his wife before he took her home for Garrett to see. Except for an occasional sniff, accompanied by a shudder, she remained quiet.

When he lifted her off the horse in front of the jail, she balked and tried to pull away from him. Dammit, he'd had enough of this. He tossed her over his shoulder and walked into the jail with her pounding on his back. The minute he sat her feet on the ground, she took his arm and the next thing he knew he was on his back in the floor. He rolled and reached for her foot but missed. Pete caught her at the door.

Royce scrambled to his feet. "Put her in a cell."

Pete gaped at him.

"You heard me, put her in number one." His deputy didn't look happy but did what he'd been told.

The carpetbag the woman had been carrying sat

on his desk. He opened it and pulled out a packet. It was addressed to Tom Syler, one of Waco's many lawyers. Pete came out of the holding area and locked the door. Royce tossed him the packet. "Take these down to Tom, will you? Tell him if he needs to talk to me, I'll be here a couple more hours."

"Sure thing, Marshal, but I'm here to tell you right now I don't appreciate the way you're treating your wife. It's disgraceful."

Royce ignored the comment, and Pete stormed out of his office. He continued to search in the carpetbag and pulled out two dresses he recognized. They were Pearl's, as were the shoes and nightgown. The gown still carried her sweet lilac scent. At the very bottom, he found the tintype of them on their wedding day.

He sank heavily into the swivel desk chair. If this woman wasn't his wife, how had she gotten hold of these items? She could've killed her and was now trying to pawn herself off as Pearl. Well, dressed as she was, she sure as hell wasn't getting off to a good start.

With a sigh, he stuffed the items back in the bag, everything except for the tintype. He slipped it in his shirt pocket. For several years now he'd feared in his soul Pearl was dead, but had never given up hope. And now, here was this woman who looked almost like her twin. People changed over time, he knew that, but... Could he have forgotten the color of her eyes, the tilt of her nose, the shape of her face? He didn't think so.

The tintype was a good likeness but didn't reveal her facial characteristics or the color of her eyes and hair. If only she'd been smiling, but her face was as sober as his own. Too bad Pearl didn't have a mole or birthmark for identification. He studied the tintype again hoping for something to erase his doubt.

By God, he wanted some answers. He opened the steel door to the holding area and went inside. She jumped up off the cot and stared up at him belligerently. His heart thumped with emotion at the tears pooled in her eyes. He wanted to open the door, take her in his arms, and comfort her. And hell yes, he wanted to kiss those sweet lips, run his fingers through that thick mane of hair, and become reacquainted with her beautiful body.

He pulled the chair from the corner in front of her cell and sat down. "Who are you? Why are you carrying my wife's things?"

She lifted her chin. Her eyes drilled his. "I'm Texanna Keith. The carpetbag, clothes, and picture belong to your wife Pearlina Baines Dyson Thompson who is ninety-four-years-old. I call her Miss Pearl. She lives next door to me in San Antonio. I've spent a lot of time at her house learning to paint. I love her dearly."

He snorted and shook his head, then thought. Ninety-four would be the age of Mrs. Baines' mother. Did Pearl have a grandmother still living? Not to his knowledge. A year after Pearl's disappearance, her mother passed on. Her illness and the shock of being unable to find her daughter broke her heart. Mr. Baines followed shortly after. To his knowledge, their three sons were the only family left.

"Pearl didn't have a grandmother named Texanna." He'd bluff the truth out of her. "So try again."

"I know that. My neighbor, Pearlina Baines Dyson Thompson was your wife. She left here on June 15, 1876, to see about her mother in San Antonio. When she arrived, it was 1936. For years she tried to get back to you and Garrett but couldn't."

He balked. How could she know the date Pearlina left unless she was his wife? Her story got crazier by the minute. Doubt and worry made his belly clench. No, she was plain out lying.

He tried to keep his eyes above her shoulders but the needy things dropped for a minute, and he saw the locket, the locket he'd given Pearl when Garrett was born. It held the piece of turquoise that had been in his family for generations. On Garrett's second birthday, they'd had his picture taken to put inside.

"She traveled forward in time."

At her words, he jerked his eyes back to her face. Did she think he'd buy that bit of nonsense? At the sheer absurdity of her remark, he threw back his head and laughed. He couldn't stop himself.

She strode forward and grabbed the bars. "Laugh, you fool, but it's the truth."

He rose from his chair. "That locket is Pearl's. Give it to me."

She covered the locket with her hand drawing his attention to the wedding ring on her left hand. Voice harsh, he ordered. "Give me the locket and the wedding ring."

She backed away from the bars. "No, Pearl gave them to me. I didn't believe her ridiculous story about time-travel either, but she wanted me to wear these. Guess to help make you believe."

"Fine, keep 'um, but when I charge you with theft, you'll wish you'd handed them over. May charge you with murder, too."

"Murder?" Her shrill screech echoed off the bare walls. It was hard to keep a straight face. "I'll have you—"

"Marshal." Pete appeared in the doorway.

"Yeah."

Pete handed him the packet he'd just sent over to Tom. "Tom says these are for you." He coughed. "From your wife."

****

Royce read and reread the letters from Pearl. The handwriting in the one, supposedly written on June 15, 1940, was undeniably similar to Pearl's. The paper was yellowed with age and delicate. The script in the other, dated June 14, 2008, was completely different, shaky and uneven. The writing paper was unfamiliar. It felt different between his fingers as he rubbed, trying to find a clue to this dilemma.

He picked up the first letter and reread her parting words.

Forgive me, my love. I've tried multiple times without success to return to you. My only means of survival in this crazy modern world is to marry. I'll always love you and our precious child.

Tears sprung to his eyes at the hardships the woman described, but it was a story, fiction, not word from his wife. Time travel wasn't possible. Royce tossed the letter aside and picked up the crisp new sheets.

I've lived a good life, learned to love my husband, but had no children. Yet you and Garrett were often in my thoughts. When John passed on in 1980, I began to research time travel and ten years ago learned the turquoise in the locket was the key. I won't go into all the details, but felt I must send word to warn you.

The woman in his jail cell was allegedly Pearl's neighbor's child, or so he was supposed to believe. She was here to warn him about a bank robbery in early August of this year where he'd be shot and killed. Lord, this was the craziest situation he'd ever run across. This was nothing but an elaborate scheme to...to what? He wasn't rich. Yes, he could provide a good home to a woman, but not finery, world travel. Or, was the woman in his cell truly his wife, and this was her way of explaining away the years? Was she ashamed to tell him the truth?

****

Texanna curled up on the cot with her face to the wall. Her lip trembled, and she bit it to keep from wailing. This had to be a nightmare. She'd wake up any minute.

At the sound of the steel door opening, she rolled to a sitting position and wiped the tears from her face. Royce stood outside her cell with a cup of coffee and a plate of food covered with a dishtowel.

"Pete brought you something to eat."

She stood up and walked to the bars. He passed the plate through the available slot and handed her the cup.

"Thank you."

"You're welcome." He turned and left the room but didn't close the outer door.

The food smelled delicious, and, despite the anxiety that churned in her stomach, she was hungry. Pearl had gotten her into a crazy mess, and she'd need all her strength to cope with it. She wouldn't let Royce have the locket and ring. The locket was her ticket home. She placed her cup on the floor and sat on the cot with the plate in her lap. Her stomach growled in response to the mouth-watering aroma of the fried chicken, mashed potatoes, green beans, and cornbread on her plate. She took the wooden-handled fork and started eating. It was filled with fat and calories, but she didn't care.

When Royce returned, her plate was clean except for the chicken bones. He took it away and returned with the coffee pot. After filling both their cups, he sat down in the chair he'd left and placed the pot on the floor.

She inched back toward the cot and plopped down while keeping her eye on her cup. He didn't speak but watched her, his brows furrowed. Damn his hide, he was good-looking, his blue eyes dark with concern. According to her wristwatch, his five o'clock shadow had turned into nine o'clock darkness. It only added to his stark sex appeal.

Texanna started when he stood. He took papers from his breast pocket and walked toward her, hand outstretched. "Read these."

She sat her mug on the floor, half-rose, and reached out to take them. There were two letters. One appeared old, the paper yellowed, and she opened it first and started reading. It was dated 1940, just before Pearl married Mr. Thompson. Her words were poignant, and by the end of the first page, Texanna brushed tears from her cheeks. On the last page, her tears turned to sobs of grief for what the woman endured.

Royce watched her carefully. He had to admit her tears appeared genuine. Either that or she was a damn fine actress. He cleared his throat. "Read the other letter."

She carefully folded the fragile paper and slipped it into the envelope before opening the other letter. As she read, her tears stopped, and at one point, a look of resignation crossed her face. Lips pinched, she finished the letter and handed them back through the bars.

"So, what am I to believe? You look a lot like my wife."

She sputtered. "Didn't you read the letters? How can you have any doubts after reading Pearlina's words?"

Whoever she was, she showed spunk, and he liked that about her. His wife didn't have near the grit, but people did change, and it's possible she'd had to. He studied the woman before him—her clear complexion, blue eyes, and strawberry blond hair. He didn't like it cut short. It didn't even reach her shoulders. The lack of weight made it curlier, an aspect he did like. It curled around her face, emphasizing her eyes, making them look larger and mysterious. Well, hell, she was mystifying for a fact.

"Yes, I read it, but don't think I can accept as truth that my wife traveled forward in time, or that you're from the year 2008. I don't believe in time-travel."

She jumped up and gripped the bars, her voice harsh and loud. "Well, hell, neither do I, but here I am in this one-horse town, in a jail without an indoor toilet or running water, talking to a man who looks like a pirate."

"Watch your tongue, young woman." She lifted her chin but kept her mouth shut. "If you need to visit the outhouse, just let one of us know, and we'll take you. I'll bring you some water so you can wash up and your bag so you can put on some decent clothes."

"I'm not wearing those tacky clothes. They're awful."

Royce couldn't restrain the snarl that rumbled from his mouth. "You'll put them on, or I'll put them on you. You're not going to display your wares like some common strumpet."

"You wouldn't dare."

"Try me." He scratched his chin and made a slow perusal of her body, his eyes lingering on her breasts. "From what I can see from here, it would indeed be a pleasure."

Chapter Three

Royce opened the cell door and tossed the carpetbag on her cot. “You’ve got five minutes to change into one of those dresses.” He turned his back, and she yanked the dress that buttoned down the front out of the bag and slipped it on over her clothes.

“I’m finished.”

He turned around. “Good.” His eyes surveyed her from head to toe. “Come on, I’ll take you to the outhouse.”

“I think I can find it on my own.”

His grin made the dimples pop out in his cheeks. The sight fascinated Texanna, making her wish circumstances were different. “I just bet you can, but it wouldn’t be gentlemanly to allow you to go outside unescorted when it’s almost dark.”

She watched as he coughed into his hand. “Plus, I figure you’d want me to check for snakes before you go inside.”

Was he trying to scare her? Probably, but she wasn’t going to take a chance. Kicking her skirt out of her way, she left the cell. He took her elbow and escorted her past the empty cells to another steel door.

****

Royce left town shortly after nine. The sun had set, taking most of the day’s heat with it, yet the air remained heavy with humidity. His mind flashed over the previous few hours. He’d grieved for Pearl for four years and accepted the fact she was dead. It was time to live again, find someone else to love.

His attraction to the woman who called herself Texanna was undeniable, everything about her—her scent, the tilt of her chin, and her persnickety attitude, called to his masculinity. Her manner of dress and vulgar mouth appalled him. He wanted to take her across his knee and wail the daylights out of her. He shifted in the saddle. Hell, he should've gone to Josephine's earlier. Then he wouldn't be as randy as an old goat.

He stopped by Aggie's and went inside to get Garrett. His son slept in the bedroom next door to Aggie's. He scooped him up, carried him outside to Samson, and stepped back up into the saddle. Garrett stirred, grinned at him, and mumbled in his sleep, "Hi, Pa." Then he quieted again.

Aggie, dressed in her robe and gown, followed him outside and handed Royce a bundle of clothes. "Lots of talk going around about the woman from the train. Is she your wife?"

With a sigh, he tilted his hat forward and rubbed the back of his neck. "I wish I knew for sure. She looks like Pearl, but acts different, like she's from another country." He'd have to make a decision soon. She couldn't roam the town telling wild stories about time-travel. She'd have to be watched closely until he solved the mystery. Keeping her close would let him decide if she was his wife or an imposter. The idea she'd time-traveled was cockeyed. He'd never believe such nonsense.

"If she's suffered abuse, she's gonna be some different, but her underlying nature will be the same. Give it some time."

He nodded. "I expect I'll know soon enough. I'll bring Garrett by in the morning. Good night, Aggie."

She waved from the porch. Rather than ride back up to the road, he cut across the field between their houses, a path worn from constant use. The moon shone brightly, giving Samson enough light to maneuver safely.

Before rubbing down Samson, he took Garrett upstairs and tucked him in bed. He sat for a while and looked down at his sleeping son, smoothing the hair back from his forehead as he did so. His little face echoed his own features, but his smile was Pearl's. He needed a mother, one to cuddle him and teach him how to be tender and loving. A father could only do so much in that area. The boy longed for brothers and sisters. If he had anything to do about it, Garrett would have them in time.

Royce lay in his bed staring at the ceiling. If Texanna was his wife and he denied her, he'd never forgive himself. Then again, if he claimed her and she wasn't, was a thief, a prostitute, or worse, a murderer, he could be putting Garrett in danger. Hell, what was he talking about? He'd be in more danger than Garrett. She'd probably murder him in his sleep. Truth be told, he didn't sense she was a threat. He'd come up against enough evil to recognize the signs.

How on earth had she thrown him on his butt tonight? Good thing Pete was the only one to see it. Jason would ride him for months. He shuddered at the thought. Nah, he wouldn't. He'd get ribbed enough himself about what she'd done to his arm. Where on earth did she learn to do those things?

God, what a mess. What kind of man couldn't identify his own wife?

Before dozing off, he made up his mind. Texanna's story about time-travel and delivering a message from his wife was too crazy to be true. Plus, she had no proof. He snorted. How could a person prove something that wasn't possible?

She did wear the locket he'd designed for Pearl and the wedding ring he'd put on her finger. The letter dated 1940 was too close to her script for him to easily deny. Could this be an elaborate ruse to cover up what she'd done to survive? Had she been abused, forced into prostitution or worse and was now afraid of his reaction? He'd never hold those things against her. He'd help her recover. God, what if she was crazy? He'd see she got good treatment, find a private treatment place for her.

If it turned out she wasn't his wife, he'd get to the bottom of where she'd gotten Pearl's things. She could've found them somewhere. Just because they were in her possession didn't mean she'd murdered his wife. Hell, maybe she was his wife and in a few days or weeks she'd say or do something to give herself away one way or another.

Tomorrow he'd bring Texanna home, but he needed a plan.

****

Texanna tossed and turned on the hard cot, the God-awful dress causing her all sorts of discomfort. The long skirt tangled around her legs constricting her movement. She'd put the dress on but kept her jeans on underneath and her tennis shoes. Swaddled in two layers of clothes, she felt like a roasting duck, a self-basting one as sweat covered her body. Without a breeze in the small hot cell, it felt like an oven.

Before he'd left, Royce escorted her to the outhouse. She'd refused to go in without a light, so muttering angrily he'd marched her back inside to get a lantern. That's what he got for scaring her with his remark about snakes. After a thorough search for spiders, she used the stinky place and exited.

Finally, exhaustion set in, and she dropped off to sleep. She woke to the sound of a rooster crowing and lay still trying to figure out where the heck she was. The brick wall several inches from her nose wasn't familiar. Then it dawned on her and she groaned. Nineteenth-century Waco, Texas. The hair on the back of her neck stood on end. Someone watched her. She could feel their eyes and the tension in the room. She rolled over and stared into a pair of blue eyes on the other side of the bars. For a minute she thought it was Royce, but on closer inspection saw a younger version. It was the young deputy whose arm she'd hurt yesterday.

"Who are you?" He had to be a relative of Royce's.

His smile didn't quite reach his eyes. "I'm your brother-in-law, Jason. Don't you recognize me?"

She sat up and studied him. He was a good-looking kid, tall and thin, hadn't put on the muscle his brother carried. "You know I don't." He didn't say anything, just stared. "How's your arm?" She hadn't meant to hurt him, but fear made her irrational.

"A bit sore, but I'll live."

"I'm really sorry. In a week, it'll be good as new."

He shrugged. "You're not my sister-in-law, are you?"

"What has Royce told you?"

"That you claim to have traveled back in time to deliver letters from his ninety-four-year-old wife." He snorted. "Never heard such a cock and bull story."

She stood up and lifted her skirt so he could see her shoes. "Look at these. Have you ever seen shoes like these in your lifetime?" She bounced for him a couple of times. "Best running shoes money can buy."

He looked at her as if she'd grown an extra head. "I admit they're weird looking and quiet when you walk." He cleared his throat. "And you bounce real good, but that doesn't prove anything."

Arm stuck through the bars, she said. "How about this watch? Runs off a battery, you never have to wind it." She shrugged. "Of course, you do have to buy a new battery on occasion."

He ignored her comment, scratched his chin, and studied her face. "You're either crazy as a loon, or a shyster. Whichever, I don't give a damn, but I want you out of this town. My brother's just got his feet back under him, and some kohl-painted, opportunity-seeking woman is not going to mess that up."

Hands on her hips, she sputtered. "Look, I don't want your brother or to be here in this one-horse town. It's hot, dusty, and smells like horseshit. And I hate these clothes." She kicked the skirt out of her way as she paced the small cell.

His jaw tightened. "You've got an ugly mouth on you, ma'am. The Pearl I knew would never use vulgarity. And she'd never strut around in her chemise and men's pants."

"May be, but the Pearl I know does, or I should say did when younger. She's pretty much wears loose dresses and pant suits now."

He watched her for several minutes, a variety of emotions transforming his face. Something was on his mind, and Texanna didn't think it'd be long until she found out what.

He stood up and approached the bars. "A train leaves for San Antonio at eight o'clock this morning. I want you on it and out of my brother's life."

Hope lodged in her throat. "I don't have any money for a ticket."

"I'll buy your ticket. Listen, and listen to me good. Don't ever come back, else I'll make your life a living hell. I'll prove to Royce what a lying conniving bitch you are."

"Now wait a minute. I'm not a liar, and did not invent this situation. I've said nothing but the truth."

He held up a hand. "Save it for someone else."

Fine, she'd leave. There was nothing she wanted to do more. But, she owed it to Pearl to make sure

Jason understood the danger Royce faced.

"All right, I'll leave on one condition."

"Don't see as you're in any the position to bargain." He rocked back on his heels waiting for her answer.

She ducked her head to hide her expression, sat back down on the cot, and folded her arms across her chest. "I can refuse to leave."

His young face hardened, the lines around his eyes and mouth deepening. Evidently, the young deputy had seen enough of life to embitter him. "What do you want?"

"Promise you'll look after Royce. Sam Bass and his gang—"

He snorted in disgust. "I know...Sam Bass and his gang will attempt to rob the First National Bank of Waco in early August. Royce will be killed."

She nodded.

"That's the stupidest thing I've ever heard. But you don't have to worry, we Dysons always watch out for each other. Now get ready to leave." He took a woman's tattered straw hat from the potato sack on the floor beside his chair. "Put this on."

She took it and settled it on her head. When she got home Pearl would get her ears scorched. The outfit she wore was humiliating.

Texanna heard Jason talking to the other deputy. "Pete, I'm gonna take the prisoner to the outhouse. When I get back I'll go to Maybell's and get her some breakfast."

"Good." Texanna peeked through the steel door left ajar. Pete folded his arms over his chest and grinned. "I'm hungry as a bear. Soon as our shift is over, wanna catch some breakfast together?"

"Sure thing. Be back shortly."

Jason opened her cell door. She grabbed the carpetbag and followed him out the back door. "Go around the corner of this building and head straight for the depot. Keep your head down and your mouth shut. Try not to be noticed."

She nodded.

"I'll go back in and leave by the front door so Pete won't be suspicious. Wait for me on the bench on the track side of the station."

****

Royce heard the train whistle as it headed out of town, puffs of black smoke billowing behind it as it traveled south. It was on time this morning. Over breakfast, with Garrett chattering like a magpie, he'd decided Texanna would stay here until he decided what to do. For safety's sake, Garrett would stay with Aggie until he knew what the hell was going on. Josie, the old horse they hitched to the buckboard, plodded along behind as he rode into town. She'd be plenty safe for Texanna to ride home. He tied her and Samson to the hitching post in front of the jail. Inside Pete sat at the front desk, feet propped up as usual.

"Morning, Pete. Any problems last night?"

"Nothing but the usual, a few fights at the saloons. At Hans' place, Hans used the butt of his shotgun on the brawler's heads and locked them in the back room. Guess he didn't want to lose their business. The other two were down at the Reservation. I rattled their noggins' a mite and gave them a good warning." He coughed. "Didn't want to put them in the back with the Missus. Wouldn't be decent."

"Good decision. Appreciate your consideration."

He mumbled something under his breath that sounded like, "At least somebody around here was thinking about the poor woman."

Royce ignored him. "Where's Jason? Surely he hasn't left already."

"Nope. Came in from checking on the prisoner and headed for Maybell's to get her some breakfast."

"Good. Think I'll go in and check on her." The steel door stood ajar. From the entry way he could see the cell was empty. He swung around. "Where the hell is she?"

Pete stood up, stomped to the door, and peeked in the cell. He pointed. "Right there the last time I saw her."

"Exactly when was that?"

"I checked on her about four this morning. She was sleeping fine."

The front door opened, and Jason walked in without breakfast. Royce's heart dropped at the look on his brother's face. It was etched with determination and without a drop of remorse.

Dread made his belly clench. "What have you done, Jason?"

Jason looked him square in the eye. "What I thought needed to be done. I put her on the train back to San Antonio."

Royce punched him before he realized he'd moved a muscle. Jason went down hard but quickly regained his feet. "Come on, big brother. Punch me again if it'll make you feel better." The blood pounded in Royce's head, and he swung again, but Jason dodged and landed a blow to the side of his head. "She's not your wife, Royce. Pearl would never act like that woman."

He charged, and they both hit the floor, rolling and punching until Pete pulled him off Jason. "Stop it, Royce. You're going to seriously hurt the boy."

His breath came in deep gasps as, hands fisted, he stared down at his baby brother, appalled at what they'd done to each other. Jason's nose was bloodied and one eye was already swelling shut. He reached out and helped him up. Voice hoarse, he mumbled. "It wasn't your decision to make, brother. It was mine. Mine alone, dammit."

Jason didn't flinch. "She's not Pearl, Royce. I

was trying to protect you." Royce and his brothers were close, their folks saw to it they always stood up for each other. He couldn't fault Jason's motive, but while trying to protect him, he'd failed to think about the ramifications of her leaving.

"If I don't know whether she's my wife or not, you sure as hell can't know for sure she's not. I'm a grown man and can protect myself. Furthermore, I'm the marshal here, and if I don't catch the train, I'll never know how she ended up with Pearl's things. You just interfered with an investigation. I should fire your sorry butt."

He grabbed his hat off the floor. Shoulders stiff with rage, he strode out of the office. The street was filling with people, stores beginning to open. To the South he could see a trace of what he hoped was smoke from the train. If he rode hard enough, he might catch the train. He vaulted into the saddle and kicked Samson into a fast trot. Just south of town, he turned the horse loose and let him run. The wind whipped at his face threatening to remove his black felt hat from his head.

He hadn't gone far when he realized the chase was useless. It'd be impossible to catch the train. Samson responded to the pull on the reins, but reluctant to end his run, danced sideways as he slowed to a stop. Royce slumped in the saddle and stared off in the distance. The horse snorted and stamped his feet in impatience. "Sorry boy, she got away." He patted his neck. "I'll let you run on the way back to town."

Texanna, the mystery woman, may have eluded his clutches this time, but San Antonio wasn't too far away. He'd wire the sheriff and have him keep an eye out for the redheaded female. Their business wasn't finished, and he wouldn't rest until it was.

Chapter Four

Texanna breathed a sigh of relief when she righted herself after being thrown around the small lavatory of the train car. She'd probably have a knot on her head from hitting the mirror. It would go nicely with the one she'd gotten the day before. With the nineteenth-century dress and straw hat stuffed in the carpetbag, she exited the restroom. Uttering a sigh of contentment at the comfort of the air-conditioned car, she found a vacant seat, leaned back, and tried to relax. Her foot tapped out a staccato beat on the floorboard. Relax? Hell's bell's, she'd just traveled back and forth in time, she might never unwind.

When the train pulled to a stop, she jumped up and rushed to the exit, anxious to get to Pearlina's house and talk. Lord, she was so wound-up she might never shut her mouth. She snorted with derision. Her loving Miss Pearl would learn what her precious Royce had done to her. Actually, she didn't quite blame the man. The entire experience was too weird to believe.

The sun blazed down on her car. As she unlocked the door and slid inside, the heat stole her breath. It must be one-hundred-twenty-degrees. She started the engine and turned the air conditioner on high. The interior cooled to a tolerable temperature, and she backed out of the parking slot and headed for the exit. As she accelerated to merge with traffic on the freeway, she thrilled at the T-bird's powerful response. She patted the steering wheel affectionately, grateful to be back in modern 2008.

Today a haze hung over the city, the modern world's smog. So the air wasn't fresh and clear like in 1880, but it didn't smell like horse manure either. It was a nice summer day, not a cloud in the sky, and she was home. Life couldn't be better.

The street in front of Pearl's house was lined with cars as was her folk's house. When her mother answered Pearl's door, Texanna knew something was seriously wrong.

Madeline Keith was born into one of San Antonio's oldest families and made sure everyone knew it. Texanna couldn't ever remember seeing the woman without her makeup or not impeccably clothed. Dressed in her designer suit and pearls, she'd have looked perfect on *Texas Monthly Magazine.*

Mother grabbed her arm and as she pulled her into the wide entry hall and hissed. "Where've you been? We've been trying to reach you since early yesterday afternoon."

Dread inched up her spine. "I've been in Waco talking to a client. What's wrong, did Miss Pearl have another heart attack?"

"Why didn't you answer your cell phone?"

"Sorry Mom, I forgot and left my cell phone at home."

Anxious to avoid anymore questions, she pushed her way past her mother to see her father and Pauline sitting close together on the sofa. Pauline was crying. Texanna's throat closed, and she had difficulty getting words out. "Daddy, is it bad?"

Andrew Keith was tall, and still a handsome man with his auburn hair streaked with gray. His face twisted with concern as he rose and came to her. He placed both hands on her shoulders. "I'm sorry, baby. She's gone."

Her eyes darted to the staircase. "Oh no, Daddy.

I didn't get to say goodbye." She fell into his arms, and he patted her back as she cried against his shoulder. "I should've been here with her, I shouldn't have left town."

"Don't say that, honey. None of us knew she'd go yesterday. Pearlina was ready, sweetheart." Texanna had known for years that Pearl asked Daddy to settle her affairs when she passed. She had no living relatives, but the possibility of Pearl dying didn't seem imminent to Texanna. Yes, she was ninety-four years old, but...

His words, meant to comfort, only made her sob harder. She felt hands on her back and turned to see a smiling Pauline, Pearl's friend and companion, her bright blue eyes sparkled with tears. "Come here, my girl, Pearl died a happy woman." She captured Texanna's face between her hands and nodded. "You made her very happy. Yesterday she talked for an hour about the joys of her life. You were one of them. She'd want you to celebrate her life, not mourn."

Texanna nodded and stepped into the older woman's arms. They clung to each other and cried until Pauline pulled back. She sniffed and wiped at her tears with a lacy handkerchief. "Now, that's enough. You need a cup of hot tea and a couple of my teacakes."

She looked toward her father, who stood with her mother in the big entry hall, seeing visitors out. Ladies from Pearl's church bustled around in the large dining room, so Texanna allowed herself to be led away. Nothing was more comforting than food and talk in Pauline's kitchen.

The tea was strong and hot, just what Texanna needed to fortify her system. Pauline took an envelope from her dress pocket. "Pearl dictated this to me after the train left yesterday."

Her hand trembling, Texanna carefully opened the letter.

My dearest child,

If you're reading this, I've passed on and you've returned to the twenty-first century. You've been the joy and hope that's kept me alive these past twenty-two years. The night you were born I dreamed of the woman you'd become. As you grew and filled my lonely hours, I felt you'd been sent to me for a special purpose. Of late, I've wondered if God had a plan when he sent me forward, if maybe I was just the catalyst for something to come. I think you were his target all along. God keep you...

Texanna didn't know what to think. God's target? What on earth did that mean? Before she could ask, Pauline reached out and clasped Texanna's hand. "She was so happy, honey. I can't tell you how long she's waited for Royce to hear from her."

"Pauline, you haven't even asked if the theory worked or not."

"Well, did it? Did you see Royce and talk to him?"

"Yes, but he locked me up in jail. The arrogant man accused me of stealing Pearl's things, even threatened to charge me with her murder. He wouldn't believe I'd traveled from 2008 even after reading her letters."

Pauline covered her mouth with a hand. "Locked you up? Oh, dear, Pearl would have a fit if she knew." She reached for Texanna's hand. "Did you give him the message?"

Texanna explained both Royce and Jason's reaction to her news about the bank robbery. She prayed they'd take her words seriously and prepare for Sam Bass's arrival. Before she could tell her how she got out of jail, her parents entered the kitchen ending their opportunity to discuss her trip further. Pauline stood to get two more cups while Texanna tucked the letter in her jeans pocket.

****

Pearlina Dyson Thompson was buried the following day. The church overflowed with people who came to pay their respects. Until five years ago, when her health deteriorated, she'd been active in her church and the community. Evidently, she'd not been forgotten. Flowers blanketed the wall behind the pulpit creating a natural backdrop for the mahogany casket covered with a spray of yellow rosebuds and white lilies.

The pastor's words soothed Texanna. "I'm reading from the book of Isaiah, chapter 43, verses 1-3.

Fear not, for I have redeemed you, I have called you by your name and you are Mine. When you pass through the waters, I will be with you; and through the rivers, they shall not overflow you. When you walk through the fire, you shall not be burned nor shall the flame scorch you. For I am the Lord your God, the Holy One of Israel, your Savior...

"I pray these words give you comfort for I know they did Pearlina. One of her favorite scriptures was Isaiah 40, verse 28. It had special meaning for her."

As he read, the preacher's melodic voice washed over Texanna like warm water over a cold back.

"Have you not known? Have you not heard? The everlasting God, the Lord, the Creator of the ends of the earth, neither faints nor is weary. There is no searching of His understanding."

Texanna stifled the sobs that threatened. Pearl fought her fate in 1936, but she'd finally given up her battle and accepted God's plan for her. What a relief it must have been.

Texanna wiped her face with a tissue from the box sitting on the pew. She sat between her father, his arm locked tightly around her shoulders, and Pauline. Pastor John, thin and frail in his long robe, looked out at them and smiled. He'd been Pearl's spiritual advisor for the past fifty years. He'd known her well. "Several months ago, over a pot of tea and a plate of Pauline's teacakes, Pearlina shared some of her precious memories." The congregation chuckled. "She told me about a journey she'd taken in her youth, one that took everything dear to her away." Texanna held her breath. Surely, Pearl didn't discuss time-travel with anyone besides her and Pauline. "When she stopped fighting against the fate God handed her, she found a new purpose in life. She reminded me how important it is not to question the journeys God sends us on, but to accept his will and enjoy the ride. Pearlina's life was rich and full. She loved the Lord and looked forward to life's final journey."

Texanna wiped tears from her face and smiled. Without a doubt, she knew the words were meant for her. *I won't forget, Pearl.*

****

Pearlina's lawyer joined them after the funeral to read the will. They sat around the long mahogany dining table covered with a hand crocheted cloth. Pauline served coffee and handed around refreshments.

Mr. Jamison cleared his throat. "Pauline, would you please have a seat so we may begin." Looking a little shocked, she nodded and moved to the far end of the table. "I, Pearlina Dyson Thompson, known to my friends as Pearl, hereby..."

He read through a bunch of legal jargon stating Pearl was of sound mind at the time she'd written her will.

"To Pauline, my faithful friend, I bequeath a monthly income of four thousand dollars for the remainder of her life. My home, with an allotment for its upkeep, all its furnishings and my personal belongings, I leave to the young woman who's made my aging years bearable—my beloved Texanna. The remainder of my estate I leave to the University of Texas Paranormal Research Department."

Face red with anger, Madeline turned on her husband. "This house should have been left to you, Andrew. I don't know what she was thinking." The beautiful old Victorian was in a prestigious part of town, as was her parents' next door, but Pearl's house was bigger, the gingerbread and woodworking more ornate. If Mother and Daddy lived in the house, her mother would enjoy the envy of her pretentious friends.

Her father hushed her with a glare. His reprimand brooked no argument. "Texanna helped Pearl fill many lonely hours these last years of her life. She wants Texanna to have this place, and I'm perfectly happy with her decision." He turned to Pauline. "I hope you'll stay on and help Texanna with things. I hate to see her here all by herself."

Texanna quickly agreed. "Please stay, Pauline. I need help going through Pearl's personal effects. Some things I won't know whether to keep or get rid of."

"I'd like that if you're sure I won't be in the way."

Texanna stood and hugged the older woman. "You know you're as dear to me as you were to Pearl. If you interfere in my business, I'll let you know."

Pauline laughed and wiped a tear off her cheek. "I just bet you will."

****

Texanna found going through Pearlina's things emotionally exhausting. She read old letters. Some words brought laughter, others tears. Her vanity held a variety of half-empty bottles of perfumes. She sampled every one and found each fragrance brought on fond memories of her childhood. One empty container sat alone. When she removed the lid, a trace of sweet lilac filled her senses. Funny, she never remembered Pearl wearing the scent, but for some reason, the bottle held a special place on her dressing table.

Her mahogany chest-of-drawers held underwear from the forties and fifties, some still with the tags. The woman had enough shoes, purses, and hats to open a store. Texanna decided to keep the ones she liked best and donate the rest to San Antonio's Community Theatre for costumes.

By mid-afternoon, tired from a full day of packing, Texanna curled up on the old four-poster bed to take a nap. When she woke, the last of the day's sunlight shone through the lace curtains onto a book on the bedside table. It was a book on the early history of Waco, Texas. She rolled over and grabbed it. As she ruffled the pages, it fell open to two pieces of stationary folded in half. She unfolded the first and read.

There is but one philosophy and its name is fortitude! To bear is to conquer our fate. (Edward G. Bulwer Lytton—1803-1873)

The second quote was longer.

Accept the things to which fate binds you, and love the people with whom fate brings you together, but do so with all your heart. (Marcus Aurelius)

Marcus Aurelius? Wasn't he a Roman emperor back in the gladiator days? She flopped back onto the pillows. Just a month ago her life had been so simple. Now she had to deal with the fact she'd time-traveled and at this very moment sat reading antique Roman literature.

Texanna sighed and flipped through the pages to a bookmarked section about Waco's Marshal Royce Dyson. At the words in the caption under his picture, her heart sank. It described his death at the hands of the Bass gang, but it was the last several lines that chilled her soul.

Marshal Dyson's wife, Pearlina Baines Dyson

disappeared on June 15, 1876. She returned June 15, 1880 but the following day vanished. Though foul play was suspected, nothing could be proven. The situation is a mystery that's never been solved.

****

Texanna searched the Internet until she found mention of the Dyson family. Jason's great-grandson Jonathan was born in 1928. His last recorded address was in Kerrville, Texas, just a short drive from San Antonio. Directory assistance gave her his phone number. He answered on the first ring.

"Mr. Dyson, this is Texanna Keith. You don't know me, but I've been doing some research on the lawmen of the Dyson family."

"Is that so?"

"Uh, yes. I wondered if I might visit with you and ask you some questions about Royce and Jason Dyson." Her heart beat so hard she feared he could hear it through the receiver.

"Why, I'd be pleased to talk to you. When can you come?"

"Would this afternoon be all right?"

The drive to Kerrville sped by pleasantly and took her just under an hour. She followed the winding drive to the midsized ranch-style, brick home sitting on several acres of rough hill country land. The yard was nicely landscaped with beds of cactus, rocks, and the occasional steer head skeleton. When she pulled to a stop, a man in his fifties came out to greet her.

He was tall and well built. His smile displayed a dimple like the one in Royce's cheek. "Hello, Miss Keith, I'm Alex Dyson, Dad's oldest son. Pop's waiting for you in the sunroom. He's been chomping at the bit all morning afraid you'd changed your mind."

She shook his hand and laughed. "Oh, I'd never do that. I'm anxious to speak with him." Her expression sobered. “I know he’s not well, so I’ll try not to tire him.”

“Don’t you worry about that now. He’s been down lately and having a chance to talk about the family history is just what he needs to perk him up.”

Before they reached the room at the back of the house, a loud voice hollered. “Is that her, Son?”

Alex grinned. “Sure is, Pop, and she’s a pretty little lady too.”

They entered the room and Texanna’s eyes lit on the older man leaning back in his recliner. He held out a hand to her, and she strode across the room to take it in a firm grasp. “Why she is at that, Son.” He motioned to the chair beside him. “Have a seat here by me.”

“Would you like some coffee, Miss Keith?” Alex waved his hand. “I know you do, Pop.”

“I’d love a cup, and please, call me Texanna.”

He nodded and left the room. “Now, young lady, what exactly would you like to know about the Dyson family?” He picked up a small pile of old books and papers from the end table. Tremors shook his hand as he lowered them into his lap. “Whatever you need to know, I’ve got the answers right here.”

“Uh, I guess I’d like to know about your grandfather Jason’s life, what it was like after his brother died.”

The older man scratched his chin. “Don’t suppose you could tell me why you’re interested, now could you?”

“I’d rather not because you probably wouldn’t believe me. It’s a really weird story.”

Alex brought their coffee and left them to talk. Mr. Dyson blew on his coffee to cool it before taking a healthy swig. “Well, I truly love stories, the weirder the better.”

She couldn’t think of a reason why she shouldn’t tell him everything. After all, the worst that could happen is he'd believe she was crazy. "A friend of mine, an elderly woman named Pearlina Baines married Marshal Royce Dyson in 1872. In 1876 she boarded a train for San Antonio and..."

Mr. Dyson didn't interrupt. His keen blue eyes watched her with interest and curiosity. As he listened, he'd nod his head from time to time. When she finished, she waited for him to make a derogatory remark, but he didn't. He settled back in his chair and studied her for a minute. "During my early years, after great-granddaddy Dyson retired, I used to sit at his knee and listen to stories. There was one in particular I begged to hear time and again. It was about a crazy redheaded woman named Texanna."

She held her breath as he continued. "Seems she told a wild story about time-travel. Of course no one believed her, but before he died in 1940, Pappy Dyson decided the woman might have been telling the truth."

He opened a diary and pointed to a specific entry. Texanna took the journal from him and read. The words were faint from age, but she had no trouble deciphering them.

August 9, 1880

Today we laid Royce to rest. My heart is heavy with grief and remorse at sending Texanna away. If only I'd listened to Texanna, Royce would be here today and Garrett wouldn't be without a father. God forgive me for I'll never forgive myself. Nor did Royce.

Texanna looked at the front of the journal. It belonged to Jason Dyson.

Voice gravelly, he asked, "Is that what you needed to know?"

Blinking back a tear, she nodded and passed the open book back to him.

"Great-granddaddy never got over his brother's death. A week before, his oldest brother Matthew's wife delivered twins. The baby girl was healthy, but the boy never took a breath. Lots of babies died back in them days. Doctors didn't know near what they do today." He closed the journal and lovingly ran his hand over the cover. "Then when the boy Garrett died, he took his death to heart as well. Jason Dyson was a fine man, a good lawman, too. Unfortunately, he carried that guilt all his life, put a damper on his happiness."

"That'd be a hard load to bear. How old was your great-granddaddy when he died?"

"Eighty-two, died just one year after his wife Sally passed on."

"Thank you, Mr. Dyson for sharing this with me." She stood to shake his hand.

He reached for both of hers. His large hands swallowed hers as he squeezed gently. "You're welcome. I enjoyed our visit." His blue eyes bored into hers—a wealth of knowledge radiated from them. "God keep you and bless you." He winked. "Safe journey, Texanna."

****

It was clear what she must do. The robbery wouldn't occur for just over a month, but she feared if she didn't go now, something might prevent her from going back. She needed to be there to make sure Royce lived.

Texanna called her father to let him know she'd be vacationing and be gone probably a month. Pauline dropped her at the depot, and carpetbag in hand, she boarded the train for Waco. Just before the train reached Austin, she went into the restroom, sat down on the toilet seat, and leaned back with her tennis shoes braced against the adjacent wall. She focused her mind on June 29, 1880 and clutched the turquoise locket. Though expecting it, the jolt still rattled her bones and her head bounced off the back wall.

She changed clothes before leaving the lavatory. Dressed in her gray serge Victorian dress and the ratty straw bonnet, she rejoined the other passengers. Hands trembling slightly, she folded them in her lap and concentrated on stilling her galloping heart.

When the train slowed and pulled into the station, she waited until everyone else disembarked before getting up. The streets and sights were the same as she remembered them. Taking a deep breath, straightening her shoulders, she struck out across the street toward the marshal's office. Men tipped their hats, ladies smiled and nodded, but no one spoke and called her Pearl. But some looked curiously at her, and she saw heads together whispering. A few people fell in behind her.

Jason sat at the desk in the jail's outer office. His brow wrinkled as he squinted trying to read the words on a small poster. She cleared her throat, and he looked up. His mouth fell open in shock. It quickly turned to anger and settled on resignation. His face was blue from fading bruises, and one eye was purple.

"What happened to you?"

He stood up and came around the desk. "My brother wasn't particularly happy I let his prisoner get away. Didn't take kindly to having his brother betray him and not follow orders."

"Why I never..." She was too shocked to say more.

Ignoring her search for words, he took her arm and led her toward Royce's office. Jason knocked once, opened the door, shoved her inside, and quickly closed it behind her.

"What is it, Jason?" When Royce didn't receive an answer, he looked up and saw Texanna. His eyes widened in surprise, and then he grinned. "Well, well, what have we here? My errant wife has returned once again." He stood up and walked around the desk.

"Your wife my ass."

Chapter Five

Texanna dropped the carpetbag and plopped her hands on her hips, her face red with anger. Her breasts heaved with righteous indignation. Lordy, she was pretty with her dander up.

"What do you mean by hitting that boy out there? The only reason he let me go was to keep you from getting hurt. He tried to help you—the big brother he dearly loves."

"That *boy* is a deputy of the state of Texas and paid to do what I tell him to do. He's lucky I didn't fire him for helping you. May yet."

She snorted. "That'd be a shame. He's going to be a good lawman, almost as good as you. I—"

"I don't want to hear it." That's all he needed—another cock and bull story that didn't make a lick of sense. He walked around the desk and stood in front of her. His closeness unnerved her, and she moved back a step. The knowledge pleased him. "What prompted you to come back?"

"You wouldn't believe me if I told you, so I'll just keep my reasons to myself."

He couldn't hold back a grin. "Ahh, you're anxious to resume our marriage. Missed my loving, huh?" The expression on her face was priceless.

"Why you puffed up buffoon." She poked him in the chest emphasizing each word. "It'll be a cold day in hell when I enjoy your loving." He'd maneuvered her back against the wall. She shoved at him. "I'm here to save your life, and that's all, so keep your hands to yourself."

Hands to each side of her head, he looked down at her pink lips. They called to him, and he wanted to bend down and taste them. He cleared his throat and pulled back. "Since you're not my wife, just where do you plan to live while you're doing this life saving? Who's going to pay the bills?"

Texanna couldn't think with him so close. The heat from his body, along with his bay rum aftershave settled over her making her woozy. His nearness was just a little too tempting.

The gleam of amusement in his eyes doused her desire. Smiling sweetly, she said. "I'll get a job doing something. If the bank will give me a loan, I'll paint portraits."

His eyes lost their humor. He stepped back. "You paint?"

"Yes, I'm relatively well-known for my portraits in San Antonio. As a matter of fact, I'm acquiring clients all over the state now, some in other states. My latest portrait commission paid five thousand dollars."

His snort of derision said he didn't believe her.

"Buy me some paints, and I'll prove it."

"Why didn't you bring money or supplies with you?"

"You know why. I couldn't bring money from the future back here. People would think it was counterfeit. They'd think I was crazy or have me arrested."

He shook his head. "You are crazy woman, or you're up to something. Until I find out why you're here, where you got Pearl's things, and what you're up to, you'll be staying at my house as my wife."

"I'll do no such thing."

"It's either with me or here in a jail cell."

What had she been thinking coming here without a way to support herself? She could have scoured the antique stores, located some old money, and stayed in a boarding house. Shoot, Royce probably would've arrested her anyway.

"I'm not sleeping with you, Mr. Dyson. If I come, it'll be an 'in-name only' situation."

"Suit yourself." He looked her up and down. "I'm glad to see you're suitably dressed today. The marshal has an image to keep up, you know."

The man was baiting her. She smirked at him. "As long as I'm here, I'll be a model housewife and not embarrass you. But I'm here to tell you, I don't know how to cook."

"We'll see about that." He grabbed his shotgun and hat, and taking her arm, escorted her out of his office. Jason sat at the desk, a look of resolve on his face. "I'm taking Texanna home. Send someone for me if there's trouble."

"Will do, Royce."

Outside, the street was full of curious people. Royce ignored them as he stowed his shotgun and tied her carpetbag onto the saddle. He lifted her onto Samson and mounted behind her. Before they rode off, he turned her face around to meet his and kissed her. A roar of approval vibrated around them. When she caught her breath, she hissed, "What was that for?"

"Why darlin', I'm letting the town know my wife has returned."

****

From inside Millie's Hat Boutique, a pair of hazel eyes narrowed as they focused on the doings in front of the marshal's office. As Marshal Dyson and the woman rode off, Danielle bit back her tears and looked down at the hat hanging limply in her hands. She'd have to buy the damn thing now. It was twisted beyond recognition.

"Millie, put this on my tab, please. I'm in a big hurry so no need to bother wrapping it up." She headed for the door.

Millie seemed shocked at her rushed purchase—in truth she usually tried on every hat in the place, but now she just wanted to leave. The shopkeeper grabbed the finest hatbox in the store, and asked, "Are you sure? It won't take a minute."

"I'm sure." And she was out the door, the bell ringing at the vibration of the slam.

Danielle passed the storefront and tossed the hat into the nearest garbage barrel. How dare that man come calling on her, invite her to the July Fourth dance, and then pick right back up with that woman the minute she comes back in town. Her face burned with mortification. She'd already told her friends she had a date with Royce. Being dumped by him for that redhead the first time was bad enough. How would she get past being humiliated again?

****

They rode along in silence. Texanna tried to sit up straight and not lean against his broad chest, but finally gave up and relaxed. One of his arms circled her waist while the other held the reins. If the close contact bothered him, he didn't let on.

From the road she could see the Brazos River winding along through the trees. As the road neared the river, large sandstone rocks bordered it to keep wheels or horses from getting too close. She peeked over the edge to see boulders, dirt, and scrub brush blanketed the descent all the way to the water.

A small white farmhouse sat back from the west side of the road. "Who lives there?"

"Agnes Farley. Most folks call her Aggie. She's a widow lady and takes care of Garrett when I'm working. He'll spend the night there tonight, so you'll meet him tomorrow or the next day."

A short distance down the road, he turned down a lane that led to another white farmhouse. It loomed larger, with two stories and clapboard siding. Twin rocking chairs sat on a porch running the width of the house. Lilac bushes grew at each corner of the porch and several old oaks shaded the front and back yards. It was a picturesque view. Texanna could see Pearl living here.

"This is nice. Bet Pearl used to have lots of flowers in that front bed."

He didn't comment, but dismounted and lifted her down. "Go inside. I'll put Samson away for the night."

Inside, Texanna walked into the wide center hall with transoms above the doors at each end. She stepped into the parlor. The furniture was sparse and plain but pillows and crocheted doilies brightened the room. She fingered a delicate scarf and imagined Pearl sitting in one of the chairs crocheting by lamplight. She stepped across the hall into the dining room. It held a beautiful oak table with six chairs and an open hutch. She examined the china lined up across the shelf. Pearlina's dishes were delicate, painted in pastels, and dust free. Someone had been cleaning for Royce.

Royce watched Texanna run her finger over the waxed wood and trace the pattern of the china. Her look was one of reverence, and her awe further confused him. He cleared his throat, and she turned and smiled. A tear sparkled in her eyes. "I just couldn't resist exploring."

He nodded. "Come on into the kitchen, and let's find something to eat." She followed him, her carpetbag still clutched in her hand. He took it from her and sat it on the end of the table. "We've got some leftover ham and fresh bread. How about a sandwich?"

"Sounds good." When he offered her a glass of milk, her lip curled, and she shook her head. "I'd prefer water."

They ate in silence. Royce watched her as she inspected the room and the items in it as if she'd never seen them.

"Where've you been since you left here?"

"Why, back in 2008 San Antonio, of course."

****

The long skirt twisted around her legs threatening to trip her as she walked down the stairs. She kicked it aside and kept moving. Men's voices echoed from the kitchen. The deep rumble of Royce's voice made her stomach jump into her throat.

"I don't know what to think, Matthew. She still claims to have time-traveled from 2008."

"Do you think she's your wife? Is it possible she's lost her memory?"

"Hell, I don't know what to think. But, last night she told me she's a portrait artist. Made five thousand dollars on the last one she did."

One of them whistled, probably Matthew, whoever that was. Ah! Probably the older brother.

"That's a lot of money. She must be mighty good. Just one more thing she has in common with the Pearl we knew and loved."

She walked through the open kitchen door. Both men rose to their feet.

That the two men were related was immediately evident but Matthew was a big man, several inches taller than Royce and more muscular. His biceps were as big around as the trunk of the tree in the front yard. Texanna mentally compared them. Both were handsome, but where Royce's dark hair fell to his collar, Matthew's was longer and tied back with rawhide. Royce was clean-shaven, but his brother had a beard and mustache.

Royce asked. "Find everything you needed upstairs?" He looked at her tennis shoes but didn't comment.

"Yes, thank you."

Royce nodded and held a chair for her. "Sit down

and let us wait on you this morning."

Texanna eased into the chair, warily watching both men as they moved around the kitchen.

Royce stood by her shoulder. "Coffee?"

"Please."

He poured them each a cup while Matthew fetched the cream and sugar. Royce placed the pot on the stove and returned with a platter of scrambled eggs and ham. Matthew gingerly grabbed hot biscuits off a pan and piled them onto a plate.

Royce took the chair at the end of the table, and Matthew sat across from her. Each reached for one of her hands and waited for her to take it. Royce bowed his head.

"Father, we thank you for our many blessings—our family and friends, and for returning Pea...uh Texanna to us. Heal her, Lord, and restore her memory. Bless this food to the nourishment of our bodies. Amen."

Restore her memory? There wasn't a thing wrong with her memory, nothing a one-hundred-twenty-eight-year jump in time wouldn't fix.

Both men looked at her, waiting for her to begin. She picked up the beautifully embroidered napkin and ran her finger over the fine stitches. Pearl was gifted at needlework. Had she done these? She'd tried to teach Texanna, but her fingers wouldn't cooperate.

Royce moved the cream and sugar where she could reach it. "Don't you want to sweeten your coffee?"

"I drink mine black." He studied her a minute then returned the bowls to the center of the table. The two men exchanged looks and cast her sideways glances. Evidently Pearl didn't drink her coffee black in this time period. She didn't in 2008 either. Texanna sipped the brew. It was more than a tad too strong for her taste, but the caffeine worked wonders at revving her up.

The men had big appetites, but their manners were perfect. Every time she looked up, their eyes immediately fled her face. Feeling awkward, she studied the kitchen while she ate. It was clean and neat. The wood floors gleamed with polishing, and the red, gingham check curtains at the windows added a cheery touch, as did the checked oilcloth on the table.

Unable to bear the silence and their scrutiny any longer, she blurted. “The food is delicious, especially the biscuits, and my goodness, real butter.”

Matthew looked at her in question. “Real butter? Is there another kind?”

Oh, boy. “What I meant was, this is really good butter.”

Matthew nodded and Royce just looked at her, one eyebrow raised. “How do you like the jelly?”

“It’s the best I’ve ever eaten. Apricot is my favorite.”

Royce nodded and smiled at his plate.

“You can thank Matthew for the biscuits. He took to Ma’s lessons better than Jason and I.” Royce’s expression held affection for his brother. Then he turned to her. “Pearl put up the jelly. This is the last jar. Thank goodness we still have apricots and plums on the trees so you can make some more.”

Texanna gaped at Royce. *He expects me to make jelly*? She was more the take-out food kind of girl. There were a few things she could cook that were edible, but not many.

Royce watched her, waiting for her to say something. “I don’t know how to make jelly.” She looked over at the big cast iron cookstove. “Or how to operate that stove.”

Royce eyed her suspiciously.

Matthew spoke up. “I’ll come by one day to help

you with the jelly, Texanna. The day before you start canning, ride out to the farm and let me know. Molly would love to see you."

"Who is Molly?"

Royce looked irritated but Matthew hurriedly spoke up. "Molly's my wife. She's big with our child and can't ride anymore until after the babe is born."

Her heart sank. This was the brother whose infant died. "Oh, you shouldn't leave her there alone then."

Matthew's smile warmed her. "She won't be alone. Several families live on the farm, and someone will always be within calling distance." His gaze searched hers. "It's nice of you to be concerned."

His comment pleased Texanna, and she smiled in response. "I love to ride and can't wait to meet your Molly."

Riding was something Texanna could do. She'd taken lessons from the age of ten. Her mother wanted her to ride English style, but Texanna wouldn't have it. She insisted on western style and for once, she got her way.

Texanna turned to Royce. "Is there a horse I can ride?" Royce didn't like her question. He frowned. If his eyebrows got any closer together, he'd look like he sported a mustache on his forehead.

"Josie is in the field behind the house, but I don't want you riding until I have a chance to go out with you." He grabbed her wrist. "Are we clear on that?"

"Clear as a bell."

Her sarcasm wasn't lost on Royce. He gentled his tone. "Texanna, do this for me, please. I'd worry about you while I'm in town."

His expression of concern was hard to miss. "All right, I'll wait." And she would, for a while. She didn't intend to hang around the house all day.

Texanna stood. "Since you guys cooked, I'll wash

the dishes. Sit, have another cup of coffee."

She looked around the kitchen. Okay, there stood the sink. A dishpan sat underneath. In a drawer, she located dishrags and towels. Now, where did she get hot water?

"Where's the tea kettle so I can heat the water?"

Royce stood and carried the dishpan to a metal box attached to the side of the stove. He turned a spigot and to her surprise, steamy water ran into the pan. *Pretty neat invention,* she thought. At the sink, he sprinkled in powdered soap and then added cold water from the pump. "Don't forget to add water to the reservoir or you won't have hot water for the lunch dishes."

Matthew stood. "I better get home and get to work."

Texanna turned. "Thank you for breakfast."

His smile emphasized his dimples. "You're welcome." To her surprise, the big man caught her in a bear hug. "And, Texanna, I'm so glad you're home."

Texanna shot Royce a look that demanded he explain the situation to his brother. He just grinned. Afraid to speak for fear of ranting, she nodded.

Royce grabbed an apron off a hook on the wall, slipped it over her head, and tied it in the back. When his fingers moved to the buttons on the back of her blouse, she stiffened.

"Looks like you had some trouble buttoning up this morning." That was putting it lightly. She'd felt like a contortionist trying to fit the small buttons in the tiny holes.

Goosebumps rose on her flesh as his hand brushed her skin, but she tried to ignore the delicious sensation while he did up the buttons she'd been unable to reach. He was so close she could feel his warm breath on her neck. The room was hot from the cookstove, she pulled on the choking neckline trying to get some air.

He patted her shoulder. “There you go. All done.”

It was about damn time. She took a deep breath as he stepped away. “Why didn’t you explain our situation to Matthew? He thinks I’m Pearl, and you know I’m not.”

“No Texanna, I don’t know that for a fact. I suspect you’re not, but I could be wrong. That’s what I’m trying to find out.”

“I’ve told you I’m not. Why would I lie?” She whisked dishes off the table and dumped them into the soapy water.

“Maybe you don’t know who you are, have lost your memory.”

“That’s ridiculous.”

He ignored her and walked to the coat rack by the back door. “I’ll be home around noon for lunch.”

“Don’t you eat lunch in town?”

“Nope. You always prepare a big lunch, and we have leftovers for dinner.”

“In this heat? I’ll roast in here.”

“Why, it doesn’t really get hot until around noon.”

Texanna looked around frantically. “Where’s the icebox? I’m not sure what to cook.”

“Just look in the larder. I’m sure you’ll find something that will do.”

The larder? What the heck is a larder?

He strapped on his gun belt, put on his hat, and moved to the door. He stopped and looked at her for a minute. Texanna felt like a doe caught in a spotlight. The tension grew so thick she could hardly breathe. In two long strides his arm was around her waist, holding her against his lean hard body. Before she could object, his mouth covered hers. His kiss was slow and sweet as he tasted and teased her mouth. The feelings of desire and joy his lips invoked terrified Texanna. She could not fall in love with this man. She would be going home in a few weeks.

Chapter Six

By nine a.m. Royce wanted to lock the jail doors. Half the population of Waco stopped in to see about Texanna. What they actually wanted to know was if she'd put up a fight and he'd had to cuff her. Due to all the hoopla, he couldn't get any work done. Plus, his mind wandered to images of how Texanna would react to Garrett and interact with him.

Royce stopped by to see Garrett on his way into town. The boy had been full of questions, and Royce promised him they'd talk tonight. What would he tell him? How did you tell a child you don't know if the woman staying in your home was his mother or not? *Lord, what a mess.*

The woman at his house was very different from his wife. She was more outspoken and self-confident—a little too mouthy to his way of thinking. She needed to learn to curb her tongue. Where had she learned to talk like that? Pictures of unsavory places and situations ran through his mind tormenting him. If he discovered her behavior was due to abuse, he'd find the individuals responsible and see they paid.

Yet he couldn't deny the resemblance to Pearl. Her hair was a little redder, her eyes darker blue, and the face that had once been fuller was now leaner as was her body. It had been four years. People changed physically over time. He shook his head in consternation and turned back to the papers in front of him.

Just when he thought he'd shoot the next person

who walked into his office, Edna darkened his door. Mrs. Edna Murphy, the top hen in the pecking order of women in Waco, could handle any man, woman, or beast in town. He'd butted heads with her and lost more times than he'd like to admit.

Royce stood and escorted her to the chair by his desk. "I can't tell you how glad I am to see you."

Edna cocked an eyebrow and looked at him with suspicion. "I believe this is the first time I've been welcomed into your office."

She was right. His joy at seeing her was a mite unusual. The stiff-necked matron had pestered him about several things in the last couple of years—the saloons, the brothels, and those hooligan boys who kept tearing up her flowerbeds.

"Well, yes, that's true. But I just realized how valuable you can be in helping Texanna settle in after her experience."

Edna's eyes crackled with interest. "Really, what makes you think that?" She leaned forward in her chair, all ears.

"You know she claims she's not Pearl, nor my wife, and insists on being called Texanna."

Hands gripping the drawstring handbag in her lap, she nodded.

"She hasn't revealed where she's been the past four years. As a matter of fact, she doesn't remember me, Garrett, or ever living here in Waco."

Her jaw dropped, and she clapped a hand over her mouth. "Oh, you poor boy, I'm so sorry to hear that."

He was quiet for a minute, thinking about strategy—how to get the older woman to help both him and Texanna. The crowd traipsing in and out of his office was bad enough, but he didn't want them flocking to his home to quiz Texanna either. Edna would be perfect at keeping folks at bay. If Texanna was his wife, he wanted her privacy respected, if she wasn't, he didn't want her story colored by other people's opinions.

Edna waited for him to speak, but not patiently. The feather in her hat twitched like a dog's rear end with its tail wagging.

"I need someone to be an example for the community, someone who can lead the others to not gang up on Texanna and ask her a bunch of questions. Let her memory return in due time."

Edna clasped her hands over her non-existent bosom. "She doesn't remember a thing?" Royce shook his head. "Oh, the poor dear." She drew herself up in the chair. "I can assure you, Marshal, the job will be taken care of as of this minute."

Royce scratched his chin. "There's one other thing you can do that will help me immensely."

Thrilled at the opportunity to be in the spotlight, Edna took up residence in front of the jail. In a rocking chair he borrowed from the general store, she sat and turned away the curious. If they didn't heed her advice and move on, she whacked them with her umbrella to get them moving. Royce was finally able to work. But no matter how busy he got, a strawberry-headed woman wasn't far from his mind.

He was studying an arrest warrant for Sam Bass and his gang when a knock sounded on his door, and Jason stuck his head in. "Danielle Stokes would like to see you."

****

Texanna stepped out onto the wide front porch that ran the length of the house. She eyed the rockers and imagined sitting here in the evenings, listening to the night sounds. A white picket fence enclosed a small front yard. She could make out Mrs. Farley's house a short distance away.

Back in the kitchen, she opened a door she'd not noticed earlier and found a room with windows across one wall. In a corner, an easel held a painting covered by a drop cloth. The hair on Texanna's neck stood on end. Pearlina's painting studio. Even in her previous life, she'd painted. Texanna reached out to remove the cloth, and then drew back. Would Pearl resent her looking at her work?

Unable to stop herself, she uncovered the painting. The cloth fell to the floor. It was a child, a small boy, perhaps three to four years old. His hair was dark, his eyes blue and the pure smile on his face reached inside and twisted her heart.

"That's me when I was little."

Texanna yelped and jumped away from the easel. A boy stood in the door, a mischievous smile making his blue eyes dance. *Garrett.*

Hand over her heart, she took a deep breath. "Whew. You scared the dickens out of me."

His face fell. "I'm sorry."

"Hey, it's okay. Bet I looked funny, huh?"

His head bobbed, and the smile returned.

"You must be Garrett."

"Yes, ma'am." He chewed his lip and studied the toe of his boot. "Are you my mother?"

Oh, God. *What now, Texanna*? If she said yes, I'm your mother, Garrett would be hurt when the time came for her to leave. But what did she tell him now?

"Uh, no, Garrett. I'm not."

"Oh." Tears gathered in his eyes. "Who're you then?"

Good question. Who the hell am I? Or, at the least, what can I tell this kid and other people when they ask? Everyone believed she was Royce's wife. How would they react when they found out she wasn't?

Texanna heard someone call, "Garrett." She supposed it was Mrs. Farley looking for him. The screen door in the kitchen squeaked.

"Garrett. Where are you?"

"He's in here, Mrs. Farley. Come on in."

Mrs. Farley crossed the kitchen and into the adjoining room where they stood looking at the painting. "Oh, dear. I didn't intend for Garrett to come over and be underfoot today. You need time to settle in."

"Oh, he's not a bother." Texanna smiled down at Garrett. "However, young man, you need to always tell Mrs. Farley when you leave her yard. Otherwise, she'll worry. Understand?"

"Yes, ma'am."

He rushed to Mrs. Farley and hugged her abundant waist. "I'm sorry, Aunt Aggie. I forgot." She dropped a kiss on top of his head.

"Just try to remember next time." Mrs. Farley's gaze met Texanna's over Garrett's head.

"How are you today?"

"I'm good." She turned back to the painting. "It's beautiful, isn't it?"

Texanna could see Mrs. Farley studying her as she bent to look closer at the painting. She seemed pleased at her interest in the portrait. "Yes, it is. Do you think you'll finish it now?"

Texanna's eyes lit at her question. "I'd love to, Mrs. Farley, but I don't have any paints."

"No paints? Why, the entire cupboard is filled with paints and stuff. Royce let you buy all the supplies you wanted, and Texanna, you always called me Aggie. Please do so again."

Texanna smiled and nodded.

"Good." Aggie bent and whispered in Garrett's ear. "Show her the supplies." He grinned and opened the cupboard door.

Texanna eyes widened as she looked from Garrett to Aggie. "Oh, my, this is wonderful."

Texanna examined the tubes of paint and pulled brushes out to inspect the bristles.

Garrett stood at Texanna's side, his face turned up to watch her. Texanna smiled down at him and put an arm around the boy's thin shoulders. Garrett leaned into her side. A lump formed in her throat.

"What do you think, Garrett? Should I finish your painting?" He nodded. "Good, we'll get started as soon as I figure out where the food's kept and how to work the stove."

She saw Aggie shake her head. "I'll be happy to help you, dear," she said.

Aggie hustled Texanna into the kitchen. They collected potatoes, onions, and carrots from the root cellar and set about peeling and paring the vegetables.

An hour later, they had a good fire burning in the cookstove and a stew bubbling, its rich aroma filling the house. Aggie wrote down a recipe for corn bread and mixed the dry ingredients for the first batch. All Texanna had to do was add the fat, egg, and milk just before baking.

Texanna bit her lip. She wasn't sure how to stoke the fire to heat the oven properly. She guessed she'd learn from experience.

"Garrett, come on home with me until your pa gets home." The boy's face fell.

"Oh, Aggie, let him stay. He won't be any trouble." Texanna ruffled Garrett's hair. "Will you, sport?"

"No, ma'am, I sure won't. I promise."

****

Royce swore at his bad luck. He didn't want to face the woman right now, but it seemed he didn't have a choice. When she breezed into the room, he stood and rounded his desk to offer her a chair.

"That won't be necessary. I'll just be a minute." Her lips were pinched, her face pale. Dressed in a navy blue, Sunday dress with a matching bonnet, she appeared formal and cold. Well hell, he didn't blame her.

"Please, Danielle, sit down for a minute and let me explain."

"I don't see there's anything to explain. Your wife returns, and then disappears *again*. You come calling and convince me the woman is not your wife but an imposter."

"Look, I—"

She held up a gloved hand. "No, no. Let me finish. I accepted your invitation to the July Fourth dance. And now, after the entire town knows we have a date, the woman returns, and this time you claim her as your wife."

He couldn't deny he'd put her in a bad situation. "I'm sorry, Danielle. I'd never hurt you intentionally."

"Well, you have, Royce Dyson, *again*. This time I intend to get even." She turned on her heel and left the room, slamming the door loudly behind her.

****

As soon as Royce rode into the yard, he smelled something burning. He jumped off Samson and ran to the back steps. His mouth opened to call out, but the words remained trapped in his throat. Texanna's voice rang sweetly around him. She was singing. It was a song he'd never heard before, but the words and melody were haunting.

"My prayer...is to linger...with you."

He could see them through the open window. Royce removed his boots as he listened to her lovely voice. Quietly—he needed to oil the damn squeaky screen door—he entered the kitchen and removed the burning food from the oven. The door to Pearl's studio was partially closed, so she hadn't seen him enter the house. He padded in sock-clad feet to the door to watch, his heart in his throat.

Texanna sat on a stool, hidden behind the large canvas, paints splattered across the board in her hand. Garrett sat on the floor facing her, a sketchpad across his knees.

"Tilt your head up for me, Garrett," said Texanna. "Ah, that's good. I like that smile. Has anyone ever told you you're a carbon copy of your father?"

"What's a carbon copy?"

Her laugh of pleasure squeezed his heart. "It means you look just like your father."

Royce cleared his throat. Both heads swiveled in his direction. Garrett jumped up and ran to him. He caught his son in a quick hug.

Texanna slid off the stool. "Oh, goodness. I forgot the time." She picked up a cleaning rag and started wiping her hands.

"Don't hurry. Go ahead and clean your brushes."

"Hey, Pa. Look what I'm drawing. Texanna's teaching me."

"Texanna, huh?"

Texanna avoided his eyes.

"That's what she told me to call her, Pa." His frown showed concern he'd done wrong.

"That's fine, Son." Royce looked down at Garrett's sketchpad. "Let's see what you've done." It was a rough drawing of Texanna at the easel. Not bad for an eight-year-old. Clearly he'd inherited some of his mother's talent. It certainly hadn't come from his side of the family.

"It's not very good, is it?" Garrett's voice was resigned but his expression hopeful.

"I think it's mighty good for a beginner. You may be as good as your moth... as Texanna with a little practice." Garrett's face broke into a grin, and he stood up a little straighter.

Texanna flushed at his near-slip and finished cleaning her brushes. She studied Garrett's sketch. "Your father is right. It's very good, sport. I think this afternoon we'll have drawing lessons. Would you like that?"

His face lit. "You bet."

Royce saw her nose twitch—her sense of smell was no longer blocked by paint and turpentine. "Oh my gosh! I've burned the cornbread!"

"It's fine, Texanna. I took it out of the oven. It's overdone but edible."

Her face registered disgust. "I burned my first batch of cornbread. Oh! What about the stew?" She dropped her cleaning rag and hurried to the stove. Her face relaxed. "It looks okay. It may be too thick, but I can add some water."

"Looks fine to me, I like my stew thick." Royce put his hand to Garrett's back and locked eyes with Texanna.

"Sport? Come on, sport. Let's wash up." *What kind of name was sport?*

Texanna's face colored, and he swallowed the laugh that threatened.

****

Texanna watched through the window as the man and boy washed their hands at the water pump just outside the barn. A towel hung on the handle. Sport, indeed. She'd better choose her words more carefully as Royce picked up every small detail. However, what did it matter? He needed to learn she wasn't from this time period.

She pumped water into the pan and washed her hands. Why didn't Royce and Garrett wash up in here? Maybe it was a habit because if they worked outdoors, they'd be clean before coming in the house. She located bowls and plates and placed them along with spoons on the table. Now, where were the napkins? She found them in a drawer of the Hoosier. The supply was quickly dwindling. As the so-called lady of the house, she'd be washing and ironing a lot to keep them stocked. Yeah, like washing and ironing was her favorite thing to do.

She took another peek out the window. Here they came. Royce had folded his jacket over his arm. Texanna leaned forward to watch them approach. Royce's shoulders looked so broad in that white dress shirt. She jumped away from the window. Oh, no. Surely he didn't expect her to wash, starch, and iron those white shirts. If she remembered correctly, spray starch hadn't been invented until the 1950's. Drat! She didn't have a clue how to make starch.

The food was already on the table when Royce and Garrett entered the kitchen. Royce carried in a pitcher of milk from the larder and placed it on the table. Stew was in their bowls, but they'd slice and serve the cornbread at the table.

Royce picked up all the napkins. "Don't you want to save yourself some washing and ironing? Unless it's Sunday or a special occasion, we share a dish towel." He reached back and snagged the towel off the sink.

He's a thoughtful man. And here she thought all nineteenth-century men were brutes who wanted to be waited on hand and foot. "Thank you."

Royce nodded and reached for her hand, then bowed his head. Garrett's hand felt so small in hers, Royce's so big. Royce's thumb stroked hers as he gave thanks. Texanna felt a chill. Seeing this man and child here at the table in prayer, reminded her of the simple pleasures in life, things taken for granted today. Well, in her time period.

Someone milked a cow this morning to provide this milk—milk she wasn't going to drink. She liked milk, but not the raw kind fresh from the cow. But the fresh butter was a different story. Who'd churned it for Royce and Garrett?

"Texanna?" Royce had asked her a question. She looked up to see she still held their hands.

"I'm sorry. I was a million miles away. What did you say?"

"Pass the cornbread." He cut it into squares and tried to lift a piece from the pan. It fell apart.

Texanna groaned. It wasn't just overdone—it was a mess. "I'm sorry. I must have forgotten one of the ingredients." Darn, why hadn't she taken home ec in school and learned to cook?

"It's fine. We can crumble it in our stew." Royce scraped some out of the pan into Garrett's bowl, then hers and lastly his. "Stir it up and it'll be perfect."

She took a bite. It didn't taste bad at all.

Royce asked. "What do you think you forgot?"

Texanna looked at the Hoosier. "The egg." How could she be so stupid? She'd been in a hurry to paint. "I'll do better tonight. I promise."

"It's okay." Royce patted her hand. "There's enough left for supper tonight."

Thank you, God. The thought of heating the kitchen again made her cringe. It was already so hot she'd begun to sweat. She didn't know which she missed most—air conditioning or indoor plumbing.

"Be sure and keep water in the tank so I can wash when I get home. I'm filling in for Jason tonight and won't be in until around midnight." She groaned. There went any hope of the kitchen cooling off. "You don't have to get the fire hotter, just add more water after you and Garrett have bathed."

She nodded. The heat issue resolved, she remembered his comment about Jason. Royce was working for Jason tonight.

"Tonight? Did you say you're working tonight? We need to talk tonight." Texanna couldn't believe it. She needed to tell him all she'd learned about his future and Garrett's and Jason's.

"Yeah, Pa. You were gonna talk to me tonight, too." Garrett was a miniature version of his father with his blue eyes and dark hair. But he had his Uncle Matthew's dimples. What did he inherit from Pearl? Maybe he got her love of art.

"We'll get to it Garrett. Don't forget your chores this evening and mind Texanna."

"Yes, sir."

Texanna bit her lip. "Is Jason's arm still hurting?"

His eyes twinkled. "Nah, didn't take long for the soreness to go away."

Thank goodness. She hadn't meant to hurt anyone, but at the sight of the dirt streets, horses and mules pulling wagons, a scene right out of *Gunsmoke,* she'd panicked.

Royce stood. "The stew was good, Texanna."

"Thank you, but I can't take the credit. Aggie made it."

"You're not afraid being out here alone, are you?"

Afraid? Of what? "No, but you probably should show me where the guns and ammo are just in case."

He cocked an eyebrow. "How much do you know about guns?"

"A lot."

"What's that supposed to mean?"

"Whatever you've got, I can probably load and shoot it. I'm a pretty darn good marksman if I do say so myself."

Royce studied her for a minute. Four years ago, Pearl would pick up a gun if necessary, but the only one she knew how to use was the 20-gauge shotgun. And she certainly wasn't comfortable with it, and he didn't trust her to use it if she had to. On the nights he worked, Jason usually came out to stay so she wouldn't be afraid. He sighed. Here was yet another mystery for him to unravel. He didn't know whether to believe Texanna or not, but a cattle drive came through town today, and the men and cattle were camped on the Brazos. He couldn't leave her and Garrett here defenseless. After seeing her with the boy, he didn't worry she'd hurt him or be unkind to him. But, could she really protect Garrett and herself?

"Garrett, scrape the dishes, and take the scraps out for the chickens."

He took Texanna's elbow and escorted her upstairs to his bedroom. A gun cabinet stood next to the washstand. The key hung on a nail behind the wardrobe. As soon as he opened the door, Texanna reached in and pulled out a rifle. "Oh, my, God. An actual Winchester Repeating Rifle." She looked at the patent markings, and then opened the chamber and sighted down the barrel. "An 1873 model short rifle."

The woman stupefied him. He'd never seen one so interested in firearms. He muttered. "Hold that rifle in position, and let me see if you're strong enough to actually use the thing."

She weighed it in her hands for a minute. "I think I'm strong enough." A smile of pride lit her face. "I used to shoot in the small-bore rifle competition in my 4-H Club. We went all the way to nationals one year. I used a .22, but I think this is a little heavier." It weighed less than eight pounds, but the barrel was twenty-inches long. He watched as she held it in place for sixty seconds, more than enough time to be able to fire off the ten rounds in the chamber.

After she'd had a chance to look it over, Royce took the rifle and put it back in the cabinet. Head in the gun case now, looking at his weapons, she whistled. "Wow, is that a genuine Peacemaker?" She flashed him a quick glance over her shoulder and asked. "Were you in the Army?"

He nodded. The 1873 .44-caliber Colt single action revolver was standard Army issue today, but it wasn't the one he'd used then. He'd been issued an earlier model.

She picked it up, an expression of awe on her

face. “Heavier than modern revolvers, but in a pinch I could hit something with it. Daddy inherited Granddaddy’s Colt but never would let me fire it.”

Modern? His weapons were about as up to date as a person could get. He shook his head as he watched her test the gun’s weight, open the barrel, and spin the cylinder. Damned if she didn’t look like a gunfighter. The thought didn’t ease his mind any, just made him worry more about what the hell was going on.

He yanked the Colt and holster from her hands and handed her the 12-gauge double-barreled short shotgun. It was his favorite for dispersing a crowd. He liked it so well, he’d bought one to keep at home. Just hearing the breech snap closed would scare off most intruders.

“Let me see you load this scatter gun.”

She opened the breech, plucked two shells from his hand, popped them in the barrels, and closed the breech. The butt of the gun rested on her hip, muzzle pointed toward the ceiling.

He nodded. “Good.” Her ability to load it didn’t surprise him. Most women knew how to use the pepper gun for protection.

“Bet this thing kicks like the devil.”

He grinned. “Yes, it does. But it can save your life.”

“Yeah, I know.” She stuck her chin out. “I’m not afraid to use it if I have to. Probably be bruised as all get out, but I won’t let anything happen to Garrett, I promise.”

Royce’s heart twisted at her words. He gauged her sincerity and didn’t doubt for a moment she’d do her best to take care of his boy.

Voice gruff, he muttered. “Don’t get these out unless it’s absolutely necessary. We’ll go out in a day or two, so you can get the feel of the shotgun and the rifle.”

"How about the Colt? I'd like to give it a try."

He swallowed his laughter. The gun would knock her on her butt. "I'll bring home a smaller handgun for you to use if necessary."

"I really do need to get in some practice tomorrow. I don't have that many days to practice. Maybe I could set up a target out back and practice while you're at work."

"You'll do no such thing." The woman was a puzzle. "What do you mean, you don't have days? I want to know what's going on in that head of yours, woman."

She stuck her nose in the air and walked toward the door. On her way down the stairs back to the kitchen, she turned and tossed him a haughty look. "You will, as soon as we have our talk."

He followed her. "Dammit, if the town wasn't going to be full of drunken wranglers tonight, I'd stay home so we could talk. But I can't let my deputies work short tonight." He wouldn't take a chance on the town's safety.

She frowned. "I'm sorry. You're right. I can wait until you have time."

At the back door, Royce watched her as he slipped into his jacket, strapped on his gun belt, and stood with his hat in his hand. This was one damn awkward situation. This woman, whoever she was, had fired his blood. Without knowing her identity, he wanted to make love to her. Damned if he'd leave without kissing her again.

Casting glances over her right shoulder, she watched his every move from her position at the sink, her hands in soapy water. Her eyes conveyed apprehension and caution, but not fear. When she met his eyes, she started shaking her head.

"Royce, this is not a good idea."

"What's not a good idea?" He couldn't keep from grinning.

She moved from the sink and put the table between them. "You know what. Kissing." She made flapping motions with her hands slinging soapsuds around the room. "Just go on to town."

He couldn't help it. Laughter erupted. He faked a lunge to the left and caught her as she moved to the right. Arms locked around her waist, he grinned down at her. Then sobered when he remembered what she'd done to Jason and how she'd thrown him on his butt. That was just one more thing they needed to discuss. He leaned down and kissed her forehead.

"I won't be home for dinner tonight. I'll get something at Maybell's Restaurant."

"Good."

"Think you'll miss me?"

She snorted. "Miss you my as..."

Never one to pass up an opportunity, he seized the moment and kissed her, plunging his tongue into her mouth. Just when he was beginning to enjoy her taste, she bit down with just enough force to hold him captive. He tried to pull back but she wouldn't turn loose. Thank God she didn't draw blood. She fluttered her eyes at him.

The vixen was asking for it. And he was here to oblige. With both hands he grabbed her buttocks, squeezed, and jerked her against him. She shrieked in rage. His tongue escaped unharmed.

On the way out the door, he flashed a grin. "Don't wait up for me, darlin'. I'll wake you when I come to bed."

Her screech of fury followed him out the door.

Chapter Seven

Royce was tired to the bone. He'd broken up two fights between wranglers, and put one of the cowboys in jail for shooting the poker dealer at Cotton's Saloon. On top of that, he was covered with dirt from lending a hand to old Jeb Mason who was driving his straggling steers off Clay Street and out to where his herd was grazing. Tomorrow he'd have to hand Jeb a bill for the damage his steers had done to the buildings. The scared cattle had bumped porch posts, causing the roofs to collapse.

He curried Samson and turned him into the pasture to forage until morning. The night was too nice for the animal to be cooped-up in the barn. It wouldn't be long until he'd have to find a horse for Garrett. When he'd decided to build on the edge of town, he'd bought as much acreage as possible. Horses need space to run, and at the time, he'd hoped he and Pearl would have several children needing horses. Many hopes died the day Pearl disappeared.

The memory of kissing Texanna after dinner made him smile. She was a gutsy woman. He admired that about her. Four years ago, he wouldn't have grabbed Pearl's butt as he'd done today. She would have died of embarrassment and said, "Royce, it's the middle of the day!" But then again, she wouldn't have avoided his kiss. This woman, who looked so much like his Pearl, was as different from her as night and day. Look at the way she'd handled his guns. Yes, she was definitely changed, and he was anxious for them to have time alone to talk.

He carried the round tin tub in from the back porch to the kitchen. Ah, Texanna remembered to fill the reservoir so he had warm water to bath. He sank into the tub with a sigh of pure enjoyment. Soon he'd order a real bathtub. One you could lean back in and soak. Maybe they could find a place in the house where they didn't have to move it around, some place close to the kitchen and hot water. He'd put in a wood stove so they wouldn't freeze in the winter.

Had Texanna taken a bath tonight? He bet so, and his body tightened at the thought of her sweet smell. Anxious to get to bed, he scrubbed the soap in his hair into lather and washed his body. With the extra bucket of water, he rinsed his hair, and with his hands wiped out the excess water. He dried off and tied the towel around his waist.

Royce emptied the tub and stood it up to dry on the back porch. The oil lamp from the kitchen cast just enough light for him to see the clothesline stretched from one porch post to another. A couple of items hung there and swayed in the light breeze. He couldn't figure out what they were. Curious, he took the objects down and into the kitchen to inspect them in the light. Both were pink, soft, and silky, and when he held them before the lamp he could see right through them. He rubbed the material between his fingers to feel their softness. One item looked like it might be a hair net of some kind, but it had three openings, one bigger than the other two. He dropped it and picked up the other article. Solid lace, it had boning in it to form a fullness shaped to fit... He shook his head. Nah, it couldn't be. Turning it this way and that, he finally figured out how to connect the small hooks and eyes.

This time when he held it up there was no mistaking what it was shaped to fit. Breasts...it was the perfect size for Texanna's small and shapely breasts. It looked like a corset that had been cut up. His heart thundered with trepidation as he turned his attention to the other garment. When he held it up by the larger opening, his mouth went dry. Oh my God, no. If this was what he suspected, a pair of pantaloons, they were even more indecent than the upper thing. They would barely cover her private parts. Texanna wore French underwear. Only whores wore the scandalous stuff. Hell, he wasn't an expert, but he didn't think even they wore anything this skimpy.

Had she been forced to work in a brothel? Forced? He knew some women chose the life, women like Josephine who owned a well-run business. But, he couldn't see Pearl or Texanna making such a choice willingly. Was it shame that made her flee two weeks ago?

Garments crushed tightly in his fist, he took the oil lamp and walked upstairs. His chest drawer rasped as he pulled it open. He stuffed Texanna's things back behind his long johns. Tossing the damp towel in the corner, he blew out the lamp and climbed into bed. What if someone had ridden around back in the morning before Texanna had brought her French underwear inside? He couldn't imagine explaining its presence to anyone.

He beat his pillow into a comfortable lump, turned on his side, and tried to relax. God, he was bone tired, but he couldn't get that underwear out of his head. To his consternation and growing discomfort, he imagined Texanna wearing them. Dammit, the woman would be the death of him.

The thought of her or Pearl working in a brothel weighed heavy on his mind. As farfetched as the whole idea sounded, he'd much rather believe in time-travel than learn either woman had been abused.

The softness of the bed felt like heaven, yet he

couldn't close his eyes. Moonlight cast shadows on the ceiling. Their movement from the breeze kept rhythm with the thoughts beating around in his head. The silhouettes appeared as mysterious as this entire situation. Lightening flashed across the sky, illuminating the room for a second. In its wake, the rumble of thunder sounded in the distance. Hopefully, they'd get a little rain before morning. His eyes grew heavy and he drifted into sleep.

The sound of cannon fire woke him. He was suffocating. Gun smoke mingled with the stench of death. Fear filled him, choking him. Bodies, mostly in gray, littered the ground. The realization that he'd contributed to the horrific scene filled him with loathing and self-hatred. That it was his job as a union spy didn't ease his abhorrence. Nothing could. They were his Southern brothers. He'd intercepted the Reb's battle route and led the Union Army to cut them off. His soul would suffer until death.

****

Texanna heard Royce thrashing about next door. He groaned and coughed. She started to get up to see if he needed help, but heard him laugh. Must be a nice dream she thought. She lay back down. He was talking to someone, though she couldn't hear their words. She'd almost dozed off when the bellow of "Nooooo," echoed through the house.

Before she could move, she heard the patter of bare feet on the wood floors and Garrett's voice soothing his father. "Pa, Pa, wake up, Pa. You was dreamin' again."

Through the walls she heard Royce groan. "Sorry, Son. I'll be okay now. Get on back to bed."

"Can I sleep with you awhile? Promise I won't squirm around."

Royce chuckled. "Sure thing. Close the door and crawl in." For just a minute she heard the murmur of Royce's deep voice and Garrett's giggle. Then they were quiet.

****

It seemed like just minutes later when Texanna heard Royce moving around the room next door. Darn, it was barely light out, but she got up and pulled on the lightweight robe she'd found yesterday. Barefoot, she went down stairs to get her underwear. It was gone from the line on the porch. There was only one person who'd know where they were.

Royce, buttoning his shirt, walked into the kitchen and grabbed the coffee pot. "Come here. I want to show you how to make coffee."

"I know how to make coffee. With a Mr. Coffee." She almost laughed at the look on his face.

"Well, I'm *your* Mr. Coffee so come here and pay attention."

"I want to know where—"

"Come here and watch." He grabbed her around the waist and pulled her to the sink.

"Okay, okay." She'd watch, but then he'd better have some answers.

"Fill the pot with water up to here." He showed her a line formed from mineral deposits. "Then add a huge scoop of coffee and some egg shells." He reached into a bowl in the cabinet of the Hoosier and gathered a small handful. "Every time you use an egg, wash the shell and put it in that bowl." He crushed them, and then dropped them into the pot. He stoked the fire, added wood, and closed the door. "Now, when the coffee starts boiling, let it boil a couple of minutes, and then move it from the flat iron. That way the coffee won't taste burned."

Texanna nodded. She could do that. "Okay, I think I can do that." Stepping back from the stove, she crossed her arms under her breasts and asked, "Now, where's my underwear?"

The face that had been smiling sobered. "What

are you talking about? Do you mean those unmentionables you left hanging on the porch for anyone to come along and see?"

"Those would be the ones."

"I burned them. They're indecent."

She wanted to screech like a banshee but kept her voice down. "You're lying. Where are they? They're all I've got to put on."

"You have a drawer full of bloomers and chemises upstairs in the wardrobe."

"I want my underwear, not those tacky things in the drawer upstairs."

"They're not decent. You're not going to wear them again."

"Well, I'm sure as hell not going to wear those ugly things upstairs. I'll go bare-assed first!"

"Now see here, woman. That's no way for a lady to talk."

"Who said I was a lady?"

Royce's face turned red. He was ready to blow. To avoid his anger, she turned and ran upstairs to get dressed.

****

Texanna stood at the stove scrambling eggs—one thing she was able to cook. Frying ham hadn't been a problem but no way would she try to make biscuits. Royce had them ready to put in the oven by the time she was dressed and downstairs. The look he'd given her when she returned was one of fury. His face wasn't red any longer, but the few words he'd muttered had been through clenched teeth.

Garrett came in with a bucket of milk, face freshly scrubbed and smiling. "Morning, Texanna."

"Good morning to you. You've already milked the cow? Wow, you must be a lot of help around here."

Garrett's chest puffed out, and he stood a little taller. "Yes, ma'am, my pa started teaching me when

I was young. Wants me to be responsible."

"Sounds like your pa is a smart man and a good father."

Royce flashed a glare that asked, *what're you trying to pull?* He took the pail and strained the milk into a crockery pitcher. She dished up the eggs and ham and placed them on the table.

Royce's biscuits weren't as good as Matthew's but a heck of a lot better than what Texanna could have put together. "The biscuits are good."

"Thank you. So are the eggs."

She grimaced at the first swallow of coffee. No wonder Pearl had put cream and sugar in it. That was probably the only way she could drink the stuff. When she started making it, she'd make it less strong. Both Royce and Garrett drank milk with their meal, but after breakfast, Royce remained at the table drinking coffee. Garrett took the scraps out to the chickens while Texanna washed dishes. Royce stood, grabbed a dishtowel, and started drying plates.

"Thank you."

"You're welcome."

When everything was put away, Royce and Garrett walked over to Mrs. Farley's. The roof of her house sat a good distance away but was visible through the trees.

Texanna sat in a rocker on the front porch with her coffee. It was early enough to still be cool—maybe seventy-five degrees but the temperature would rise quickly. She closed her eyes to the sun and thought of Pearl sitting here in this very rocker, just as she was today. What did she think about back then? Probably about her child, what to fix her husband for dinner, or she may have even liked poetry back then. One of the quotes from Pearl's book came to mind.

Accept the things to which fate binds you...

The fact she was here in 1880 still amazed Texanna. She was on land that in 2008 was probably a commercial building, a parking lot, or possibly houses built in the thirties and forties. Nothing seemed real—it felt like a dream. One in which she'd wake at any moment and find herself back in her apartment in San Antonio—her air-conditioned apartment. The thought of being stuck in this time period made her panic. Her heart raced, and she closed her eyes to will the worry away. What would she do if she had to remain in this century forever? Would she make the most of what life had given her? Marry and have a family like Pearl had done?

She heard the back screen door creak as Royce entered the house. A minute later his footsteps echoed through the hall as he approached the front porch. It was a reassuring sound and eased her panic somewhat. He came outside with his coffee and sat in the rocker beside her. As he'd done the past two days, he wore a starched white shirt. It enhanced his dark good looks. Her stomach flipped and felt fluttery. The whiff of bay rum that drifted her way on the light breeze just fed the fire.

"Where's Garrett?"

"He's with Aggie for the day. He's used to staying with her and you need time to settle in."

She nodded and they sat quietly, enjoying the peaceful morning. The grass was tall in the area around the yard. His horses and cow had plenty to munch on since Royce didn't farm his land. It was late June and the grass was dry and brittle.

"Did you talk with Garrett this morning?"

He nodded.

Her heart skipped a beat. "What did you tell him?"

"That you might be his mother, but you're so different I'm not sure. I told him you'd lost your memory. He cried, but I think he understands."

Oh, the poor kid. And it wasn't the truth. She should've talked to Royce sooner, before he'd talked to Garrett. Anger and hurt brought tears to her eyes.

Her voice was thick. "That's not the truth and when he learns that, it'll just be harder on him. You should've let me talk to you first."

He didn't answer for a minute, just drank his coffee and looked out across the fields. Finally he said, "Then what is the truth?"

Okay, this is it. This is what she'd come here to do. She breathed deeply to control her fragile emotions. Talk to Royce and tell him everything. She cast sideways glances at him, anxious as to how he would react. Would he believe her?

"Texanna, you better get started. I have to leave here after the noon meal."

"Okay, just a minute more." The early morning light painted the white house and porch with a rosy glow. Royce looked relaxed but sober, waiting to hear what she had to say.

"Please understand. This is hard for me. Especially since I never believed I'd be sitting here today. I know you don't believe in time-travel. You think I'm crazy and have concocted some elaborate scheme. To do what, I don't have a clue." He tensed and looked at her with one eyebrow raised. "I understand your distrust, your disbelief."

"Do you?"

"Of course. If circumstance were reversed, I'd feel the same way. When Pearl mentioned time-travel to me, I thought she'd lost her mind. I got on that train over two weeks ago just to pacify her." Now that the time had come for their talk, she'd give anything if someone stopped by to postpone it—one of his brothers, a stray cow, a rabid dog—anything or anybody.

She sighed. "My neighbor and dear friend, Pearlina Baines, was born in 1854. In 1872, at the age of eighteen, she married Royce Dyson. Their son Garrett was born in 1873. When the child was born, you presented her with this locket. Garrett's picture was added when he was two years old."

Royce's eyes watched her closely. At the mention of the locket, his eyes focused where it lay against her breasts. Feeling his gaze, flustered, Texanna covered it with her hand. "I don't know what she was like as a young woman, but the woman I knew was a tough old broad."

Just thinking about Pearl made Texanna grin. Royce's mouth twitched but didn't lift in a smile. "From her letters, you know how she lived out her life. I know it's hard to believe she traveled forward in time. I don't know if my father or mother knew. The only people I think she trusted with her past were her husband, John Thompson, and her friend and housekeeper, Pauline." She had his full attention, he watched her intently.

"In 1940, when she accepted the fact she was stuck in the twentieth century, she married but never had any children. By the time I was born, she was a widow living alone in a big house with Pauline and her paints."

She couldn't help but remember the first time she'd found her way into Pearl's studio. "Pearl visited us from time to time, but other than her church activities, she mostly stayed to herself." The wide expanse of glass windows fascinated Texanna. "One day, I knocked on the back door and said I wanted to see the glass room." She smiled at the memory. They'd had teacakes and lemonade. "That day I began art lessons. Pearl was my teacher."

By now Royce was leaning against a porch pillar, his back to her. "I am *your* Pearl's next door neighbor. I'm the child she didn't have, someone for her to love and dote on."

She watched Royce's rigid back. He didn't move

a muscle. "Pearl sent me so you'd know she didn't abandon you and Garrett and wasn't killed in some horrible way. She wanted to set you free to go on with your life."

He whirled around to face her. "You expect me to believe you traveled back in time to give me this message?"

"Yes, but I also—"

Curses spewed from his mouth. "Give me some proof. I want proof."

"What about my shoes and clothes?" She stood up and with her finger punched him in the chest. "And my underwear? I still want it back."

"It's indecent. No woman but a whore would wear such." He grabbed her shoulders and forced her to look up at him. "Have you been working in a brothel? Did someone kidnap you and force you into that type of slavery?"

Texanna was shocked speechless. Furious, she tried to knee him in the groin. When he jumped back she smacked him across the face before he had a chance to deflect her blow. "You think I'd work in a brothel? Why would you think such a stupid thing?"

He swore and muttered. "That damn French underwear. What do you expect? No decent woman would wear such skimpy unmentionables."

"In 2008, all women wear underwear like mine. And they swim and sunbathe in public places in bathing suits that look much like *my* underwear."

If the situation weren't so serious, she would have laughed at the look on his face. His mouth opened and closed trying to say something. He was so red in the face she thought he might explode at any minute.

Finally, he bit out, "I don't believe you. No lady would go out in something so shocking."

"Well, I'm not a lady, at least that's what I thought we'd agreed upon in the kitchen."

His eyebrows furrowed, and he looked at her breasts. Why, the man was straining to see if she wore a chemise. She backed away from him. His eyes flashed up to hers. She turned and dashed into the house. He was on her before she made it through the door. Turning her in his arms, he locked hers down by her sides. Pressed against his chest, his forehead touched hers.

"Don't do it, Royce. I'm warning you." His hand grasped a handful of her skirt and gathered until she felt air on her bottom. Tears pricked her eyes. "Please, don't do this."

His big, warm hand cupped her bare buttock—her flesh quivered, his touch evoking feelings foreign to her. At her body's response, his hand stilled, and then he groaned low in his throat and covered her mouth with his. Unable to resist, she returned the kiss, clutched his waist, and pressed her body into his.

Texanna was melting, her body screamed for more of this man's touch. And she wanted to touch him in return—reach inside his shirt and run her fingers through the hair on his chest, feel the muscles of his back and his taut butt.

So, this is what it's all about—the fire that ignites between two people. She shoved at his chest. "Stop. We can't do this."

He froze and moved his hand to her head and held it to his chest. Voice hoarse, he rasped. "Why, Texanna? Tell me why." He forced her to look at him. "You want me too, I know you do." He planted soft kisses on her cheeks, her lips, and under her jaw. "Say it."

She swiped at the tears on her cheeks and cried. "Yes! I do. You're the only man who's ever made me feel this way, but it can't happen."

"Give me a reason, dammit."

"Because I'm not your wife, and you don't love

me."

His face buried in her hair, he spoke softly in her ear. "You could be my wife. I need proof you're not. You're so like her, yet so different." He yanked her head back and fixed her with a stare. "What does it matter anyhow? In a brothel, one customer is as good as another."

Blood pounded in her head, and flashes of light danced in front of her eyes. Shrieking like a mad woman, she struck out at him with both hands. Faster this time, he caught both fists and shoved her back, not releasing her hands.

"Stop it. You're acting like a child."

She jerked free and batted at the tears on her face. "The only proof I have I'm not your wife or a whore is the fact I've never been with a man. I may not be a lady, but I'm a virgin."

Holding in her sobs, she moved toward the door, and then turned back toward him. "Stay the hell away from me."

Chapter Eight

Royce sat on the front porch pondering Texanna's words. Her declaration left him flabbergasted, and he'd been unable to come up with a rebuttal. Was it possible Texanna was a virgin?

He shook his head. No, time-travel wasn't possible. It had to be a made-up story, fiction like that book by Jules Verne, *Journey to the Center of the Earth*. That's what Royce wanted to believe, but doubts worried him. If folks thought he'd even considered her tale, they'd think him crazy as a loon. What scared him the most was her cock and bull story began to make sense.

Ah, hell. Sitting here worrying about it wasn't going to change things. He stood and started for the door when he noticed the book on the table between the rockers. The title read *Early History of Waco, Texas 1837-1955*. His eyes must be playing tricks on him. He picked it up and flipped it open to read the publishing date—1962.

Legs feeling like rubber, he eased down into a rocker. The book could be a fake. It wouldn't take much to put the wrong date in a book. He ran his finger over the dates on the cover, noting the frayed edges of the book.

Heart hammering in his chest, he sat the book in his lap and let it fall open to a place marked with a photograph. He picked it up and immediately noticed it was clearer and sharper than the tintypes he'd seen. A man and woman stood together, his arm around her shoulders. She wore a two-piece suit with the skirt hitting just below her knees. Her hair was short like Texanna's and curled around her face. A hat with a feather sat cockily on her head. She looked amazingly like Texanna, but with a fuller figure. Even the smile on her face was similar. He turned the picture over. Written in ink were the words—*John Thompson and Pearlina Baines Dyson on the courthouse steps on their wedding day, September 21, 1940.*

Hands shaking, he turned to another section marked with one more likeness. An older woman, her pink scalp showing through her thin white hair, sat in a high-backed chair in front of a fireplace. Though wrinkled, her pale face had added color with paint on her cheeks and lips. His stomach clenched in alarm. The blue eyes that stared out of the photograph were Pearl's.

****

With the book tucked under his arm, Royce ambled into the kitchen where Texanna stood looking through a cookbook. Her back was to him, and she didn't turn. From the square set of her shoulders, he knew she was still upset. He suspected she'd been crying, which made him feel lower than a skunk.

He cleared his throat. "I'm sorry for those things I said. This crazy situation has got me flummoxed."

She turned and nodded. "I can understand that."

"I found this on the porch." Her eyes followed his hand as he laid the book on the table. "Saw the pictures, but I'm not ready to believe my eyes. My mind just can't grasp it." He pulled out a chair and sat down.

"I need to tell you something else."

Royce propped his elbows on the table and clasped his hands. "Oh, Lord. What now?"

Her expression was sympathetic. He saw a glitter of tears in her eyes. "When I returned to my time, Pearl had passed on. We buried her two days later."

He didn't know what to say, how to respond, or how to feel. A month ago, before Texanna's arrival, if Pearl's body had been found, he'd have known how to grieve. Her death was a fact he'd lived with for four years. But this was different. If the woman in the picture was his wife, how could he deal with it?

Texanna asked. "Did you look through the book and find the pictures of you and Garrett?"

"No." He stood shoving his chair back. "I didn't get past the pictures of Pearl...the pictures of the woman." He couldn't deal with anymore right now. He wasn't sure which was worse, accepting Texanna's story of time-travel or thinking the woman in those pictures might be Pearl.

Grasping to change the subject, he muttered. "You want to take those guns out back and give 'um a try? See if you're as good a shot as you claim?"

"Really?" Her eyes rounded with hope.

"Sure, why not?"

"What about lunch? You need to eat before you leave."

"I'll help you throw something together when we finish, then you can ride into town with me."

"You mean it?"

"Of course I mean it. Find a hat and some gloves while I fetch the guns." He looked at her skirt. "And put on your riding skirt and a chemise. You can't go into town with nothing under that blouse."

Her chin raised an inch, and for a minute he thought she'd decline his invitation. Then she turned and walked ahead of him to the stairs.

"If you don't want to have chapped legs, you better put on those bloomers."

At his statement, her step faltered, but she continued up the stairs. His eyes locked on the movement of her hips and rounded butt, and he couldn't keep from noticing she had a fine-looking rear end.

He stood at the back door with the Remington and the Colt, cartridges for each in his pockets. A feed sack filled with empty cans sat by his feet. Since he and Garrett had been alone, many of their meals came from tin cans. They'd stacked them in a box on the porch.

Texanna flew into the kitchen in a whirl of red hair, gloves and hat in her hand. Her face was rosy from rushing, and her blue eyes danced with excitement. She was so naturally beautiful, and her cocky attitude enhanced it. He could only stare and soak up the warmth she radiated.

Her smile faded. "What's wrong? I put on that tacky underwear if that's what's bothering you."

"Just lost in thought there a minute. Let's go."

Royce made sure the horses and the cow weren't in the line of fire and set five cans in a row about twenty-five yards from where he and Texanna took up position. He handed her the Colt and six cartridges and watched her load the Peacemaker.

"Alright, let's see if you can hit one of those cans. Remember, it's gonna have a hearty kick."

She nodded and took aim using her left arm for a brace. When she fired, the can popped into the air, and she stumbled back several steps. He reached out to catch her before she fell.

Laughing, she grinned. "Wow! That was awesome."

"You did good."

"Thanks. Piece of cake."

"You want cake?"

She chuckled. "Uh, no, that's just an expression. It means that was easy. You know, a piece of cake."

"Uh, huh." No, he didn't understand, but decided to drop the subject. "You want to shoot the rest of those cans or move on to the Winchester?"

"I think once is enough with the Colt." She removed the remaining cartridges and dropped them in his hand before handing him the firearm.

He took the Colt and handed her the Remington Repeating Rifle. She loaded the rifle with ease and sat it on her hip, barrel facing skyward until he returned from moving the cans farther back. When he returned, she lifted the rifle to her shoulder and fired. From fifty yards, she hit all five cans and immediately turned the barrel skyward. Someone had taught her well. Not only was she a good shot, she was careful.

"Who taught you to shoot like that?"

"I learned in the 4-H club. By the time I entered high school, I was competing across the state with other kids my age."

"Hmm. What is this 4-H?"

"It's a club where kids learn all sorts of important skills like shooting, judging animals for competition, cooking, sewing, and archery to name a few."

"Guess you didn't take to the cooking and sewing part, huh?"

She shrugged and blushed. "Didn't interest me."

"Why don't you take the guns up to the house while I saddle the horses? Put some ham on those leftover biscuits. We'll eat along the way." For once she didn't argue. "And bring my jacket and shotgun on your way out."

He had Samson and Josie saddled by the time Texanna returned, her stride long and purposeful as she walked to the barn. The gun belt, holding the Colt, riding her shapely hips was hard to miss. She'd tied their lunch in a dishcloth. Reins in his hand, he met her halfway.

She handed him his jacket and waited until he had it on before turning over the shotgun. When he had it securely in his scabbard, he turned and looked down at the belt riding low on her hips, a tad too low. It needed more holes punched. He'd add them for her another time, find her a more suitable pistol, and she could wear it when she rode out to see Matthew.

"You are not wearing that gun to town." He saw that mulish look on her face.

"Why not? You're loaded down with them. And don't think I didn't notice that .32 revolver in your boot, either."

"How observant of you. Did you notice the Bowie knife in my other boot?" Aha, he'd gotten her there. "I am the Marshal of Waco, you know. I'm expected to be armed."

"Yeah, well, I know that, but there might be a time when I need to protect your back. I want to be prepared."

"Thunderation! I'm the protector here. There will never come a time when you need to watch my back. That's what my deputies are for. Give me that damn gun belt or get in the house." His wife or not, she wasn't going into town looking like a gunfighter.

She started to argue, then bit her lip and removed the belt. On his way back from the house, two canteens slung over his shoulder, his step faltered as realization hit him. He'd never used foul language around Pearl, but in the past three days, Texanna had him spouting all sorts of obscenities—hell, damnation, and no telling what else. That had to stop. Though she irritated the hell out of him at times, she was a woman and deserved his respect.

They rode at a leisurely pace, munching on their biscuit sandwiches. Texanna's eyes were alert as she took note of her surroundings, seemingly seeing it for the first time. They passed Aggie's house, sitting a half-mile off the road. Her dog, Pepper, came down the lane at a run. Royce tossed him a bite of ham.

"How far are we from town?"

"About two miles from the court house. Actually, we're on the outskirts. I wouldn't be surprised if in a year or two more houses spring up around us. Town keeps spreading in all four directions." He'd already begun to wonder if he'd bought too close in. At least he'd had the foresight to buy fifty acres.

Texanna continued to watch the passing countryside but from time to time would cast sideways glances his way. The third time, he muttered. "What is it? What'da you want to ask?"

"Why do you wear a coat everyday? It's hot out here. And what about those white shirts? You don't expect me to wash and iron them, do you?"

"I wear a coat because it's expected of me."

"By who?"

"The city council. And don't worry about the shirts. I take them to the Chinese laundry in town."

"Whew! What a relief. I was afraid you'd expect me to wash and iron them. I'd hate for you to have to wear scorched shirts."

Yeah, well, he'd hate it too. So, ironing was something else she didn't remember how to do, or maybe he should say hadn't learned. Hell, these were skills all young girls in this neck of the woods were taught early in life. How could she have grown up without learning how to do home chores?

"You do have to wash the sheets and the rest of our clothes."

"They may not look good the first time or two until I get the hang of it." He'd never expect perfection, and he bet she'd do just fine.

"Royce, how can you afford a house like yours on a marshal's pay?"

His house did look better than most with its wide porch and second story. He'd built it, with the help of Matthew and Jason, during his spare time, often working past dark. It had been a labor of love for his soon-to-be wife, Pearl.

Before this morning he'd have wanted her to say *our* house, but after seeing the pictures, he felt pretty sure she wasn't Pearl. Until he figured out what to do, they'd have to keep up the pretense.

"Jason and I own part of the farm. Matthew pays us a small percentage of what the farm produces in return for using our sections. My pay as marshal is more than enough for us to live on." And what they didn't need they banked for hard times. He wanted Garrett to get a college education if the boy wanted one.

"And from time to time you sell a painting."

"Really?" She looked surprised.

"Folks around here love your portraits. They press you to do a painting of their kids or their families."

A smile hung on the edges of her mouth. He wondered what was going on in that head of hers.

"How about Aggie? How does she manage?"

"She has her house and a garden in the summer. It always produces well, so she puts up vegetables, pickles, fruit, and chow-chow for the winter. And folks around here help her out. We take turns making sure she has firewood and help with any repairs needing done."

"That's good. I'm glad. You're a nice man, Royce Dyson."

He couldn't respond. What could he say? What kind of man wouldn't help out a widow in need? People took care of each other when times were hard. But her comment touched him and pierced the sturdy shield around his heart.

He coughed to clear the emotion that had a hold on his throat. "For the rest of the summer, I'd like for Garrett to visit Aggie from time to time. That way she won't feel like she's accepting charity when I pay her what she's been used to making."

She nodded.

"It'll give you time to paint and learn how to cook and do laundry.

Her snort made him grin.

They rode quietly for a while. She watched him from the corner of her eye and appeared to be mulling something else over in her mind. Why couldn't she just spit it out? Before he could ask, she pulled Josie to a stop. He paused beside her, curious at the concern in her eyes.

"Ah, I...I heard you last night."

His jaw clenched. "Just what did you hear?" His nightmares were private and none of her business.

She studied her hands on the pommel. "I just heard a bunch of muttering and then you yelling, 'No," real loud." Her eyes lifted to his face. "Then Garrett woke you. I'm sorry, Royce. Were you in the war? Does it still haunt you?"

He couldn't keep the anger from his voice. "It's none of your concern, so forget it."

Her hurt expression shamed him, but he wouldn't go baring his soul to this woman. "Anything else you want to know?"

Shoulders rigid, she spat. "No, nothing that's any of my business, that is." She kicked Josie into a trot, and he stayed behind and let her lead.

When they neared town, he drew up alongside of her. "I'm sorry for being surly."

"No problem. I assume I'll adjust."

Damn, she wouldn't let him off the hook easily. Fine with him. He sure as hell wasn't going to walk on eggshells around her. He'd say his mind like he'd always done, and she'd better get used to it.

As soon as they reached the center of town, the sidewalks began to fill. Hats were lifted, hands waved, and greetings shouted.

Sam Howard left his barbershop and headed for the hardware store across the street. "Howdy, Marshal. Ma'am. I'm needin' to buy a new broom today."

Royce shook his head as folks poured from the hardware store, the feed store, and Maybell's to greet Texanna. As gracious as a queen, she replied to their many questions. Her responses were perfect and left them smiling.

****

Texanna felt like she'd been plunged into a history book. Dirt streets, false front buildings, and the clothes. When she'd stepped off the train, she'd been too shocked to take in much of the surroundings. Now she couldn't wait to see every inch of the town. Then the people filed out to greet her, and the buildings and landmarks faded into the background. Tears pricked her eyes at the warmth of these nice people. Oh, how Pearl would have loved this welcome.

Then the First National Bank of Waco loomed before them. The bank was a two-story building. It sat on a corner, and the street that ran alongside was narrow. She reached out and touched Royce's leg. He looked at her in response.

"I'd like to see the First National Bank of Waco."

"We just passed it."

"I know, but I'd like to go inside and look around."

"We don't bank there, Texanna. Why would you want to go inside?"

Good question. Why did she want to when the shoot-out after the bank robbery would take place on the side street by the bank? It was important to check all angles and positions. "I'm interested in the architecture. I might want to do a painting with it in the background."

He gave her an odd look but didn't ask questions. "Maybe Jason can take you over to look around."

"That'd be great. I'd like to see the store, too.

And the library."

"Do you need something at the store? Charge anything you need."

Yes, she needed some things, but she didn't think the store carried the items. Underwear would be nice. She'd buy "grannie panties" and not complain.

"No. I just want to explore." And get the lay of the land.

They stopped in front of the jail. Somehow word had preceded them, and a small crowd blocked the hitching post.

Royce said, "'Scuse us, folks." They parted so he could tie his horse.

Texanna started to jump down but decided to wait and see what was considered proper dismounting etiquette. With a hand on Josie's hindquarter, Royce moved around the horse and helped her down.

"Welcome home, Pearl," said a young woman with a toddler on her hip.

"Howdy, Pearlina. Glad you're home."

Smiles and words of encouragement echoed around her.

"Be sure and come to the quilting bee Monday."

She stumbled, and Royce caught her arm before she fell. Voice thick with emotion, she said, "Thank you all for the warm welcome."

These good people were Pearl's friends and neighbors. What would they think if they knew the truth, and how would they react when she disappeared again? More importantly, what would Royce think? Surely Pearl thought about the repercussions before hatching her plan? Maybe she thought Royce would accept her message at face value so Texanna could return home without complications. No, that wasn't right.

"Are you all right?" His breath was warm on her

ear.

Texanna flashed him a smile and hoped he didn't notice her tears. "I'm fine."

They stepped inside the jail's front office. A deputy jumped to his feet. "Howdy, ma'am. It's sure good to see you."

"Hi, Pete."

He eased his tall, lanky frame around the desk to shake her hand. She had to crane her neck to look him in the face. His dark eyes twinkled. "Glad you came back."

A snort came from the other side of the room, and she turned to see a young man walk toward her. In his early twenties, Jason was a younger version of Royce, yet his self-confidence made him appear older. His hair was dark, but not black, and his eyes were brown. Right now they were crackling with humor.

His good spirits were confusing considering he'd told her never to come back. Before she could respond, he grabbed her around the waist and swung her around the room. When he sat her feet on the ground, he held her close a minute and whispered in her ear. "I'm glad you returned. I don't know why, but I think helping you leave was a mistake."

Texanna was relieved he felt that way. She didn't want him to think she was Pearl, but then again, she didn't want him to be filled with remorse for the rest of his life.

Royce untangled her from Jason's arms. "What are you whispering in my wife's ear, runt?"

"Runt? Who're you calling runt, old man?" Jason pummeled Royce on the arm, and, before he'd gotten in his second punch, Royce caught him around the neck. Both men were laughing when they broke apart. "I told her since she's home maybe you'd be decent company."

"Don't count on it."

Texanna enjoyed the warm exchange between the two. She was glad Royce wasn't holding a grudge against Jason for helping her leave.

He turned to Jason. "Texanna wants to tour the First National Bank, the store, and the library. Think you can do that and see her home?"

"I can get home by myself. Jason has better things to do."

Royce cupped her chin. "Don't argue with me on this." His blue eyes flicked to her lips, and for a second she saw heat blaze there. Unwillingly, her body responded, and she stepped back to cover her confusion.

"Alright. We'll stop and get Garrett on the way." She knew how and when to choose her battles, and this one was of little importance. He wouldn't like it if she defied him in front of his deputies.

Jason strapped on his gun belt and grabbed his hat. "I'll have her home by six o'clock."

Royce cocked an eyebrow at his brother. "Why so early?"

Jason blushed. "I'm seeing Sally tonight."

Royce frowned and shook his head. "If you marry that girl, you'll regret it. She's too mule-headed to make a good wife."

Texanna gasped and turned on Royce. "What a male chauvinistic thing to say."

All three men stared at her. She sputtered. "You know, macho, machismo." She pounded her chest and called out, "Ohooo, uh oh, oh, ooh. You Tarzan, me Jane." She stomped her foot. "Bossy, bull-headed, know-it-all men."

Royce cleared his throat, "Well, uh..."

Texanna grabbed Jason's arm. "Let's go."

****

The First National Bank of Waco occupied the corner of Austin Avenue and Fourth Street with

Miller's Hardware across Fourth. Both possessed a steady flow of traffic, as did the barbershop facing the bank. The McLelland Hotel took up the corner on the diagonal block.

When they walked into the bank, a clerk jumped up from his desk near the entrance and started toward them. Jason raised his hand. "Keep your seat, Hershel. Texanna wants to look at the architecture for one of her paintings."

The young man approached anyway. "Well, that's fine, ma'am. Just take your time. We're honored you are interested."

Since the bank building was narrow and deep, the main entrance was on the corner, and another opened onto Fourth Street. Texanna wondered if there was a back door. Yeah, there had to be.

"Excuse me," she glanced at the nameplate on his desk. "Mr. Brown, would it be possible to see the back?"

"Well, that's highly unusual. But, I don't guess we have to worry about the marshal's wife robbing the bank. Haw, haw, haw." Herschel's laugh came out like a donkey's bray.

As he led them back to the teller enclosure, she noticed the staircase along the back wall that led to the upper story. Behind the barrier where the tellers worked, she could see the vault and, yes, there was the back door.

She shook his hand. "Mr. Brown, thank you so much for showing me around. This is a beautiful building."

"You're very welcome."

Outside, Texanna looked up and down each street, making a mental note of where windows and doors were located. She didn't know anything about robbing banks, but could see the robbers would have a variety of places to station themselves until they struck. They could easily blend with the crowd and be harder to spot while making their escape.

Texanna flinched as a dog's pitiful yipping split the air. "My, God, what's happened? What's wrong with that dog?" She turned in the direction Jason faced.

He shook his head. "Bull Tate probably kicked the poor thing again. One of these days someone is going to see he gets a dose of his own medicine."

She stared at a large man's back as he walked farther away down the street. An ugly, long-haired dog, tail between its legs, followed a few feet behind. People moved aside to let the man pass. She shivered.

"We better get started home. You don't want to keep Sally waiting this evening."

Jason blushed. "What about the library? I thought you wanted to see it."

"I do, but it can wait until another time."

Texanna stopped at Aggie's to pick up Garrett. Obviously excited, Garrett talked non-stop to his uncle all the way to the house. The two of them groomed Josie. Then, after helping Garret milk the cow, Jason rode back to town.

Texanna fixed scrambled eggs to go with the ham and leftover biscuits. She needed to figure out something else to cook—their diet was becoming monotonous.

Garrett balked at having to take a bath two nights in a row and went to bed in a pout. It was hard to keep a straight face as he scowled and stomped up the stairs to bed. He looked so much like his daddy.

She sat at the kitchen table with a sketchpad and drew a diagram of Austin Avenue, Fourth Street, and the buildings on each corner. Her memory was good, and she felt she'd remembered the correct placement of windows and doors. All the buildings, except the bank and hotel, were one story.

Now, where was the best place to station herself? Pearl said Royce was shot in the back, which didn't make sense. The jail was up a block and on the opposite side of the street from the bank. From the description in the history book, the gunshot came from the corner of the hotel.

She chewed on the end of her pencil, thinking. Then horror overwhelmed her. Oh God. It wasn't the bank robbers who killed him. It was someone close to him, someone he knew and trusted, or someone with a grudge. Or worse yet, one of his own men. Her mind catalogued the people she'd met today. Would one of them prove to be a murderer?

Chapter Nine

Royce had washed, and with a towel around his middle, walked upstairs. He stepped softly down the hall to look in on Garrett. The boy was sprawled across the bed on his stomach, his nightshirt up around his knees. He was so beautiful, this child of his. His heart twisted when he saw Garrett and Texanna together. She was a natural at mothering, and Garrett was crazy about her. Their closeness made him long for her to treat him with the same affection. She could deny being his wife, but her fondness for Garrett was obvious.

He eased the door open to her room. As he placed the package he'd carried up under his arm on top of the bureau, a smile teased his lips. He couldn't wait to see her response to his gift. The store had been just about to close when he'd dashed in to make his purchase.

Back in his bedroom, he tossed the towel into a corner, started for the bed, and then froze. Should he put on a pair of drawers in case he had to get up and check on Garrett? It wouldn't do to shock Texanna. He reached into the chest to get a pair and touched Texanna's silky underwear. So soft and delicate, they were indecent, yet he'd love to see them on her. His chest wasn't the best hiding place. Tomorrow he'd find a better one.

He grinned and crawled into bed naked. Shocking her was so much fun. His humor vanished. Pearl had been modest and, before her disappearance, would have pretended to not notice his body, but not this woman. She'd most likely look at his bare ass and chew him out. The thought was arousing. He groaned and turned his head into the pillow. Lord, could his life get anymore complicated? His thoughts turned to the history book on top of the night table. He needed to face whatever was in it.

****

The sound of rustling next door woke Texanna.

Royce stuck his head in her door. "Get out of that bed, sleepy head. Today is Sunday, and church services start at ten o'clock."

Oh drat. She didn't want to go. Then she remembered her mission. Today she'd have an opportunity to watch people and see how they acted toward Royce. Maybe she'd spot whoever hated him enough to commit murder.

"There's a parcel for you on the chifforobe." He grinned and walked back into his room.

Curious, Texanna jumped out of bed and picked up the package. It was wrapped in brown paper tied up with string. Whatever was inside was soft.

She folded back the paper to reveal a blue dress, the color very close to her favorite, turquoise. It was the one she'd admired in the department store window while walking with Jason. "Oh, it's beautiful. How did you know?"

From the other room, he answered. "Jason told me it caught your eye yesterday."

His thoughtfulness touched her deeply. She slipped on a robe and walked next door. He stood at the mirror brushing his hair, the shirt pulling across his broad back as he raised his arms. She laid her cheek between his shoulder blades, wrapped her arms around his waist, and squeezed. "Thank you."

He froze, then sat the brush down and covered her hands with his to stroke her forearms. Voice gruff, he said, "You're welcome."

She suddenly realized her breasts were

flattened against his back and pulled away.

"Hurry and get dressed so we can have breakfast. Then you can try it on."

Downstairs she stoked the fire and put on the coffee, using a little more than half the amount of coffee Royce had used. Royce brought milk and meat in from the springhouse. She sliced the sausage and started frying patties. By the time Royce and Garrett were finished with the outdoor chores, she had the table set and the eggs ready to scramble.

She could hear Royce's deep voice as they walked from the barn, but not what he said. It sounded like laughter. As they neared the house, she heard Garrett's voice.

"But Pa, she made me take a bath two nights in a row. Ain't that a waste of water?"

"No, it's not, and it helps keep the sheets clean, so you mind her, you hear?"

"Yes, sir." His answer wasn't enthusiastic.

Royce's eyes were twinkling when they entered the kitchen.

She grinned and shrugged. "Wash up. Breakfast is ready."

They washed in the pan of hot soapy water at the sink.

"Everything looks good. Where'd you get the bread?"

"Jason and I stopped at the bakery yesterday, and I got a couple of loaves. I hope that's all right."

He took a bite and nodded. "Of course it is. I like toast, especially the way you fixed it."

"Yeah Texanna, it's good." Garrett had jelly smeared across his face.

Their compliments touched her. It was a first for her when it came to cooking. "I'm glad you both approve."

She watched as Royce sipped his coffee and looked from his cup to her. He raised an eyebrow.

"I made it weaker. Do you think it's awful?" Tasted ten times better to her but...

"It's good."

When they finished eating, Royce stood and covered the leftover toast and sausage with a dishtowel. "Let's get a move on." He helped Garrett put the food scraps on one plate and poured the sausage drippings on top.

Texanna hurried to finish in the kitchen, and then ran upstairs to try on the new dress. Since she didn't have a choice, she put on a chemise and bloomers. Lord they were ugly. She slipped on the skirt of the two-piece dress and found it a bit snug. It fell straight in front but the back was full, longer, and made of five panels, resembling un-gathered curtain valances. The bodice buttoned up to a v-neck with a wide collar and elbow-length puff sleeves.

She heard Royce coming upstairs so stepped out into the hall. "Look." She tugged on the bodice trying to get it to lay flat. "This dress doesn't fit me right." It was too large in the bust, and, at the waist, the facing for the buttons gaped some.

"Turn around and let me see." He looked her up and down, and then tugged on the bodice where it dipped low in the back. His eyes focused on the vicinity of her breasts. "You need a corset." His lips twitched before he turned.

She snorted. "I'll just wear something else."

Before she reached the chifforobe, he blocked her way and put his hands on her waist. "Please, wear this for me today. The color is so pretty on you."

Well, she didn't have anything else to wear. And he had asked nicely. "Alright, I'll put on the damned corset."

His face flushed with anger. "Watch your mouth. Garrett doesn't need to hear language like that coming from his mother."

"I am not—"

He gripped her chin, and his eyes bored into hers. "I don't want to hear it. Whether you are or not, he's crazy about you and thinks you hung the moon." His gaze dropped to her lips, and her tongue darted out to moisten them.

She pulled away and walked to the chifforobe. "You're right, of course. I usually only swear when I'm angry or scared. And since you're the only person to rouse those emotions in me..." But lately she'd been out of control. Shame coursed through her. She'd make a conscious effort to do better.

His hands caressed her shoulders, and he murmured into her hair. "I can understand the anger, but why on earth would you be afraid of me? I'd die before I hurt you."

Should she lie or tell him the truth? She chewed her bottom lip, and then made up her mind. "For one thing, the fact I'm standing here in 1880 is almost more than I can comprehend. That's scary as all get out." She paused, trying to decide whether or not to be honest with him. "You stir feelings in me that are foreign, and I have no right to feel."

"What feelings? Tell me." He turned her to face him.

Her bottom lip trembled, and she bit it to keep it still. "Desire so strong I want to make love to you. Kiss every inch of your gorgeous body." His blue eyes burned with a fire that caused Texanna's stomach to lurch and her heart to pound. "A first for me. You see, in my time period I'm considered odd because I'm still a virgin at twenty-two. Many women have had several lovers by that age. My last *fiancé* broke up with me because I wouldn't have sex with him."

His expression was unreadable, yet she thought she saw uncertainty in his eyes. He dropped his forehead to hers.

"I never wanted to share my heart and body

with anyone until I met you. But I don't belong in this time period, and I'll be leaving after the bank robbery. Plus, your feelings for me are confused with those you have for Pearl."

He pulled her close, his embrace so tight she could hardly breathe. But she didn't care, just hung on savoring each moment.

Voice thick, he said, "We need to hurry and finish dressing." He held her at arms' length for a moment, and then dropped his hands to his side.

****

"Pa, how do I look?"

The boy was growing as fast as a weed and already his new pants were a minute away from being too short. "You look fine, Son. You think you could sit up here and hold the reins while I get Texanna?"

"Sure, Pa. Tell her to hurry or we're gonna be late."

"I'll do that."

Texanna was walking down the stairs when he entered the hall. "You look beautiful." She flushed and smiled. "But, we need to find you a hat and a parasol."

Royce found a box of hairpins, and Texanna pinned her hair back and sat the straw bonnet with flowers on her head.

He tilted it to a better angle and added pins to hold it in place.

"I feel stupid in this hat."

"You look lovely, and it matches your dress."

She examined herself in the hall mirror. "Maybe."

He handed her a white parasol. "This will have to do. It's the only color that matches. Next time you're in town, pick up a new one."

As they walked to the buckboard, he looked to see how the dress fit. The corset had pushed her breasts up to fill out the bodice and it fit like a glove down to her waist.

"Wow, Texanna. You look purty."

She smiled at Garrett's compliment and curtsied. "Thank you kind sir. You look mighty handsome yourself. And what a fine carriage you're driving. I feel like Cinderella going to the ball."

"Who's Cinderella?"

"Oh, she's just a girl in a storybook. I'll tell you the story sometime."

"Hop in the back, Son."

"Aw, can't I sit up here?"

Texanna raised her shoulders. "It's fine with me."

"Okay, but be still."

She put her arm around Garrett and pulled him closer to her. "Give your father a little more room. He's a big man."

"You reckon I'll be as big when I'm growed up?"

Royce's lips twitched. "I expect so. Look how big Uncle Matthew is. You might take after him."

His eyes got big. "Yeah."

Royce looked up to see Texanna smiling at him, and his heart lurched. "You're mighty quiet."

"Because I'm doing good to breathe."

"That bad, huh?"

"Would you like to try wearing it for awhile so you can know firsthand?"

"I'll take your word for it," he said and laughed.

She snorted. "Chicken."

He shook his head. She was something else. Her confession this morning had humbled him. That she desired him soothed many hurts, yet raised more questions.

Women in 2008 have sex without marriage? It happened in this time too, and Doc delivered an eight-pound premature baby on occasion. The women at the brothels exchanged sex for money but didn't mingle with decent folks. He knew a couple of men who visited some of the widow ladies on a regular basis. Maybe their bodies plagued them for sex like a man's did. He didn't understand the physical needs of women that well. He knew before her disappearance Pearl had enjoyed the marriage bed, but he'd always felt she held back a part of herself.

His body flushed at the memory of Texanna's words earlier. "I want to kiss every inch of you." His body tightened, and he gritted his teeth to keep from groaning. The Pearl he knew would never have told him of her desire, much less act on it.

It was a puzzle. He didn't know what to think anymore. No one could make him believe time-travel was possible. But, maybe he was a fool. One thing for sure, this woman beside him was under his skin. His desire for her was totally different from what he'd experienced with Pearl. He'd adored her and treated her like a fragile flower. With Texanna, if they ever made love, there would be nothing delicate about their coming together. He sensed their passion would ignite like a flame. Already he dreaded the day she'd leave.

****

Royce pulled the buckboard to a stop before a white frame church with a tall steeple situated above the front door. People in their Sunday best mingled on the lawn as they made their way inside.

"Are we late?"

"Not yet." He lifted her from the buckboard.

Texanna smoothed the front of her dress and wished she could ease the flutters in her stomach the same way.

They hadn't made it quite past the door when people turned to look, and the room began to buzz.

Texanna felt her face heat. Royce ignored the congregation and directed her to a pew half way down the aisle. Garret slid in before her, and Royce sat at the end of the row. He stretched his arm across the back of the pew, laid his hand on the back of her neck, and gently squeezed the tendons. She glanced at him and saw him try to control the twitching of his lips. It was all she could do to keep from reaching over to pinch him. He was enjoying the spectacle they were making.

The preacher approached the podium carrying a well-worn Bible. He wore a three-piece suit as did many of the men in the room, and sweat beaded his brow. Why did the men dress so in this heat? Better yet, why was she tied up in this corset? She felt like a turkey ready for the oven. Most of the other women were decked out in similar outfits, but a few wore cooler, more comfortable dresses made of gingham checks and soft solids. It didn't look like they were wearing corsets either.

"Folks, let's everybody take a seat so we can get started."

The chatter quieted as people settled on the pews.

"Let us bow our heads in prayer. Heavenly Father, today is indeed a wonderful day. Not only did you send us beautiful weather, but you also returned Texanna to our flock. We thought you had called her home, that we'd never see her again. Thank you for this wonderful blessing. We are eternally grateful, Lord."

Amen's echoed around the room.

Texanna tried to scoot lower in the pew, but her body wouldn't bend. Royce squeezed her neck. He was going to pay for this. He could've warned her. She tried to catch his eye, but he refused to look at her.

"And you returned another to us, Lord, one who was lost but now is found. He lost faith in your love and mercy, his burden was heavy, and the weight bore him down. But you've lifted him up today, Lord, and we thank you. Welcome home, Royce, we've missed you, son."

Royce nodded.

The amens grew in volume and number.

The words hissed from the side of Texanna's mouth as she tried to whisper. "What is he talking about?"

"I haven't stepped foot in a church since I gave up the search for you three-and-a-half years ago."

Texanna closed her eyes in hopes darkness would help her not think about the agony Royce must have felt. And Pearl—did she lose her faith somewhere along the way? No, she'd been strong and faithful in her convictions all Texanna's life. Prior to that, she couldn't say.

"Jesus, let us learn from this situation. We don't always understand why tragedy strikes us, and we grieve and ask, 'Why, Lord, why me?" We fight against the restraints you put upon us and want problems to be resolved immediately," he pounded his chest, "on our schedule. Help us to remember, Lord, that your plan will be revealed to us in a matter of time. Amen."

The preacher's words reminded her of Pearl's note just before she died. What kind of special purpose could God have for her? If saving Royce's life was His goal, anyone could have come back and changed history—well, they could if they knew the secret of time-travel. *What are you thinking? They'd have to possess the magical stone in the locket.* You'd think God would have prepared her by seeing to it that she knew how to prepare something decent on that old iron cookstove.

A giggle escaped her lips to be nipped in the bud by the pinch of her corset, making her choke. She started coughing and gasped for air trying to stop. Royce looked at her with concern and pounded her on the back. If she didn't stop, the strings on the device choking her would snap and she'd bust out of this dress. With both arms, she hugged her waist.

Hell, this whole affair didn't make a lick of sense. Oh, shit...darn...here she was, after vowing to do better, cussing in church. *Forgive me, Lord.*

Chapter Ten

After the closing hymn, folks began to file from the pews. A crowd formed around them, greetings for Texanna coming from all directions. With his arm around her waist, Royce moved them along with the group.

A voice from the back rose above the others. “Move back. Let me through.”

Royce couldn’t keep the grin off his face when Edna Murphy swooped down on Texanna like an eagle protecting its young.

“Ya’ll stand back now, you’re crowding the girl.” Edna pushed through the crowd and took Texanna’s arm. “Come on, sugar, let’s get outside, and then you won’t feel so confined.”

Texanna turned to Royce with pleading eyes. “Here, Edna. Let me help you.” He closed in on the other side of his wife, and they jostled their way to the door.

They stopped for a minute, and Edna leaned in to whisper something to Texanna. Afraid he’d miss something important, Royce put his head close to theirs, but the feather from Edna’s plumed hat tickled his ear. He swatted it away like a fly.

“Don’t you worry about a thing, child. I’ve made sure everyone in this town knows you’ve lost your memory, so don’t be afraid to say ‘I don’t remember.’“

Royce saw Texanna visibly relax and a smile begin on her face. “Thank you, ma’am. That was very kind of you.”

Edna snorted and gave Royce the evil eye. “Well,

it's the least I could do." Her face flushed. "I wasn't very nice to you before. I'm sorry."

"How come?"

"How come I'm sorry, or how come I treated you poorly?"

"Why weren't you nice to me?"

"Cause I was a snooty, old woman. Thought I was better than everybody else. Still do in some ways." She eyed the group of people waiting to join them. "But the Lord has delivered my comeuppance, and I've changed my ways. Most of 'um least ways."

She flashed Royce a smile. "And when the marshal here asked me to try to stem the gossip," she lowered her voice, "which really surprised me because we haven't always seen eye-to-eye, I felt it was my opportunity to make amends."

Preacher John Riley huffed his way toward them, his face red from exertion. "Why Edna, you just whisked this young lady by me so fast I didn't get a chance to say hello."

"John, she looked faintish, so I wanted to get her outside."

The preacher looked at Texanna, then back to Edna. "Well, she looks fine now. Royce, bring your wife over, and let folks say hello."

As they approached, the group stopped talking and pressed around them. Royce received his share of handshakes and slaps on the back, but the folks wanted to talk to his wife. He stepped back and watched. They were all good people, and he was grateful they were glad to see Texanna.

He felt a hand on his shoulder and turned to see Matthew with Molly, his arm around her shoulder. His sister-in-law was petite, too small, in his opinion, to be having a child with Matthew. He worried about her and knew Matthew did also. His brother had fought his love for Molly, but the woman persisted and they'd married. She looked like a ripe watermelon ready to pop.

"Hello, darlin'. How's my favorite sister-in-law?" He hugged her gently and placed a kiss on her forehead.

"How do I look?" She held up a hand. "No, I don't want to hear that line one more time. I *am* not glowing. I'm fat and ugly, and I'm your *only* sister-in-law." Her voice broke on her last words, and her face scrunched with threatening tears.

But to Royce she was radiant. Her dark brown hair held a sheen that enhanced her creamy skin and brown eyes. Matthew's hair was almost black so their baby would be dark-headed, but would it have her brown eyes or Matthew's blue ones?

Royce knew from experience the last month of pregnancy was hard on a woman. Pearl had been so hard to live with right before Garrett was born; he'd wanted to leave the state. Molly needed a distraction, something to keep her mind off her burgeoning body.

"Molly, I'm sure Matthew told you Texanna doesn't remember any of us. She may need you to help her learn some things, like needlework and cooking."

She hiccupped and then giggled. "You mean she's forgotten how to cook? How can anybody forget something like that?"

"I don't know, but she's also got some weird behaviors. Don't be offended at some of the things she says." He stuffed both hands in his pockets. "And just so you know, Garrett calls her Texanna, not Ma."

Their shock was obvious, but Matthew merely nodded and turned to Molly with concern. "Come on, honey, you need to get off your feet." He turned to Royce. "Collect Texanna and Garrett, and meet us at Maybell's. Jason's bringing Sally." His face split into a grin. "Should be a lively meal with Sally there."

Royce snorted. Lively was right. The girl was a handful, and if Jason married her, he was afraid she would lead his young brother around by the nose.

The crowd around Texanna was dwindling. She'd probably scorch his ears for leaving her by herself. He moved into the group and took Texanna's arm. "We need to leave, folks. We'll see you all at the July Fourth picnic."

Just as they moved away, Royce glanced up to see Danielle Stokes standing in their path. His step faltered, but he quickly recovered and moved Texanna forward. *Might as well get this over with.* Hopefully, the woman wouldn't make a scene. From the pinched look on her face, it was doubtful.

He nodded. "Hello, Danielle, is your father with you?"

Her eyes never left Texanna's face. Her expression remained brittle. "No, he wasn't feeling well this morning."

He turned to Texanna. "Sweetheart, this is Danielle Stokes, Judge Stokes' daughter."

Texanna extended her hand. "Hello, Danielle, it's nice—"

"Don't think for one minute you can pull the wool over my eyes," she spat. "Just when Royce starts paying attention to me again, you show up. I'm not fooled by your ridiculous story, and before long the rest of this town will know the truth too."

Royce felt Texanna stiffen. She snapped her parasol closed and squared her shoulders. "Just what are you saying?"

Danielle drew herself up to her full height, chin in the air. She stood several inches taller than Texanna. "You've been off whoring, and now you're back and want to take my man—"

Texanna jerked free of his grip, and before he could yank her back, she'd grabbed a handful of Danielle's bodice and pulled her face down level with hers. "Who are you calling a whore?"

Danielle shrieked and shoved her attacker away. The sound of ripping fabric made Royce cringe. He stepped between them. "Stop it, both of you. You're making a spectacle."

Texanna struggled to get around him and get at Danielle. If he wasn't so embarrassed at her behavior, he'd laugh. He was tempted to turn Texanna loose on the hateful woman. Lord, the woman was deluded—her man? He'd just asked her to a dance.

Edna Murphy witnessed the scene, as did a few other shocked church members. Edna hustled over from her buggy to collect the sobbing Danielle and drew her away. She looked back at Royce, rolled her eyes, and grinned.

Texanna crossed her arms and refused to budge. "Just what was that all about?"

Before he could answer, Garrett ran up. "Gol-leee, you showed her, Texanna. Guess she was jealous 'cause Pa's been courtin' her some."

"Courtin', huh?"

"Yeah, but that was before you come back, huh, Pa?" Royce ushered her toward the buckboard, lifted her onto the seat, and Garrett climbed up beside her. "You're much prettier, and he likes you lots better. I can tell."

Royce wisely didn't comment, just climbed in beside her and twitched the reins.

****

Danielle sat in the buggy beside Edna Murphy. The old woman had thrown a shawl over her shoulders to cover her torn dress. Mortified beyond belief, she hid her muffled sobs behind her handkerchief.

Edna slapped her on the leg making her jump. "Stop caterwauling right this minute. You're lucky you got off with just a torn dress. Could've lost some of that hair you're so proud of."

Too stunned to respond, Danielle stared at the old biddy for a minute. Finally, she found her voice. "Royce would've married me if she'd not come back, I know he would have. He was taking me to the July Fourth dance."

"But she did come back, and your behavior today didn't endear you to anyone in this town. You'll never land a husband with your hateful ways."

"I don't want just any man, I wanted Royce. He's going to pay for treating me like he's done."

"Young woman, there is nothing you can do to Royce to hurt him. You'll just make a bigger fool of yourself."

That's what you think, old woman. I've already got revenge on Pearl, Texanna, whatever the hell name she went by. Hiding her smirk behind the handkerchief, she crushed it in her hand, the locket hidden in the folds biting into the tender flesh of her palm.

****

Texanna was surprised when they walked into Maybell's to find Matthew with his wife and Jason with Sally at a table waiting for them.

"Texanna, you remember Molly, Matthew's wife?"

Molly's smile was warm and welcoming. She was pretty and dainty, probably not much over five feet tall. Her body was round with pregnancy. "Hello, Molly."

"It's so good to see you. Royce, I do believe she's prettier than she was before she left."

Color flooded Texanna's face. To make matters worse, Royce stood there and studied her. She had to restrain the urge to stick her tongue out at him.

Texanna turned to Jason and the pretty young woman at his side.

He stood, hugged Texanna, and kissed her

cheek. “My, you look lovely in that dress.”

“You and Royce have nice taste in ladies’ clothing.”

He grinned. “Well, thank you, ma’am.”

Jason introduced Texanna to Sally, and then she and Royce took chairs beside Jason.

So this is the pretty, blue-eyed blonde Royce called mule-headed. Texanna swallowed the giggle that threatened to erupt. What Royce meant was she wasn’t all sugar and spice. She had a mind of her own.

Sally extended her hand. “Hi, Texanna. I’m glad to meet you at last.”

“Thank you. You too.”

Garrett bounced in his seat. “Uncle Jason, you shoudda seen Texanna whup—”

Royce put a hand on the boy in mid-bounce. “Not now, Son.”

“Ah, Pa, can’t I tell.”

“No, you cannot.”

Texanna thought she’d sink through the floor. Her face burned with embarrassment, but by golly, the woman called her a whore. She met the curious glances of the others at the table. “I’m sure Royce will fill you in later.”

“Marshal, don’t you think every woman should know how to handle a gun?” Sally’s blue eyes nailed Royce’s, and he looked at Jason. Texanna was grateful everyone’s attention turned to the cute blonde.

Jason, brow puckered, looked hard at Royce as if begging him to say no.

“Call me Royce, Sally. Yes, I do think at some point a woman should learn the use of firearms.”

Garrett piped up. “Pa lets me shoot sometimes. When I get a little older he’s going to buy me a rifle of my own.” Royce winked at his son and was rewarded with a snaggle-toothed grin.

Sally pressed the issue. "See there, Jason. I told you so. Molly can use a gun, and I bet Texanna can too."

"Sally, you're just eighteen-years-old. You need to be more mature to handle a gun."

Sally's face turned beet red. "I'll have you know—"

Texanna coughed to hide her chuckle. "I think what Jason means, Sally, is using a gun requires a certain amount of strength. Strength you might not have yet."

Jason nodded. "Yes, that's it exactly. Guns are heavy." He pulled at his shirt collar as if it'd suddenly grown too tight.

"I'll tell you what. Come out to the house some morning, and we'll see if you're strong enough. I'll let you fire a couple of rounds so you'll have an idea of what's involved."

Texanna turned to Royce. "If it's all right with Royce."

"Really?" Sally reached across Jason and grabbed Texanna's hand. "Thank you."

Nodding at Sally, she added. "Maybe Sally can teach me to make biscuits."

Royce considered for a minute. "You can teach her how to load and hold the Winchester, but no firing."

Texanna started to argue but didn't. She turned to Molly. "When's your baby due?"

The petite woman moaned and touched her belly. "In about ten minutes."

Matthew kissed her cheek. "Don't tease us, little mother." He smiled at Texanna. "He's due in four weeks, sometime in early August."

Texanna couldn't resist asking. "He? You know it's a he?"

The big man shrugged and grinned sheepishly. "Doesn't matter, boy, girl, we'll be happy with either."

What would they think if they knew about ultrasound and discovering a baby's sex before birth?

"Is there a hospital in town where you'll have the baby?"

No one spoke. They looked at her as if she'd lost her mind.

Royce took her hand. "We have a hospital, but most babies are born at home. Doc comes to the house and delivers them."

She searched Molly's face, looking for fear or worry, but she didn't appear to be afraid.

Molly's smile was sympathetic. "Don't look so concerned. All the women at the farm have had babies and could probably deliver this one themselves."

All she could do was nod. Texanna knew that's how it was done in the old days. But she'd never been living it before. She feared for Molly and the baby. But Pearl had managed with Garrett.

"Pa, I'm hungry. When are we gonna eat?" Garrett's question broke the tension.

"Right now, young man." A large, gray-haired lady stood beside the table and nodded. "Howdy, Marshal, folks. What can I get ya?"

The meal was hardy, good, and full of cholesterol. Hungry as she was, Texanna's middle was so pinched she couldn't eat more than a few bites. She'd better start running again next week. As she picked at her food, she scanned the room. No one stared at Royce with animosity. She hadn't seen anyone at church who came across as a threat either.

Texanna peered around Jason to study Sally's waistline. Sally's blue check dress fit her nicely, but she appeared comfortable.

As they left the restaurant, Molly pulled her aside. "Get rid of the corset."

She giggled and whispered. "Is my misery that obvious?" They walked in front of the men, and Texanna glanced back to make sure they weren't heard. "Royce wanted me to wear this dress and it's a little too snug without it."

Molly winked. "Bring it out to the farm, and we'll let the seams out."

"Oh, I think I love you."

Molly put her arm around Texanna's waist. "Matthew will be out next week to help you make jelly. You have those apricots picked and ready, and your day will go faster."

Texanna threw her arm across the petite woman's shoulder. "Thank you."

"You're welcome." Molly leaned in close and whispered. "Now, are you going to tell me who you whipped at church?"

She made sure the men weren't paying them any mind, and then regaled Molly with the judge's daughter's accusations.

"And you ripped her dress?"

"I didn't mean to, but she called me a whore."

Molly nodded her understanding. "The poor woman's been after Royce since way before you came on the scene. She about died when Royce returned from San Antonio and announced his plans to marry you." She shook her head. "Judge Stokes has spoiled her something awful."

They stopped at the buggies, and Molly turned to the men. "Royce, why don't you let Garrett come out and stay until Matthew rides over on Wednesday to make jelly?"

Garrett looked at Royce with hope written all over his face. "Yeah, Pa. Can I? I'll help Aunt Molly with her chores."

"Who's going to do your chores?"

Garrett's face fell.

Texanna spoke up. "I guess I could learn how to

do them, do you think?"

Royce was quiet for a minute. "Okay, but we need to stop and get extra clothes."

"Oh, thank you, Pa." Garrett ran to Texanna and hugged her tightly. "Thank you, Texanna. I'll show you what to do this afternoon."

Giving the boy a hug and ruffling his hair, she said, "No problem, sport."

Neither Matthew nor Molly mentioned Garrett not calling her mother or ma. Maybe Royce had explained the situation to them.

Royce helped Texanna into the buckboard. "We'll bring Garrett out later."

On the ride home, Garrett stood behind them and started giving her instructions on how to gather eggs. "Don't be scared of those hens. Just reach under 'um and swipe the egg real quick."

She heard Royce chuckle and poked him in the ribs.

"You don't think I can learn to gather eggs or milk a cow, do you?"

He shrugged. "It'll be interesting to see. I don't know many women who don't know how."

When they got home, Texanna ran upstairs and removed the dress, tossed it over the foot of the bed, and unlaced the corset. "Oh, God. I can breathe again."

****

Garrett went through the motions of showing Texanna how to gather the eggs and milk the cow. Royce had to admit, she tried, and it was interesting to see Garrett in the role of teacher. The boy made him so proud. But Royce was still flummoxed as to why Texanna didn't know how to do these ordinary chores.

They rode horses to the farm, Garrett behind Royce talking non-stop. Texanna was curious to tour the big farmhouse where he'd grown up, so Royce showed her around the place. He watched her peer in the rooms with interest like she'd never seen them.

It was close to sunset when they got back from the farm. As they saw to the horses, Royce couldn't keep the grin off his face. Texanna had been a sight that afternoon at grasping Flossie's teats. Even Garrett had laughed. You'd have thought she was reaching for a snake. But, after considerable work, she had a little milk in the bucket. It would be interesting to see how she managed the next few days.

As they walked to the house, he put his arm around her waist so she wouldn't stumble. He found himself touching her at every opportunity. Matthew and Molly were trying to give them some time alone. Not that it would change things between them. He hadn't had a chance to tell his brother that each day he was more convinced Texanna wasn't his wife.

"You want to heat up the coffee and sit on the porch with a cup and watch the sunset?"

Her smile made his heart lurch. "Yeah, that sounds nice."

It was hot, but a light breeze cooled them and carried the scent of freshly mowed hay. After dark the mosquitoes would be out, and they'd have to go inside the house.

"Were you serious about the judge's daughter?"

With the toe of his boot, he sat the rocker in motion. "I'd made up my mind to get a mother for Garrett. She seemed a likely candidate."

She snorted. "More like candidate for queen of the wicked stepmothers. She'd have made you and Garrett miserable."

"You think so, huh?" He didn't wait for her answer. "Tell me about the future."

"You believe me then?" The excitement in her voice was hard to miss. Her face was radiant, and her hair shone from the rays of the sunset. He wanted to pull her onto his lap, tuck her head under his chin, and rock with her in his arms.

He sighed. "I wouldn't say that, but I'm dang curious to hear what you're going to say."

"Strange you should ask. I was thinking earlier how our advanced medical technology would help Matthew and Molly right now. In my time, they would know if their baby was a boy or girl. They'd even have a picture of it before it's born."

He snorted. "That's not possible."

"In my time it is. Very few infants die in the United States, and it's rare for the mother to die during childbirth. I know Matthew is worried because Molly is so small."

"Yes, he's beside himself with worry." As was Royce.

As if reading his thoughts, she reached out and squeezed his hand. The tender gesture touched him, making him ache for the feel of her hands on his body. He shook the feelings away.

Her face was calm. He watched for signs she was making this all up. "Tell me more. Tell me about the modern revolver you mentioned."

Texanna's face lit with enthusiasm. "Oh, you'd love the guns available. Some carry the bullets in a clip. When you've fired all ten rounds, you remove the clip from the handle and put in another." She leaned over and put her hand on his knee. "And listen to this. You only have to cock it one time, it throws a shell into the chamber, and then you can fire all ten rounds in rapid succession. Be mighty good in a shoot out, wouldn't it?"

Well, hell yes, it would. "What is this clip?"

"It's a rectangular box that holds ten bullets. I think there is one model that holds more—like sixteen."

Lord, she had an imagination to be able to make

all this stuff up. Maybe she needed to turn to writing instead of painting. He shook his head. *She acts like she believes what she's saying.*

"The population of Waco is over 100,000 people now. San Antonio is even bigger."

"What about those clothes you had on when you arrived?"

She shrugged. "They're just plain old ordinary clothes. Everyone dresses that way. Well, actually, young women with good figures do." She grinned. "Older women are more conservative in the way they dress."

Well, at least they're not all crazy. "You mean it's common for women to go around in tight men's pants and a bodice that hugs their breasts?"

She looked down her nose at him. "Yes. Sometimes the bodices are short and their belly shows."

He could barely croak out the words. "And the underwear, that French type underwear ladies of the night wear? Why were you wearing them? Only strumpets wear 'um."

"Actually, prostitution is illegal in the modern world. Well, in the United States, that is. Even so, prostitutes are still available. If they get caught soliciting, they go to jail, as does a man if caught propositioning a hooker for sex."

Prostitution was illegal? He shook his head and cleared his throat. "What do men do when they have urges and need a woman?"

"The same thing a woman does when she needs a man. Go out and find one—at a bar, a party, anywhere—and take him home with her."

Royce knew his mouth hung open, but... He'd never heard of anything so...so...hell—he didn't know what. That was the most indecent thing he'd ever heard, and he'd heard plenty. His face heated in embarrassment and anger at the thought of

Texanna...

Clenching his jaw, he bit out, “I can’t believe—”

She noticed the look on his face and held up her hand. “Let’s don’t even go there. The modern world is a crazy place, I know. But not everyone has loose morals, myself included.”

He dropped his head in his hands and massaged his temples. A headache was forming behind his eyes. “And this modern world, you’d prefer to live there, you intend to go back?”

“Royce, I’m not your Pearl. She’s dead now. But, I had to come back because you didn’t heed my message.”

Rage, pain, and desire mixed together turned to anguish. His heart pounded and threatened to explode. God, she was driving him crazy.

“You’ve delivered your message. Why the hell are you still here, then?” He stood and pulled her against him, molding her soft body to his. Hands in her hair, he yanked her head back and lowered his within an inch of her face.

He knew his voice was harsh, but he couldn’t hide the pain. “Why haven’t you boarded that train to San Antonio and gone back to your modern time?”

He kissed her moist mouth, his lips hard and unforgiving. Angry and hurt, he wanted to punish her, but at her soft cry, he softened the kiss. He brushed his lips back and forth across hers and teased, tasted, and sipped.

With his cheek against hers, his voice filled with torment, he asked, “Are you here to torture me, to drive me insane with wanting you?”

She broke away. “No, no. I want you too. I’m afraid I’m falling in love with you, but I don’t belong here. I can’t stay. You don’t even believe I’m from the future.”

He shoved her away. “You’ve delivered your message, so go.”

She lifted her chin, their eyes met and held. "Yes, but you didn't believe me. When I returned to my time, history had not been changed. You were killed in the shoot out."

He raked his heads through his hair and cursed. "Woman, you can't change history."

"I can, and I will. You need to read the book. More than just your life is at stake. Garrett's is too."

Chapter Eleven

"How can you know such a thing?"

Royce wanted to hit something and pound it to a pulp. It was one thing for him to get shot, but the idea of Garrett being a train robber at the age of eighteen terrified him. His stomach rolled and bile rose in his throat.

Texanna stood at the end of the porch, as far away from him as she could get. He had to strain to hear her.

"From the history book Pearl had, the one I brought back with me." She stood, quiet and unmoving, then turned to him, her expression cold. "It makes no difference if you believe me or not, because I know it's a fact. History books don't lie. It'll happen August eighth, sometime around noon."

She walked to the door. "Now, if you'll excuse me, I'm tired. I'm going to bed." She let the screen door close behind her, stopped, and added. "And I'd appreciate it if you'd tell me where my jeans and tennis shoes are so I can run in the morning. I'm used to jogging at least three days a week, and I don't want to get out of shape."

Then she was gone.

Royce dropped his head into his hands. Jogging? Just one more thing to confuse him. He didn't know what to believe. Her stories sounded convincing. Lord, he was going crazy with wanting her. What if he discovered she was telling the truth, would he love her any less? Love? He groaned. Did he love this woman already, regardless of who she was? Yes, dammit, he did. And if she was telling the truth, she'd want to return to her own time.

It hurt to have her near and not be able to touch her, to... Ah shit! He stood and went inside. It didn't matter. She was leaving again anyway. He needed to put her from his mind.

He lit the kerosene lamp sitting on the kitchen table. Texanna's footsteps and drawers opening and closing could be heard from upstairs. He took his bottle of whiskey from the cabinet and slammed it down on the table. The movement upstairs stopped. Good. He hoped to hell he'd disturbed her. He took a hefty slug, enjoying the heat as it rolled down his throat and pooled warm in his belly. The sensation reminded him of the past.

When his search for Pearl ended, he'd spent an entire week drunk, wallowing in his grief. Pete stood in for him at work while he was gone. Pete liked being marshal. What could another week hurt? He'd considered letting Pete have the job permanently—until Matthew and Jason showed up at his door. His brothers spent an entire weekend abusing him—they bathed him, forced food down his throat, and then sat him in front of the portrait of Garrett and closed the door. His child smiled at him from the canvas. He'd sobbed and raged until he dropped from exhaustion. When he woke, he was on the floor below the painting.

The next day Molly rode up with Garrett. The boy clutched Royce's neck, and Royce couldn't put him down—he sensed the boys need, and he recognized his love for his son would sustain him.

Royce took another drink, corked the bottle, and put it away. The lamp lit the way as he walked upstairs. He undressed, stretched out on the bed, and opened the history book.

****

When Texanna heard Royce's steps on the stairs

she held her breath and swallowed her sobs. She listened as he removed his boots and clothes and heard the give of the springs as he got into bed. And she ached—for what she desired above all things but couldn't have and would never experience—the touch of the man who could be her life mate. A man not of her time. If only she could stay.

****

Her jeans and tennis shoes were on the foot of the bed the next morning when she woke. Texanna put on an old shirt of Royce's, rolled up the sleeves, and tied it in a knot at her waist. Then she hurried outside and started her warm-up routine. The slam of the back door announced Royce's arrival. Texanna tried to avoid his eyes as she stretched her muscles. Her heart was in her throat, the strain between them palpable.

He handed her the Colt .45. "I want you to wear this. If you need me, fire two shots into the air."

It was probably not the most comfortable thing to wear while jogging, but she'd manage. Texanna strapped it on and noticed he'd punched more holes in the gun belt so it would fit around her hips. His thoughtfulness touched her.

"Thank you."

"You're welcome. Be careful."

She nodded. "I'll be back in forty-five minutes or an hour at the most."

The sun was just peeking over the horizon. By the time she reached the turn, she had a steady rhythm going. She turned in the opposite direction from town. Hopefully, she wouldn't meet anyone and embarrass Royce.

****

She'd said no more than forty-five minutes, and it was getting close to an hour. Royce couldn't stand to wait any longer. He whistled for Samson. The horse nickered and trotted to the gate. Before he opened the gate, he looked back one more time. And saw Texanna's small figure running up the road.

He breathed a sigh of relief, rubbed Samson's ears, and patted his neck. "Sorry to disappoint you fella', but I jumped the gun. You know I love her, don't you?" Samson butted him in the chest and proceeded to nibble on Royce's ears. His hat fell, and he caught it before it hit the ground. "Yeah, I love you too." Royce walked away from the fence.

Texanna stopped in front of the water pump, dropped her hands to her knees, and drew in gulps of air. She straightened, removed the holster, and handed it to him. Royce watched her stretch her legs, one at a time, out behind her and raise and lower her heel. He shook his head. Why would anyone want to run up and down the road? She took the ladle from the hook and drank two cups full, then poured one over her head dousing her shirt—his shirt.

He turned back to the fire he was building to wash clothes. It would take a while longer for the water to be hot enough. The scrub board sat on a low table so Texanna wouldn't have to bend too much to use it. Today he'd help her with the laundry so she'd know the routine.

"Come inside. The coffee's hot, and I saved you some breakfast."

Still breathing hard, she gasped. "Okay, be there in a minute."

Royce watched from the kitchen window as she drank more water and poured another dipper full over her head. Her red curls hung straight and were plastered to her head. She was a mystery, no two ways about it. He took the warm plate from the range and set it on the table with silverware and a cup of coffee.

Texanna left her shoes on the screened-in porch and walked to the sink to wash her hands. His shirt was plastered to her body, giving him a nice view of her graceful back. His eyes traveled lower to the roundness of her butt and almost groaned when he remembered how her bare cheek had felt in his hand. The memory made him shift his weight in the chair. He picked up his coffee cup and took a drink. She dried her hands and turned to sit down. At the sight of her breasts beneath the wet shirt, he inhaled coffee and choked, gasping for breath.

She rushed around the table and pounded him on the back until he managed to say, as he wheezed, "Stop...I'm fine." From the opposite side of the table, she watched him with concern for a few minutes.

"Eat before it gets cold. I'm all right." Now that the shock was over, he looked his fill. The front of her shirt was wet, almost transparent, and molded to her breasts, defining their shape and size. They were beautiful.

"Thank you for the breakfast. You didn't have to cook for me." A lock of hair fell forward and brushed her cheek. She shoved it behind her ear drawing his eyes to the white column of her neck. He'd like to kiss her neck, right under that ear.

"It's just as easy to cook for two as it is for one." He tried to keep his eyes on her face but the damn things kept dropping to the breasts staring him in the face. "How far did you run?"

She finished chewing and took a sip of coffee. "Down to that partially burned house."

Flabbergasted, his mouth fell open, and he sputtered. "That's over two miles." How could she run that far and then back? Sure, she looked pretty tired when she got back, but...

"Why? Why would you want to run up and down the road?"

"It's good exercise, keeps my heart healthy, my muscles toned. I just run three times a week. A person can overdo it, especially women if they lose too much body fat." For some reason she looked down, noticed how exposed she was, and yanked the shirt away from her body.

Royce covered his eyes, rubbed his forehead, and pretended he hadn't noticed. He could feel her glare and peeked through his fingers. If she could shoot fire with those blue eyes, he'd be ashes about now. He struggled not to laugh out loud.

"You have a headache?" The glower he received didn't express the sympathy her voice carried.

"Yeah, didn't get much sleep last night." At least that was the truth.

"I'm sorry. I didn't sleep well either." She dropped her fork onto her plate and propped her crossed arms on the table. "Look, I need my bra back. It's not good to run without one."

His eyebrow twitched as he studied her to see where this was going. "Why not?"

"Well, would you just think about it? It keeps things from jiggling around."

His face heated. "Oh. Does it hurt?"

"No, it doesn't hurt." She averted her eyes. "I guess it could at a certain time of the month."

"Then why? If it doesn't hurt, you don't need it."

She spoke through gritted teeth. "I don't want the tissues to break down and my boobs to hang down to my waist by the time I'm forty."

"Boobs?"

"You know what I'm talking about—knockers, hooters, tits, breasts." Her face was almost purple.

He coughed into his hand to hide his grin. "Oh, I see." He sobered. Hell, he didn't want them to hang to her waist either. "Sounds like you shouldn't be running if that's the case."

She screeched. "You're the most unbending person I've ever met." Grabbing her dishes, she shoved her chair back and stood. The activity set her breasts in motion, more so when she kicked the chair under the table.

Oh, boy. What a beautiful sight. He wished her shirt were still wet. It would be a shame for them to get saggy. Unaware she watched him, he grinned. A wet dishcloth hit him and wrapped around his face.

"Ohooooo! You pervert!" She folded her arms across her breasts. "Fine then. I'll just run like this and entertain all those men who saw me running this morning. They got an especially good view when I raised my arm and waved."

She ran in place and held her arm over her head pulling the shirt tight across her right breast. "Yoo-hoo. How're you this fine morning?" She lowered her arm and kept running. "Then I'll run in place, and we'll chat for a while."

Okay, by God, that did it. She looked at his face and froze. He shoved his chair back and before he could get around the table, she lunged toward the door. He grabbed a handful of her shirt and pulled her back against him, his arms locked around her waist. His heart thundered, and he felt every breath she took. Her scent mixed with the sweat from her run teased his senses. He dropped his head to her hair, and his hand moved from her waist to cup a breast. It fit his hand perfectly. A groan rose from deep within his chest. He ran his thumb down the firm flesh to the nipple. She jerked in his arms and cried out. His hand returned to her waist.

"I'm sorry. I couldn't resist." Hell, he was torturing himself. He wanted things settled between them so he could love her half the night and then get her dander up every morning. "I was only teasing you. You can have your bra back."

"Thank you, I appreciate it."

"You're welcome." He dropped his chin to the top of her head. "I read that section you marked in the history book last night.

She turned in his arms. "I'm sorry. It must have

been hard."

Hard, hell, he'd felt like his heart was being ripped from his chest. Garrett growing up to be a train robber and then dying was inconceivable. Whether the book was real or not, he'd do his best to see Garrett lived a long, happy life.

"Yes, it hurt like hell."

She put her arms around his waist and her cheek against his heart. "I'm so sorry, but you had to know."

One hand on her head, the other on her back, he held her for just a minute. Then he stepped back. "We better get busy, or we'll be doing the wash during the heat of the day."

****

Texanna rubbed the clothes back and forth across the scrub board. This was not fun. She washed. Royce rinsed, wrung them out, and tossed them in a tub. They'd both hung them on the line. The wash and rinse water had to be changed twice. Her back and shoulders ached before they started hanging them. By the time they were finished, she was too tired to fix lunch. It was all she could do to drag her body into the house. She stood in the kitchen in a stupor.

"You want me to rub your shoulders?"

Too tired to speak, she nodded.

"Sit down at the table, fold your arms and lay your head on them."

His hands were strong, and he knew how to use them. As he kneaded her sore muscles, groans and moans escaped her. "Oh, that's wonderful. Thank you."

"It would feel a lot better if you'd take that shirt off." From his hands she could feel his body shaking with laughter.

She snorted. "You wish."

"Yes, ma'am, I do." He hit a particularly sore

spot and she yelped. “Sorry. What you need is a warm bath.” He patted her shoulder and went to the screened in porch for the bathtub. He stopped and turned back. “By the way, what’s a pervert?”

She giggled. “A...lecher, you know, a seducer...a dirty old man.”

He threw back his head and laughed. Texanna’s heart tripped at the delightful sound and the amusement on his handsome face. The man was too damned handsome for his own good.

A horse and rider galloped into the yard. “Royce! Royce!” Royce rushed out the back door.

“You gotta come quick. Miz Molly’s havin’ her baby.”

Texanna went to the door and watched Royce stride to the man on horseback. “How long has she been in labor, Jim?”

The old man’s face was etched with concern. “’Bout three hours, and she’s in terrible pain. Matthew is beside himself with worry.”

Royce patted the older man’s arm. “She’ll be fine, Jim. You run on to town and get Jason and Doc.” Jim turned the horse and kicked it into a full run. Royce hurried to the barn and emerged with his saddle in one arm and tack in the other.

Oh, God, no. Texanna’s heart dropped as she remembered the words from Jason’s journal about Molly having twins. He’d said one of them would die.

She raced to catch up with Royce. “I’m coming. Don’t leave me.” Inside the barn she grabbed her tack and dragged her saddle out the door. Royce had Josie standing beside Samson. He was saddled and ready to go. Royce reached for her saddle and lifted it as if it were light as air, then waited for Texanna to smooth the blanket on Josie’s back before setting it in place. Mounted on Samson, he looked down at her.

She studied his face. He didn’t look like he

thought Molly would be fine. His mouth was pinched and white—his eyes filled with concern. His large hand cupped her cheek.

“I’m gonna set a fast pace. Can you keep up?”

“That depends on Josie. If I lag behind, don’t worry about me. I know the way.”

She grabbed his boot before he could kick Samson into a gallop. “Royce, I have to tell you something I learned before I came back. Molly’s having twins. One of them will die.”

Chapter Twelve

Royce looked at her in disbelief and horror, and then kicked Samson into a full gallop. She didn't blame him for not trusting her words. He'd had a lot of shocks the last few days.

Texanna finished saddling Josie and mounted up. She took off after Royce, but he was just a speck on the road. When she reached the farmhouse, a man stepped off the porch to take her horse.

Matthew was a wild man, pacing back and forth in front of the stairs. He raked his hands through his long hair. The rawhide he'd used to tie it back was gone.

"I shouldn't have married her. Dammit, I knew this was going to happen. She's going to die, and it's my fault."

A scream drifted down the stairs and ended with a moan. Matthew's body froze and his face furrowed with agony. "Oh God. I can't stand to think of the pain she's suffering." Royce stood at Matthew's elbow, his arm across his brother's shoulder, his face a mask of worry. "If she survives, I'll never touch her again."

Yeah, that's what they all say. Texanna walked over to Matthew and slipped her arms around the big man's waist. He crushed her in a tight squeeze. "Women suffer during childbirth, but after Molly sees your baby, the pain will be forgotten. She wouldn't want you to think that way." At least that's what Texanna had been told by Pearl and her friends who had children.

With her arm around Matthew's waist, she led him to the sofa. He sat down and dropped his head in his hands. Her eyes met Royce's. "Where do you keep your whiskey?"

Royce made a fast escape and returned with a bottle and two glasses. He poured two fingers of whiskey in each glass and handed one to Matthew. The second he started to raise, but Texanna took it before it reached his mouth. He looked at her in question. If she were going upstairs, she'd need all the fortification she could get. She tossed it down, gasped and coughed as the searing heat flowed to her stomach.

Texanna handed the glass to Royce and wheezed. "Don't get drunk. She may need you two before long."

Matthew's eyes lit with fire. "Those damn women up there won't let me in, even when she's crying out for me."

Texanna had read stories of men being barred from the room during a birth. In her opinion, it was stupid. Husbands should share in the pain and joy associated with birthing, as they did when creating a child.

"Give me a few minutes upstairs, and then I'll call you."

She pulled Royce aside. "Where's Garrett?"

"One of the hands took him over to Aggie's." He tilted her face and kissed her cheek. "Don't worry. He's fine." He dropped his forehead to hers and whispered, "Please tell me what you told me earlier was a lie, a mistake."

Texanna shook her head sadly, turned, and started up the stairs. She felt like she was going to the gas chamber. Molly's scream had been terrifying, and Texanna would love to hide. For some odd reason she needed to be there for Molly. Why, she didn't know.

When she opened the door, both women by the bed turned. Neither looked happy at her appearance. Molly saw her and stretched out her hand.

"Please, Texanna. Stay with me."

Texanna took Molly's hand. The woman's gown was drenched with sweat, her damp hair plastered to her head. "I'll be with you, and Matthew will be up in a minute."

The oldest of the ladies opened her mouth. "Men aren't needed in..."

Texanna held up her hand. "If Molly wants Matthew here with her, she's going to have him. I want some cool water and a fresh gown." The younger woman, the one that had kept her mouth shut, ran to do her bidding.

Molly lay on a pad made of several folded sheets, with an oilcloth underneath to protect the mattress. Texanna sat beside her on the bed and stroked her hair. "We're going to clean you up and make you more comfortable before Matthew comes up."

Molly's lips trembled and produced a hesitant smile. "Thank you." No sooner had the words left her mouth than her face twisted in pain. "Ohoo...it hurts so...bad."

Texanna knew zilch about childbirth. Well, she'd taken child development class in high school and watched a birth on television. But that was the limit of her education.

Molly arched off the bed and screamed in pain.

The desperate cry raced up Texanna's spine and across her shoulders. She shivered. *Oh, God, please help us here.* The contraction ended, and Molly relaxed. "Molly, I read somewhere if you focus your mind and eyes on an object, it's easier to control the pain."

Molly looked at her as if she'd lost her mind.

The woman pushed through the door with a pan of water and a washcloth. Together they worked the damp gown up and off her body and covered her with a sheet. Texanna dampened the cloth and cooled off Molly's face and arms and body. Texanna helped her sit up so they could slip the clean gown over her head. She brushed Molly's long, dark hair and plaited it so the braids hung down on each side of her face.

Texanna turned to the ladies and thanked them. "I'm sorry; I don't remember your names. I'm Texanna."

"Lands, child, we know who you are. I'm Betty and this be Liz." The older woman nodded toward her younger helpmate.

Texanna took Betty's arm. "Come outside a minute." She turned to Liz. "Please call if you need us. We'll be back shortly."

In the hall, Texanna bent her head to Betty's. "Is something wrong in there?"

"Peers the little 'un is turned wrong."

"What'll we do?"

"When Doc gets here, he'll try to turn the baby. We might help by massaging her stomach."

Sounded like a good job for Matthew. He could touch Molly and help at the same time. When Texanna called for Matthew, he ran up the stairs taking them two at a time. He rushed to the door. Texanna caught his arm before he could enter. His eyes flashed with anger, and for just a second Texanna felt fear.

"Matthew, try to calm her. As you talk, gently massage her abdomen. Tell her how much you love her." He nodded, leaned down, and kissed Texanna's cheek.

He knelt beside the bed and caressed Molly's large belly as he kissed her. Then he laid his head on her breasts. She stroked his hair. His voice was thick with emotion. "Molly, Molly, my love. I'm so sorry, baby."

Liz came out and closed the door to give the couple a few minutes of privacy. But the door had no more than closed when the sounds of Molly's whimpers reached them.

"I'll go in," said Texanna. "You two need a break. Relax a while and I'll trade out with you in a few minutes."

Texanna went to the opposite side of the bed. "Try to focus on something, Molly, and breathe in through your nose, out through your mouth." Now where had that come from? Something else she'd heard or read.

Matthew's eyes were glued to Molly's. Ah, thought Texanna, she's decided to focus on his eyes.

"Matthew, don't forget to massage her abdomen." Texanna pulled Molly's gown up to expose her bulging belly. Matthew's big hands moved with care over the mound housing their child. When she relaxed, he leaned over and kissed the exposed flesh then returned his gaze to Molly.

It was another hour before Doc arrived. He examined Molly then drew Matthew and the women aside. "The baby's trying to enter the world foot first. I'll have to either free the other leg or turn him before she can deliver. It's gonna hurt some, Matthew. If she starts thrashing, hold her still."

Matthew looked physically ill, but Doc gripped his arm. "You've got to be strong. The nitrous oxide will help tremendously, but she may still have some pain." Matthew nodded.

Doc turned to her. "You Texanna?" She nodded. "Go get Royce. We'll need him on the other side."

Doc removed a canister from his bag and attached a mask to it. "Molly, this gas will ease your pain but you'll be awake enough to push." He patted her hand. "Try to relax. Your baby will be fine." He put the mask in Molly's hand. "Hold this over your nose and mouth."

Doc washed and disinfected his hands and arms, and then went to work. Matthew watched with concern. Royce's lips were pinched as he helped Matthew hold Molly's upper body still. Texanna held one bent knee while Liz held the other.

With his hand in the birth canal, Doc's brow furrowed with concentration. Molly whimpered and cried out as Doc worked to turn the baby. When another contraction tightened Molly's belly, Doc stilled and waited for it to pass.

After what seemed an hour, Doc removed his arm and smiled. "We've got the little bugger in better position. Labor will move along faster now."

Doc walked to the washstand and cleaned his hands.

Molly was completely relaxed and had dropped the mask.

Doc pulled a chair close to the bed and motioned for Matthew to get in it. The big man slumped into the chair, leaned forward, and propped his elbows on the bed, his eyes on his wife. He took Molly's hand and kissed the palm, then dropped his head to the bed.

Doc cleared his throat. "Let's give them some time alone."

Texanna headed downstairs with the doc and Royce, while Betty and Liz waited outside the door.

Jim, the man who'd ridden into town to find Doc came out of the kitchen. "Come on in to the table folks, I've got fresh coffee made and some sandwiches."

Texanna hadn't realized she was hungry until she smelled the coffee. But it was six o'clock, and she hadn't eaten since breakfast. Royce held her chair and sat beside her. His arm circled her shoulders as he leaned in to kiss her cheek. The expression on his face squeezed her heart, causing her throat to tighten. He was such a good man, a man who loved deeply. Seeing Molly and his brother in pain and being unable to help was wearing on him. The lines across his forehead and around his mouth had deepened. His beautiful blue eyes were dull. She wanted to see the sparkle return.

Texanna cupped his cheek and lightly kissed his lips. "She's going to be all right—Molly and the baby. We need to have faith."

They'd just finished eating when Liz called from the landing upstairs.

Doc examined Molly, and with a smile, pronounced her ready to push. Matthew and Royce took their positions at her shoulders and Texanna and Liz at her knees. They moved her down in the bed so she could use the foot rail to push.

On television, the births didn't take near this long or look as hard. Molly drew strength from Matthew, and when the pain got bad, she'd breathe more of the gas. An hour of pushing went by before Doc announced.

"Okay, Molly. I've got his head and shoulders. One more push and you'll be a mother."

Molly clenched her teeth, drew in a deep breath, and pushed. Doc caught the baby's head and butt easing it from her body. The infant immediately announced displeasure at being forced from his mother's warm body. The wail bounced off the walls and mixed with laughs of relief and joy.

"Congratulations, folks. You've got a beautiful baby girl. A little on the small side, but I think she'll be fine." Doc held her up for inspection. He cut and tied the cord, then handed her to Betty to clean. In five minutes the baby was in Molly's arms.

Matthew laughed and sniffed to cover his tears as he cradled his wife and child. Texanna tried hard to keep hers at bay, but when she noticed Royce watched her with longing, her chin quivered and tears clouded her vision.

Molly gasped and clutched her abdomen. "Ohooo, Doc... something's wrong. The pain is..." She cried out.

Doc bent over the bed to examine her. "Molly, it appears your second child is about to push its way into the world."

Matthew looked like he'd been pole axed. Molly's face was radiant with joy. Texanna caught Royce's expression of pain and moved to his side. Ten minutes later a baby boy entered the world. The room resounded with laughter then grew silent.

The baby wasn't crying. Doc suctioned the infant's throat and nostrils. When that didn't work, he held the baby by its heels and slapped his little buttocks. The room was quiet as death. Doc continued to work with the baby by blowing air into his lungs.

His face was grave and he shook his head. "I'm sorry folks, he's dead."

Molly's screams of, "No! No! Nooo," would haunt Texanna forever. As would Matthew's grief stricken face, as he gathered his wife and daughter to his heart. Royce's jaw clenched, his eyes lined with pain as he turned toward her.

Shaking, crying, Texanna's sobs turned to a scream of rage. She shouted, "Give me that baby. He's not dead. I can save him." She tried to take the baby from Doc. Royce pulled her away and wrapped her in his arms.

"He's gone, sweetheart. Let it go."

Texanna shoved him away. "No he's not. Give me that baby. Right now, dammit!" Stunned, Doc handed the baby over.

Royce watched in bewildered silence as Texanna laid the infant on the bed and knelt. She tilted the little head back, covered his mouth and nose with her lips, and blew a puff of air into his lungs, making his chest rise. Then she put two fingers on his breastbone and pushed five times in rapid succession. Again and again she repeated the cycle until Royce thought she'd drop from sheer exhaustion. Tears rolled down her face, and he stepped forward to lift her away from the infant.

Royce squeezed her shoulders in compassion, "Come on, Texanna. He's gone," but she shrugged him away. When he gripped her firmly and lifted her away, she screamed in rage and pain. She tried to struggle but lacked the energy. Her shrieks turned to sobs.

Royce turned her in his arms and held her close. "You did all you could. It just wasn't meant to be."

A thin wail broke through Texanna's muffled sobs. Royce froze and looked at the bed, as did everyone in the room but Texanna. The cry increased in volume. Doc was the first to react and hurried to pick up the mewling infant. His cries became stronger. Betty handed Doc a blanket, and he wrapped it around the child and put him in Matthew's arms.

Grin stretching his face, he kissed the infant and placed him in Molly's arms. "I can't believe it. Twins." He wrapped his arms around his family and held them. Molly dropped her head to Matthew's and cried in relief and gratitude.

Texanna continued to sob. Royce forced her to turn around. "Listen, love. Hear that loud wail? That's our nephew making his presence known."

She stopped sobbing, but her body continued to shake. She moved closer to the bed to peer at the infant.

Matthew stood and held out his arms. Texanna walked into them, and her cries of joy were muffled by his shoulder.

When she turned toward Royce, her smile warmed his heart. She took two steps, stopped, and fell to the floor in a dead faint.

Royce placed Texanna on the bed in his old room and lay down beside her. His heart hammered against his chest. She'd saved the infant's life. He was still astounded and looked at Texanna with awe and tenderness. She'd been terrified, but her strength stepped in and let her tend to the babe.

Doc waved smelling salts under her nose and she jerked away from the noxious smell. "Make her rest, Royce. When she's asleep, come downstairs. We need to talk."

Royce nodded. Doc left the room and shut the door behind him. Texanna turned toward him, her face against his chest. He stroked her back, and his hand moved under her hair to caress the nape of her neck. "Sleep, sweetheart, sleep."

When she slept soundly, Royce forced himself to pull away from her. He longed to stay on the bed and hold her, listen to her breathing, and feel her chest expand and fall. A feeling of unease filled him. He couldn't ignore the facts any longer. He didn't want to believe she was from the future, that she wasn't his wife. Texanna's actions today left little room for doubt in his mind. Maybe she'd learned the technique she'd used today wherever it was she'd been the last four years, but he didn't think so. He brushed a kiss on the side of her mouth.

How many times can a heart be broken before it shatters?

He went downstairs.

Doc and Jason sat at the kitchen table, each staring into a glass of whiskey. Jason jumped up when he entered the room. Royce grabbed his arm.

"Where're you going in such a hurry?"

"Matthew said to come get him when you came down."

Doc looked at Royce, his eyes searching. "What the hell happened in that room upstairs, son?"

Chapter Thirteen

Royce propped his elbows on the table and dropped his head into his hands. “Wait ‘til Matthew and Jason get here.” He didn’t want to have to repeat himself. Once would be hard enough.

Doc poured whiskey into a glass and shoved it toward Royce. “Drink it. You look like death.”

Hell, he felt like he was dying. Texanna was telling the truth, and she would be leaving him. He lifted the glass, tossed the liquid down, and pushed the glass toward Doc for a refill. Doc raised an eyebrow but didn’t question him.

The sound of Matthew and Jason’s boots on the stairs echoed through the house. They came through the kitchen door like a gust of fresh air—Matthew so happy and Jason laughing at the grin on his big brother’s face.

Royce stood and clasped his brother in a bear hug. “Congratulations, Papa.”

Matthew’s grin turned sober. “If it hadn’t been for Texanna, we’d be planning a funeral.” He and Jason sat down, and all three men turned to look at Royce.

Doc was the first to speak. “What happened in that room, Royce?”

“Hell, I don’t know. Well, I might know, but it doesn’t make a lick of sense.” He searched Doc’s and his brothers’ eyes. “You remember what Texanna said that first day when she got off the train?”

Jason spoke, “Sure do. She said, ‘My name’s not Pearl. It’s Texanna, and I’m sure as hell not your wife.'"

"That's right. Later she told me, 'The only reason I know you is because you were married to my elderly neighbor in 2008.'"

Jason sputtered, "That's impossible."

Royce nodded. "That's what I thought, but I'm beginning to think she's telling the truth." He took a deep breath and continued. "She has a history book that was printed in 1962 and swears she's from the year 2008."

Jason and Matthew laughed then sobered when they saw the expression on Doc's face. Doc poured Royce another drink. "Go on. What else has she said?"

Royce's chest hurt, and he rubbed it trying to soothe the ache. "That my wife Pearl boarded the train in 1876, but when she got off the train in San Antonio, it was 1936." Royce ran his fingers through his hair. "She rode the train to Waco as often as she could, trying to get back to me and Garrett. In 1940, she gave up and married, but never had any other children.

"The woman upstairs is Texanna Keith—Pearl's next door neighbor. As a child, Texanna formed an attachment for Pearl and spent many hours in her home learning to paint. It's uncanny that she also closely resembles Pearl."

He leaned back in his chair. "Everything she's told me echoes what was written in the two letters. Supposedly Pearl wrote one in 1940 and the other in 2008."

No one spoke as they mulled over what he'd said. "Do you believe her?" asked Jason.

"I didn't at first, but she has a picture of an older woman, and I'd almost swear the blue eyes of the woman are Pearl's." He scratched his head. "Doc, Matthew, you saw what happened upstairs. It was a miracle." He studied their expressions, trying to determine if they believed him.

"Doc, she said doctors can tell the sex of a baby before it's born and take pictures." Doc's eyes hadn't left Royce's face. He felt like a bug under a magnifying glass. "Guns in her time can shoot ten bullets in rapid succession after cocking it once. She called it a nine milli something."

Jason's face lit. "That'd be something to see."

"She told me Molly was having twins before we left home today and that one would die." He grasped Jason's arms. "Said your great-grandson had your journal that told about it, among other things."

All three men looked at him as if he'd sprouted horns. Should he tell them about the French underwear? Might as well make his lunacy complete. He cleared his throat. "Do you remember how she was dressed when she got off the train?"

Grinning, Jason nodded and started to whistle. Royce slapped him on the head.

"Ouch! I'm just trying to lighten the mood around here." Royce cocked an eyebrow, and Jason muttered. "Okay, I'll shut up."

"The clothes were bad enough, but you won't believe what she had on underneath." Three men leaned forward in anticipation. Royce debated whether to tell them or not. Ah, hell, he'd come this far, he might as well finish. He glared at them. "I better never hear what I'm about to tell you repeated."

Both of his brothers reached out and squeezed his arm. "You know better, Royce. We're family, and what goes on in this family stays with us," said Matthew.

Jason, face sober, nodded in agreement.

Royce turned to Doc.

"You have my word. I took an oath, and I've never broken it."

Royce felt the heat rise to his face, and he

groaned. "French underwear. Bloomers no more than a scrap of cloth and couldn't cover..." He looked up and cleared his throat. "I can't even describe what she had for a chemise. I was afraid she'd been working in a bordello.

"When I asked her if she had worked in a brothel, she got all puffed up and said, 'That would be interesting—a virgin working in a whorehouse."'

Doc scratched his chin and then studied his hands. Matthew and Jason watched Doc, waiting for him to ask. "Well, was she a virgin?"

"How the hell do I know? She won't let me touch her." He finished off his whiskey. "And since I had doubts all along that she was Pearl..."

Matthew cleared his throat and nodded. "Sounds reasonable. She's had decent upbringing." Royce was tempted to tell them about the lack of prostitution in the twenty-first century, and what men did when they needed a woman.

Matthew swirled the whiskey around in his glass. "Royce, this doesn't make sense. If time-travel were possible, why would she want to come back here, knowing she's not your wife?"

"Her reason for being here is a promise she made to the older woman, her beloved Pearl as she called her though they're not related. Texanna came to tell me why my wife didn't return and to protect me and Garrett."

"Protect you and Garrett from what?" Jason asked.

"To keep me from dying in a bank robbery on August eighth. She has a history book with my picture stating when and how I died." Pain clutched his heart. "And one of Garrett. The book said he died in 1890 while robbing a train."

"That's ridiculous!" Matthew's face reddened. "Garrett wouldn't do something like that."

Royce shrugged. "Supposedly after losing his

mother and then his father, he turned bad. Became wild." His hands clenched around his glass. "After the robbery, when she knows I'm safe, she'll get on that train and travel to San Antonio and her time."

"And how does she bring about this time-travel?" asked Doc. "Seems to me if such could happen, folks would be traipsing back and forth all the time."

Royce looked at his brothers. "You remember back when Pa gave me that piece of turquoise. I was sixteen at the time, and both of you resented the fact that he'd given it to me."

Matthew spoke up. "Did for the longest. I was the oldest. It should have come to me." He clapped Royce on the shoulder. "But, I don't any longer."

Jason just shrugged. "Didn't seem like such a big deal to me. Just a piece of pretty stone."

Royce cleared his throat. "Do you remember how he told me to always protect the turquoise, that it was part of our heritage—the Indian side?"

"Yeah, I remember," said Matthew as he finished off his whiskey.

"Later he took me aside and told me the stone had magical qualities. He didn't know what they were, but his father impressed upon him the importance of protecting the stone. It had been passed down from son to son for almost a hundred years."

"But why you and not one of us? Asked Jason.

"I don't know, he just said I was the chosen one."

The room was silent, each man alone with his thoughts. Jason was the first to break the silence. "So, you still haven't told us how she *supposedly time-travels.*"

"The turquoise is the key." He raised a hand to halt their questions. "Don't ask me how it works, because I don't understand it. When Pearl tried to come back from 1936, she couldn't because the turquoise was missing. She'd had to hock the locket."

Doc's eyes bored into his. "And you really believe she's not Pearl, that she's telling the truth?"

"At first I thought she'd just lost her memory, but things started adding up, and now this—this thing she did to bring that baby back to life. Hell, I'm so confused I don't know what to believe, but I do know she's not Pearl."

Matthew's face was pinched with worry. "What about this bank robbery? Did she give you anything to go on?"

"The Bass gang will rob the First National sometime around noon on August eighth of this year. Texanna said I was shot in the back."

"Shot in the back?" Jason slammed his fist on the table. "That's ridiculous." His eyes narrowed. "There's only one way that could happen."

Doc spoke up. "Yeah, someone besides one of the bank robbers fired the shot."

"You need to meet with your deputies so they can be prepared," said Matthew.

Jason shook his head. "No, brother. We've got to keep it quiet. Only the four of us need to know. And Texanna, of course."

Royce studied his younger brother and grinned. "I think we just might make a good deputy out of you after all."

"What do you mean? I'm a good one already."

Royce looked up to see Doc twisting his hands. "Ahem, I hate to bring this up, but if Texanna isn't your wife, she shouldn't be living in your house."

"She can live here with Molly and me."

Anger choked Royce, but he swallowed it. "Texanna isn't going anywhere. She's staying with me." Nobody had to know she wasn't his wife. He needed her with him for as long as she'd be here.

Doc peered over the top of his glasses. "Son, if folks find out, her reputation will be ruined. You don't want that to happen."

"She's staying with me and Garrett, and that's final."

"Okay. You can dry her tears when folks start snubbing her." The older man shoved his chair back and stood.

Royce flinched at Doc's words. No one would ever know she wasn't his wife. "I won't allow that to happen."

"Suit yourself." Doc clapped Matthew on the shoulder. "Keep those babies in the house until they've fattened up. And keep as many people away from here as you can. Don't want 'um catching something at this age."

"Thanks, Doc, I will." Matthew walked out with the older man.

Royce mulled over Doc's words in his mind. He didn't want to hurt or shame Texanna, but he couldn't let her go right now. She'd be leaving anyway so it wouldn't matter if the town's people snubbed her. They'd never know the truth.

Jason clapped him on the shoulder. "I'm heading upstairs to bed. You and Texanna spending the night?"

It was almost ten o'clock, and he didn't want to wake Texanna. "Yeah. You working tomorrow?"

"Yeah, me, Pete, and Ross. Don't know who else is coming in. Relax and enjoy your day off tomorrow." He grinned. "Hope it'll be less exciting. Having babies is hard work."

Royce couldn't help but laugh. The kid was so full of bull. He hadn't arrived until after the babies were born. "Isn't it past your bedtime, runt?"

Jason grabbed Royce around the neck.

"No horseplay in the house, you two." Matthew said from the kitchen door. "Whoever wakes those babies has to change their diapers."

Jason threw up his hands. "Okay, okay, I'm

going," he said and started up the stairs. Royce started to follow. He was bushed. Matthew laid a hand on his arm.

"Stay awhile longer. I want to talk to you."

Matthew could talk all he wanted to, but Texanna was staying in his house with him and Garrett. He joined his brother at the table.

"Royce, since you know for a fact the Texanna upstairs isn't your wife, do you love her with the passion you had for your wife?" Matthew asked.

The question took Royce by surprise. Even though he couldn't make love to her, she added joy and excitement to his life. He looked forward to teasing her, getting her dander up.

His voice was thick. "Yeah, I do." He dropped his head into his hands. "God help me, I love her even more than I did Pearl. I'm not sure I'll survive when she leaves."

"Then maybe you better figure out a way to make her want to stay."

Royce pondered Matthew's words as he eased onto the bed with Texanna. He slipped his arm under her head, and she turned to snuggle against his chest. His last thought before falling asleep were Matthew's words. "Make her want to stay."

****

Texanna woke to found herself in Royce's arms. They were both on top of the covers and in their clothes from yesterday. She studied him as he slept. Gone were the wrinkles in his forehead and around his eyes. His mouth was relaxed, his lips tempting as she stared at them. Black stubble covered his chin and cheeks. She was tempted to reach out and discover how it felt against her hand. *Better keep your hands to yourself.* He was too tempting lying there, and if he woke...

She eased from the bed, tiptoed downstairs, and left by the side door to visit the outhouse. The wooden cubicle gave her the willies. She checked for spiders and sighed with relief when she didn't find any. Inside the screened-in back porch she found a washstand with warm water in the pitcher and wash cloths stacked to the side. After she washed her face and hands, she used the rag to scrub her teeth. If only she could strip, wash off, and put on clean clothes. Still in her jeans and Royce's shirt, she felt filthy and exposed. She sighed. It couldn't be helped.

Betty and Liz were in the kitchen. Jason sat at the table eating eggs, ham, and fresh biscuits. Between bites he teased the women. The tantalizing aroma of the ham made her stomach growl.

"Good morning." At her voice, the women turned and gave her broad smiles. Jason stood and kissed her cheek, then held a chair for her. "Thank you, but I need to help Betty and Liz."

"Lands, child, we didn't hear you out there. Bet you'd like to wash up and change clothes." Betty wiped her hands on a dishtowel and left the room to return with a bundle of clothes. "Here, you just go back out there and wash up good and wear these. No one will disturb you."

Texanna took the clothes. "Oh, thank you. I won't be long." She rushed back to the porch. If felt heavenly to get out of the dirty clothes and wash all over. They'd even included fresh underwear—nineteenth-century of course. Right now, she couldn't complain.

When she entered the kitchen, Betty led her to a chair. "Now, you sit down and enjoy your breakfast. Liz and I have everything ready. We'll let you know if we need help." Betty made flapping motions. "Go on, sit."

Jason held the chair for her to sit. So she sat while Liz placed coffee and a plate of ham, eggs, and biscuits in front of her. She'd just finished eating when Royce entered from the back porch. He'd shaved and smelled good enough to eat. Evidently, he'd borrowed a fresh shirt from Matthew, because it hung loose on his broad shoulders.

His eyes lit on her, and the corner of his mouth tilted. He leaned over her chair, his eyes on her lips. Before Texanna could utter a word, his mouth swooped down and locked on hers. It wasn't a passionate kiss, but one of possession. She should be irritated at his behavior but instead was pleased.

He smiled while her heart thundered in her chest. "Good morning," he said as he sat in the chair beside her.

She managed to squeak out a soft, "Good morning."

Betty and Liz fussed over him as he ate, adding extra biscuits to his plate. When he finished, Texanna and Royce went upstairs to see the babies. Texanna sat in the rocker, and Matthew placed a baby on each arm. One baby was asleep, making little smacking noises. The other twin was wide-awake and studied Texanna.

"That's Nathan. He feels a kinship with you."

Her heart lodged in her throat. "You think so?"

Matthew's voice was thick. "I know so. You two have bonded for life."

His comment touched her, and tears gathered in her eyes. She struggled to speak. "They are so beautiful." A tear rolled down her cheek.

"Hey, now, don't be stingy. Let me hold my niece for a minute and then we'll switch." Royce's light comment eased the ache in her throat.

Royce lifted the infant and handled her like a pro. His eyes met hers, and the love in them washed over her like warm water. To this strong man, love and family were everything.

"What is this little one's name?" he asked.

Molly spoke, "Her name is Pearl."

Chapter Fourteen

When Royce and Texanna rode into the yard, Texanna noticed the bare clothesline. “Where are our clothes?”

“Aggie probably took them in for us.” Royce jumped off Samson and lifted Texanna off Josie before she had time to dismount. They groomed their horses and turned them loose in the pasture. When they started for the house, sunlight glinted off a large object sitting by the back door. She looked at Royce and noticed the twitch of his lips. As they neared the house, her excitement grew. It was a claw-foot bathtub. The feet were made of cast iron, but not the tub. It was tin coated with white enamel on the inside and blue on the outside. The rim was oak.

She ran her hand around the smooth wood edge. “Oh, Royce! It’s beautiful.” She threw her arms around his neck and kissed him. Before she could move away, he caught her waist. Her eyes met his, and she watched them darken. When she didn’t push away, he pulled her closer. She knew what was coming, but she didn’t care, she wanted the touch of his mouth and the feel of his body against hers. He gave her one last chance, but her eyes never left his. One arm locked around her waist, his other moved up her back. His fingers fisted in her hair and held her head steady. His mouth descended, and his lips touched hers lightly.

Texanna stood on her toes and pressed forward to make better contact, but he was intent on torturing her and leaned back. She'd had enough and with both hands, she grabbed a handful of hair and pulled his face to hers. He groaned and sealed his lips to hers. Jolts of pleasure shot from her head to her toes as desire and longing swept through Texanna. Her legs wobbled and almost gave way. Royce lifted her and held her against the side of the house with his body. His knee nudged her legs apart, and he lodged his hips between her thighs letting her feel his hard length. When he moved against her, she cried out as the contact made her lower body pulse. She pushed against him, wanting more.

Suddenly, he moved back, and she slid to the ground. Cupping her face, he leaned down and dropped a light kiss on her lips.

"A rider's coming."

****

Damn! Royce had asked Jim to come help with the tub before they left Matthew's. He didn't figure the older man would be so prompt. Hopefully, Jim wouldn't notice the tight fit of his jeans. It was down right embarrassing. He felt like a randy sixteen-year-old. Texanna ducked inside the house, and Royce waited for Jim to dismount.

"I see it came." He walked to the tub and ran his gnarled fingers over the wood trim. "Pretty thing. Was Texanna happy?" The old man's eyes twinkled with mischief.

Royce's face heated. He cleared his throat. "Yeah, she loves it."

Jim nodded. "Good. Let's get this thing in the house so I can get back to work."

Royce and Jim worked to get the tub into the house. It was heavy, but not near the weight of one made of cast iron. They moved it in front of the window in Texanna's painting room. He planned to board up a section of the screened-in porch, cut a hole for a door, and move the tub out there. It would interfere with Texanna's light for painting, but he'd work out something.

Jim chuckled and slapped his leg. "If Miss Molly sees this, she's gonna be wantin' one too."

Royce grinned at the thought. "I don't doubt it." Royce walked Jim to his horse. "Thanks, Jim. Couldn't have done it without you."

Jim waved as his horse trotted out of the yard. "Anytime."

The minute Jim was gone Texanna rushed into the kitchen to start warming water. "I've got to have a bath and wash my hair."

Dinner consisted of fried ham, boiled potatoes, carrots, and cornbread. This time the cornbread held together. Royce spent all afternoon nailing boards to the outer studs of the porch, leaving space for a high window. Texanna put clean linens on the beds, swept, dusted, and when Royce came in, she was at her easel working on Garrett's portrait.

After supper Royce and Texanna sat on the front porch with their coffee and talked about the twenty-first century until bedtime. It didn't sound like a place Royce would want to visit, though he would like to see that gun she'd mentioned. He might even be interested in seeing more of that French underwear.

****

Royce stared at the ceiling—thinking, feeling confused, and guilty. Was loving Texanna a sin? He was convinced she'd told him the truth. His true wife was dead. She'd sent Texanna here for a purpose—to let him know she hadn't deserted him and Garrett. It was comforting to know she hadn't been tortured or killed. He cherished knowing how much she'd cared, and how hard she tried to get home. Her hell must have been worse than his. She'd been alone in a new century without a soul to help her. He admired her courage and determination to persevere. Yet, he also hurt. Had he shifted his love for his wife to Texanna? Was it possible he'd finished grieving and was ready to go forward with his life? Or was he fooling himself? Hell, he didn't know what to believe anymore.

What about Texanna? She'd been engaged three times and never married. Why? She didn't seem to be incapable of love. She'd said she loved him, but still wanted to return to her time. Was it possible his wife, the ninety-four-year-old Pearl noticed her disdain for the men in her time period? Had she sent her neighbor, the young woman she'd come to adore, back in time hoping she'd find love—with him? Maybe sending Texanna was Pearl's way of gifting them both.

The door to the guest room opened. Royce held his breath and listened for footsteps. His door opened, and Texanna stood, cast in moonlight from the open window. She remained in the doorway for what seemed like an eternity, as if trying to make up her mind. His heart thundered with hope, but he remained still and silent. It had to be her choice.

Texanna walked closer to the bed. She chewed her bottom lip. "I love you, Royce. You're the only man I've ever wanted to make love with and I... don't want to wait any longer to feel your touch."

His heart expanded in his chest, making breathing difficult. Texanna's words eased his fears and doubts. "I love you, Texanna. I don't know who you are anymore, and I don't care. All I know is I need you." They were together for a reason, and he intended to see they stay together.

He sat up on the side of the bed and dragged the sheet over his lap. She moved back a step. His breath caught in his throat. *Don't leave me, love.* "Are you sure this is what you want?"

Texanna lifted the gown over her head and dropped it to the floor. She stood before him, her head high. Royce's breath left him in a whoosh. That she'd come to him in the night humbled him, but to gift him with the sight of her body was beyond his wildest dreams. Women in this era were modest, and her boldness fired his blood. He looked his fill. Her breasts were small but round, her waist flared into gently curved hips, and her legs were long and shapely. A groan rose in his chest, and he held out his arms. "God, you're beautiful."

She drew closer and put her hands in his. He kissed the palm of each and placed them on his shoulders, then caressed her waist, so small he could span it. His hands shook as he slid them up her rib cage and back down over the curves of her hips and thighs. Her skin was soft, and his roughened hands rasped against the smooth texture. He skimmed the outsides of her breasts, and then cupped their fullness. As his thumbs brushed her nipples her body jerked, and she moaned as he continued to tease them. His hands dropped to the fullness of her buttocks and pulled her closer.

Her eyes sparkled in the moonlight and a smile teased her lips. "My turn." She ran her hands up and down his arms and across his shoulders. His breath hitched. He gasped when she thumbed his nipples. When her palms eased down his abdomen, his muscles lurched. Then she knelt before him and placed kisses across his abdomen and twirled her tongue in his navel.

Royce groaned and lifted her to her feet. "No more."

"But I want to touch you."

"Later, love, later." He pulled her against him and rolled, placing her in the middle of the bed. "It's my turn now. I want to taste your breasts." She trembled when his mouth touched her nipple and cried out when he laved it with his tongue. When he stopped to move to her other breast, she grabbed his head.

"Don't stop, please don't stop."

Voice hoarse, he whispered, "Never, sweetheart. Not unless you ask me to."

Texanna gasped as Royce's hand spanned her belly and shivered as his fingers trailed down her hips. She quivered and grew taut with wanting as his hands and mouth teased and stroked her body as if he were fine tuning an instrument. Voice choked, he stoked her desire with whispered words. "Touch me, my love. Feel how my body responds to you."

She splayed her hands over his chest and abdomen, reveling at the firmness of his muscles. When she cupped his buttocks, they jumped in response. They were rock hard, but his skin was smooth and warm, beautiful. Her fingers teased his ribcage and stomach. Royce remained rigid under her touching, his body trembling as he allowed her exploration. When her hand closed around his shaft, a low growl rumbled from his chest. She smiled at his reaction, enjoying her power to please him.

Royce removed her hand and lay back, pulling her body half over his. Hands in her hair, he drug her mouth to his. Their lips joined, giving and taking as their tongues tasted and stroked. He rolled her onto her back and pushed her thighs apart with a knee.

"I love you so, Texanna." His hand skimmed down her hip and cupped her mound. "I love how you gasp when I touch you here." His hand slid lower and found her moist center. Two strokes across her sensitive flesh and Texanna shattered.

Her body arched as a low keening rushed from her throat. Royce plundered her mouth and held her quaking body as he continued to stroke her. His lips left hers and moved lower to suckle at her breasts. The tension built again, and Texanna squirmed beneath him wanting him inside her body—needing to become one with him.

Texanna reached for him. “Now, Royce, please now.”

He held her hands above her head and spoke, his breath warm against her neck. “Not yet, love, I don’t want to hurt you.”

“You won’t, I promise.”

With a groan, he released her hands and settled between her legs. He ran his fingers under the hair at her neck and tilted her head to trail kisses from her ear to her jaw, then used his tongue to trace the tendon in her neck. She shivered in response and curled her arms around his neck. He settled his shaft at her moist entrance.

“Oh, God, you’re responsive.” He grasped her buttocks and tilted her pelvis. His eyes never left hers as he drove inside her. “I love you, Texanna.”

Texanna gasped and tensed as he thrust inside. “Oh my.” There was a sharp pain but nothing unbearable. The fit was tight, and she wondered at her body’s ability to accommodate him.

Royce held himself motionless above her, his breath coming in deep shudders, and dropped his head to her shoulder. She felt her body ease and a heady sensation coiling inside her.

He kissed her collarbone. “Are you all right?”

She ran her hands down his back and clasped his buttocks. “Oh, yeah, I’m fine.” She wiggled her hips. “How about you?”

He gave a choked laugh. “I’m better than fine.” His lips found hers, and then he started to move in slow strokes, pushing and pulling away. She arched into each thrust, grasping at the building pleasure. Her body became boneless and liquid. Her muscles trembled with anticipation.

Oh, God, how had she lived this long without experiencing lovemaking? No man ever made her feel loved and desired as Royce did. She’d never been able to settle for just the physical side of sex, she wanted the emotional side too. As the tension inside her built, tears pricked her eyes, and she wanted to cry with abandon at the beauty of this moment.

Royce was dying. Her warmth enveloped him, her muscles clenched around him as he drove in and out. His love for this woman overwhelmed him. Her response and joy in their joining filled his heart to near bursting. He arched his back and bent to take a nipple into his mouth. A gentle nip with his teeth and she convulsed beneath him.

He rode the wave as her body shuddered and clutched in spasm after spasm. Oh God, she was beautiful, so beautiful. Unable to wait any longer, he dropped his face to her neck as jolt after jolt of pleasure washed over him as well.

Royce collapsed and rolled, taking Texanna with him. His heart pounded, and he sucked air into his lungs. Texanna lay sprawled atop his body, giving him full access to her back and buttocks. He explored her curves and cupped the rounded cheeks, reveling in their shape and softness. Lord, she was a passionate woman. Her enjoyment in their lovemaking made his heart soar. And she'd been a virgin. He had his proof. He took no pleasure in knowing she was from the future, but it didn't deter him from his purpose—making her love him so much she couldn't leave.

He patted her butt. "Did I hurt you?"

"Yes, a little." She lifted her head and smiled. "But it's the best hurt I've ever felt. Not too crazy about the stickiness between my legs though."

The tension left his body, he laughed and squeezed her waist. "I can fix that." He eased from the bed and padded naked to the washstand to return with a damp cloth. "This is probably going to be cold."

She jumped when its coolness touched her flesh,

but as he gently washed her, the cloth warmed to her skin. "How's that?"

"Better. Thank you." He quickly cleaned himself and tossed the rag across the room where it landed in the washbowl, sending splatters of water over the tabletop.

Texanna snuggled against Royce when he crawled back into bed. A smile tilted her lips. She'd done it. She'd finally lost her virginity at twenty-two years old, and it was everything and more than what she'd been told. Of course, Royce made the difference. He was special. They loved each other—something she'd feared she'd never experience.

Again she wondered if loving Royce was right. It felt right and good. She'd never been happier. There would be no going back now. Royce was her soul mate, her fate. He would be the father of her children. Lord, she hadn't stopped to think about birth control. It was almost time for her period so she was probably safe. She had some serious decisions to make, but they'd have to wait until tomorrow. Her eyes wouldn't stay open.

Royce stroked her back and wondered what was going through her mind. He felt her body relax and knew she slept. His heart swelled. Having her in his arms was heaven. Their lovemaking was more than he'd dreamed possible. It had sealed their fate. He wouldn't let her leave again without a fight. And it was such fun to butt heads with her. With a smile on his lips, he closed his eyes.

He dozed and woke with Texanna still atop his body, her chin propped on his chest as she watched him. When he opened his eyes, she grinned and started trailing kisses along his shoulders and arms.

"Again? Love, are you sure you're not too sore?"

She raised her head and pouted. "I'm fine, but if you're too tired..."

With a laugh, he flipped her onto her back and

positioned himself between her thighs. "What do you think?"

****

Damn, he wished he had another day off. Texanna was still asleep, her head on his shoulder, one leg sprawled across his. The sheet had dropped just below her waist, giving him a nice view of her hip. He caressed her back. She mumbled in her sleep and rolled over taking most of the sheet with her. The move pulled the sheet lower.

He pushed up to his elbow, stroked her side, and couldn't resist tugging the sheet down farther to better view her body. His eyes followed the path of his hand as he traced the shape of her side and hip. He froze and pushed up higher to get a better look. She had a picture of a flower on her butt. The only ones he'd ever seen were on the arms of sailors down at the coast. Curses spewed from his mouth.

He jumped from the bed and stood over her, hands on his hips. "Dammit to hell, woman. What do you mean by doing something like that to your body?"

"Hmm? What are you talking about?" She rolled to her back. Her eyes traveled his body and gave him a sleepy smile. "You are so beautiful."

"Don't try to distract me." He flipped her onto her stomach and slapped her right buttock. "What the hell is that?"

"Ouch, that hurt." She rubbed her cheek. "What does it look like? It's a rose."

"I know it's a rose. I want to know what it's doing on your butt and who put it there?"

She sat up and stretched, giving him a delicious view of her breasts. Her grin was wicked. She knew what she was doing to him, and his already engorged member throbbed in response.

"Don't try to change the direction of this conversation."

"Oh, all right. It's a tattoo, and the man at the tattoo parlor put it there."

He raked his hands through his hair and sputtered. "You mean you exposed your backside to some man?"

Her chin shot up. "I'll have you know I had on my bathing suit, so I didn't expose anything. A friend of mine had one put right here on her breast."

Texanna pointed to the inside slope of her breast. His mouth fell open. Lord, the people in the twenty-first century must be a depraved bunch. He shook his head. "Get up. Garrett will be here in a minute."

She jumped from the bed, "Well, I can see the honeymoon is over," and padded out the door buck naked, her cheeks undulating with the swing of her hips.

Too shocked to speak, and distracted by her nakedness, he stood with his mouth hanging open. With a growl, he charged out the door and caught her before she slammed the guest bedroom door in his face. Her body held flush with his, he kissed her. "The honeymoon is definitely not over." He nuzzled her neck. "But I've got to go to work today."

She sighed. "Yeah, and I've got to pick apricots. Hope they won't rot before I get some help to make jelly."

"They'll hold for a while in the larder."

"Wonder if Jason would bring Sally out tomorrow and help me learn to cook?"

"I'll ask him."

****

Texanna stood at the sink washing dishes when Garrett charged through the back door. His face was freshly scrubbed and alive with excitement.

"Is it true? Did Aunt Molly really have twins?"

"Yes, sir. She really did. A boy and a girl."

He mulled the news over. "Wow. Reckon we can

go see 'um?"

Texanna considered the request. Doc said to keep folks away for a while but surely that didn't apply to family. A boy needed to see his cousins.

She ruffled his hair. "Tell you what. You help me dry these dishes and pick apricots, and after lunch we'll ride over there."

Garrett found the dishtowel and dried while she washed. When he caught sight of the bathtub he wandered in to look. He didn't appear happy when he came out. "Why's Pa boarding up that end of the porch?"

"So we'll have a private place to take a bath." She explained his father's plans, and, though Garrett listened with interest, he looked at her with suspicion.

"Does this mean I have to take a bath everyday?"

"Yes, at least most days."

Garrett's shoulders slumped. "I'll go get the ladder and start picking the apricots."

It was almost lunchtime when they finished picking the fruit. She needed to fix something quick for lunch. The cookbook on the Hoosier had a recipe for potato soup that didn't look too hard. By the time Royce arrived, the soup was ready. Since it wasn't a hearty meal, she added chunks of ham. Garrett rushed out to meet his father, and they both washed at the pump and walked in together. Texanna had bowls filled with soup and a plate of biscuits on the table.

Texanna stood waiting at her chair when Royce and Garrett entered the kitchen.

"Something looks delicious." As Royce held her chair, he whispered in her ear. "The food looks good too."

Her face heated, and the fool man had the nerve to grin. His lips twitched. She gave him a wicked smile. "Thank you. I hope you enjoy it."

He ate a spoonful and looked surprised. "It's delicious." He reached for a biscuit and took a bite. It broke apart and fell in his bowl.

"Oh, drat. I followed the recipe exactly." She was never going to get the hang of cooking.

"They're fine. You probably just over kneaded them." He reached for her hand and squeezed it. "Jason's bringing Sally over in the morning."

"Do like me, Pa. Soak your biscuit in the soup. It's good."

Royce spooned up a bite. "You're right, Son." He patted Garrett on the back. "Smart idea."

****

Texanna and Garrett rode double on Josie to the farm. Excited, he talked the entire trip. She fought the long skirt the whole way, trying to get comfortable. If she had her jeans on underneath, the position of her skirt wouldn't matter.

Matthew met them at the porch. He picked Garrett up and tossed him in the air.

"So, you couldn't wait to see your cousins, huh?"

"No, sir. Texanna said they're beautiful. I've never heard of a boy being *beautiful.*"

Matthew laughed. "Well, you were mighty pretty when you were first born too." He hugged Texanna, and, with an arm around each of them, took them inside.

Molly was glad to see them and pulled Garrett onto the bed for a good hug. Texanna stood with Matthew looking at the babies. "I can't believe they're both asleep at the same time."

"Shhhhh," said Matthew. "They might hear you. This is the first time. We probably got two hours of sleep last night."

Garrett pushed his way between them and peeked into the bassinet. "Which one is Nathan?"

Texanna went to sit with Molly while Matthew

introduced Garrett to his cousins. "How are you feeling?" Having a baby might be hard work, but Molly was radiant.

"Wonderful, but Matthew won't let me up for more than a minute or two at a time." Molly teared up and grasped Texanna's hand. "We'll always be grateful to you for saving our baby."

"I'm just thankful I remembered what to do. That was my first time to use what I'd learned years ago in high school health class." She prayed she'd never have to use the skill again.

"Royce explained to the men who you are and what's going on."

Texanna stiffened. Why didn't he tell her?

"He had to, Texanna. Doc was beside himself to know where you'd learned such a thing. None of them will betray you." Her eyes were sympathetic, but steady. "Royce loves you so much. We don't want to see him hurt and broken again."

Texanna felt the intensity of Molly's words. Hurting Royce was the last thing she wanted to do. She loved him. But she also had a responsibility to Pearl. "I'd never do that on purpose. I love him too much, and Garrett too."

Molly was quiet for a long moment, and then smiled and nodded. "I can't believe I'm sitting here talking to someone from the future. One of these days I want you to tell me what it's like."

"I will, but if you don't mind, I'd like to talk about Pearl, what she was like as a young woman."

Molly was quiet for a minute. "You're very like her, you know." Texanna nodded and Molly's forehead furrowed. "But, I noticed something different from the very first and couldn't put my finger on it. I've laid here and thought about it the last two days and finally figured it out. With Royce, you're outspoken, blunt, and don't beat around the bush." Texanna grinned. Yep, that was her. "But

Pearl made her wishes known in more subtle ways. She didn't raise her voice or argue, but Royce always got the message."

Texanna couldn't imagine Pearl being mild mannered. She shook her head. "Her jump forward in time must have changed her then, because the woman I knew could put my bluntness to shame. She was a tough old broad and the sweetest person in the world." Texanna's throat tightened. "I miss her."

"What that poor woman must have gone through." Molly shook her head. "I just can't imagine turning around and finding myself in another century." She shivered.

"I can tell you, it's a real shocker. I got on that train to please Pearl, but had no idea her theory of time-travel would work."

Texanna studied her hands. Her voice was thick when she spoke. "It's the best thing that ever happened to me. I can't imagine life without Royce and Garrett." Making love with Royce eased the tension between them. As she'd lain in his arms last night, she'd considered her options. Now, in that moment, she realized there were none. Her destiny was changed forever.

Chapter Fifteen

Royce woke to the smell of coffee and bacon. He washed, using the water on the washstand, and dressed. Downstairs, Texanna stood at the stove. Snaking an arm around her waist, he nuzzled her neck until she giggled.

"It's about time you got up. You're getting lazy in your old age."

He growled in her ear. "Lazy? Honey, I'm just a satisfied man. Your lovin' wears me out."

She elbowed him in the ribs. "Sit down and eat your breakfast before I toss it out the back door." He took the plate she handed him and sat down. With a dish towel, she picked up the coffee pot and poured them both a cup of coffee.

"Where's Garrett?"

"He went next door to see if Aggie could come over and help me make jelly one day this week." She sipped her coffee. "Did Jason ask Sally to come out?"

"Yep, she'll be here around eleven o'clock this morning. Has chores to do for her mother first." He finished his breakfast and carried his plate to the dishpan full of soapy water. "You might want to stock up on sugar. It takes a lot to make jelly. Wouldn't hurt to have more flour too."

"Oh, dear. I hadn't thought about that."

"It's not a problem. You and Garrett can ride into town with me this morning and pick some up at the general store."

Garrett came in through the back door, letting it slam loudly. "Morning, Pa."

"Good morning, Son. You want to ride into town this morning?"

His face lit with delight. "Oh boy, I'll go change real fast."

Royce caught him around the waist before he could clear the table. "Have you finished all your chores?"

"Yes sir. Even took more milk over to Aunt Aggie."

"Okay. Get your hair combed while you're up there." The boy hit the stairs at a run.

"I better find something easier to ride in. This skirt makes it hard to maneuver." Texanna stood and set her coffee cup in the sink.

"There should be several riding skirts upstairs in the chifforobe."

Before she could leave, Royce took her hand, pulled her on to his lap, and squeezed her waist. "You're so much fun to tease."

"Well, you just keep having fun. I'll make a list of spots where pinches will be most effective." To make her point she pinched his underarm.

He yelped and swatted her rear. *God, he was happy*. He pulled her mouth down to his and kissed her. "I love you, woman." She twined her arms around his neck and kissed him. His free hand moved up to stroke the side of her breast. When he pulled back, his breathing was ragged. His eyes flicked to the stairs as his hand moved under her skirt to stroke her leg. "Can you think of an errand we can send Garrett on? Maybe to Aggie's to double check about tomorrow."

"That wouldn't take him long enough. He can be over and back in a flash." At the sound of Garrett's boots pounding down the stairs, Texanna stood. "I'd better hurry."

When Texanna left the house, Royce had Samson and Josie saddled. He'd added a scabbard to the saddle on Josie, and the Winchester was in it. Pleased but surprised, she looked at him in question.

"I don't want you and Garrett out alone without protection." He'd debated long and hard with himself about a pistol for her and finally settled on a .32 caliber pocket pistol. She could carry it in a holster, a pocket, or her boot. He pulled it from his saddlebag. "Here, I got you this."

She took the pistol and looked it over, checking to see if it was loaded. Smiling, she nodded and tucked it in the pocket of her riding skirt. "Thank you. It's perfect for me."

"Thought you'd like it." He stowed a box of cartridges in her saddlebag and helped her mount Josie. "You can wear it in a holster to Matthew's, but never in Waco."

"Okay. I'll remember that."

Texanna enjoyed the ride into town. The morning sun beat down on them, warming as it moved higher into the sky. Garrett rode in front of his father, and chattered nonstop. Royce stopped in front of the livery stable. He helped Texanna down and turned to Garrett. "Stay here with the horses, Son. I want to show Texanna something in the stable."

With his hand at the small of her back, Royce took her to a stall in the far back. Inside stood a pretty sorrel mare, her mane and tail slightly lighter in color than her coat. The horse stuck her head, with its white blaze, over the rail and whinnied as they approached.

Texanna couldn't resist reaching out to touch the horse's neck and mane. The mare liked her touch and smell and proceeded to sniff her shirt pocket looking for a sweet. Texanna laughed and moved back. "Sorry, girl, I didn't bring anything."

Royce laughed. "I think she likes you."

"She's beautiful. Whose horse is she?"

"She's yours."

Texanna was stunned. "Mine?"

"Yes, yours. You're a good horsewoman, Texanna. You deserve a good mount."

"Oh, my gosh." She threw her arms around his neck. "Thank you." His arm circled her waist.

"You're welcome. Her name is Strawberry." Royce kept his arm around her as they turned back to the stall. "We'll let Garrett ride Josie. When he's better in the saddle, I'll buy him a good horse."

"How on earth did she get the name Strawberry?" asked Texanna.

Royce laughed, and his voice grew husky. "I don't know, but when I saw her coloring, she reminded me of you. Then, when I learned her name, I had to buy her." He leaned in to smell her hair. "That first night you were home, your hair smelled like strawberries."

The gesture pleased Texanna immensely. "Royce Dyson, you're a romantic."

"Guilty as charged." He opened the door, stepped inside, and quickly saddled the mare.

"A new saddle, too?"

"Figured we needed one. Don't want you or Garrett riding bareback." Clicking his tongue, he said, "Come on, girl." One hand on the reins, the other at Texanna's waist, he ushered them from the stable.

At the sight of the mare, Garrett whistled. "Ooh-we, she's pretty, Pa. Whose horse is she anyway?"

"She's Texanna's."

"Who's gonna ride Josie then?"

"Figured you could until I think you're ready for a more spirited horse." Royce couldn't resist grinning at the excited boy. He jumped a foot into the air.

"Do you mean it?" Before he could answer, Garrett had his arms wrapped tightly around his waist. Royce patted his back and ruffled his dark head of hair. “Thank you, Pa. I’ll take good care of her.”

“I know you will, Son.” He gathered both Samson and Josie’s reins. “Now, you go on to the store with Texanna. I’ll take the horses with me to the jail. You can pick them up there.”

Texanna grinned up at him. “We won’t be long.”

In the general store, they purchased two ten-pound sacks of sugar, a twenty-pound bag of flour, and extra canning jar lids. While the clerk totaled up their bill, Edna Murphy marched into the store.

“I declare, Texanna. What’re you going to do with all that sugar?” Texanna was surprised the older woman was so dressed up. Her outfit was grey serge with navy trim, similar to the dress she’d worn to church last Sunday. She even had on a hat with feathers stuck out at various angles.

Garrett piped up. “We’re making jelly the day after the July Fourth doings.”

Edna patted Garrett’s shoulder. “Is that a fact? Well, I’ll be out first thing that morning to help. It’s the least I can do.”

“Oh, Edna, there is no need. It’s a long way out from town, and Aggie will be over to help me.” She wasn’t sure why, but the thought of the two women in the same kitchen made her uncomfortable. Both were strong personality types and would probably mix like oil and water.

Edna sniffed and looked piqued. From the expression on her face, the woman considered herself superior to Aggie in the cooking department. “Just never you mind. It’s not that far. I’ll see you then.” Oh dear, Texanna’s assumption was correct. With both women helping, it would be a long day.

They stopped by the marshal’s office as they’d planned. Their horses were tied out front. Inside, Royce’s door was closed, but Pete manned the front office. As usual, his big-booted feet were propped on the desktop. He unfolded his long length and stood as they walked in the room.

"Howdy, Miz Dyson." He rushed over and found her a chair. "The boss will be out in a minute." Pete grabbed Garrett and swung him into the air. "What's this I hear about you ridin' a horse, tadpole?"

Garrett yelled with glee and when on his feet again, pulled Pete outside to see Josie.

Texanna grinned at the child's joy. The iron door to the cells opened, and a young man close to Jason's age froze when he saw her. A smile grew on his face as he looked her over from her heels to the top of her head. His eyes flicked around the empty room, to Royce's closed door, then back to her. She watched him with caution as he stepped through the iron door. It closed behind him with a clang.

Texanna studied him as he locked the door. Tall and muscular, he bordered on being stocky, but that didn't detract from his good looks. His hair was almost as dark as Royce's, and though handsome, his smile made her uncomfortable.

He approached her chair and was almost toe-to-toe with her when he stopped. "Hello, ma'am, my name is Ross." He emphasized the 'hello' with a slow drawl.

Texanna leaned back to distance herself. Noticing her discomfort, he leaned in, dropped his eyes to her breasts, and then flicked them up to her face. "You are one fine-looking woman." She was ready to wipe the gleam from the man's face with a punch to his nose when a bellow sounded from the doorway.

"Ross! What the hell do you think you're doing?"

Ross straightened but didn't move away from her. Before Texanna could open her mouth, Pete had Ross pinned against the wall. The jolt to the wood knocked a picture down. It hit the floor with a bang shattering the glass. "The lady is Miz Dyson, you fool. If Royce doesn't beat the tar out of you for showing disrespect, I will."

Royce's office door flew open. "What in thunderation is going on out here?" His eyes, dark with anger, lit on Texanna and moved to Pete and Ross.

Pete shook Ross. "Speak up, man."

Ross's face was a deep red, his jaw clenched in anger, but he finally nodded in Texanna's direction. "My apologies, ma'am." Pete turned him loose and without looking at her or Royce, the chastised deputy headed for the door.

Texanna turned to watch him. Garrett stood just inside, his eyes big and round. "Come here, Garrett." He hurried to her side and slid his arm around her neck.

She pulled him close and whispered in his ear. "You're not frightened, are you? Everything is just fine. Pete is here and so is your Pa."

Royce turned and said something to whoever was in his office. Seconds later a man left. Royce motioned with his head for them to enter. With her hands on Garrett's shoulders, they went inside.

Royce's brow was furrowed, and a muscle jumped in his cheek. "What happened out there?" She didn't know exactly what to tell him. The man didn't touch her. It was the way he'd looked at her. "You can tell me or Pete will."

"He got too close. His look was suggestive."

"Pa, he was lookin' at her bosoms. That's what he did."

Texanna felt the heat rise to her face. Royce nailed her with a stare. "Did he, Texanna?"

She nodded.

Royce looked like he'd explode, but he glanced at Garrett and worked to get his anger under control. "I promise you it won't happen again." The tension left his face, and he smiled. His expression may have fooled Garrett, but Texanna knew he was fighting to keep his rage under control. "Did you two get your shopping done?" Texanna assumed he was just making small talk.

"We—"

Excited, Garrett rushed ahead. "We got the groceries, Pa, and Mrs. Murphy is coming out the day after the picnic to help Texanna and Aunt Aggie make apricot jelly."

A grin stretched his lips. "Is that so? Ought to make for an interesting day."

She snorted. "Would you like to join us?"

"Afraid I'll be busy."

Royce walked them outside. The errand boy from the store had tied the bags of sugar with a small piece of rope and secured them to Josie's saddle. He made sure they were secure, transferred the Winchester to Strawberry, and then helped them mount. It took a few minutes to adjust the stirrups on Josie for Garrett. "You mind Texanna, Son. Don't be trying to kick Josie into a gallop or do anything foolish."

"I won't, Pa, I promise." He watched as they rode down the street toward home, then spun on his heel and strode to his office. "Pete, come in here a minute, would you?" He'd had it with Ross. This wasn't the first time his behavior was less than honorable.

"What you need, Royce?"

"Find Ross and bring him in here. I want his badge."

Thirty minutes later, Ross sat in the chair across from Royce. His look was defiant and cocky. Royce wanted to beat some sense into the kid.

"What do you have to say for yourself?"

Ross grinned and shrugged. "I didn't know she was your wife. Anyhow, you should be glad other men find your woman attractive."

Royce struggled to hold his temper.

"It's one thing to find a woman attractive and another to boldly insult her."

"I didn't insult her. All I did was look."

Royce stood so fast his chair hit the back wall. Ross was on his feet by the time Royce rounded his desk. He stood nose to nose with the younger man. "You damn well better learn to keep your eyes above a woman's neck." Royce shook his head. "You just don't understand, do you? What kind of manners did your mother teach you?"

Ross bristled. "My mother was a whore. All I learned from her was how to survive."

It was no wonder the kid didn't know how to act around decent women. Despite his faults, he had some good qualities Royce would like to see developed. Royce was tempted to give him another warning but decided against it. He'd already talked with him because of his over friendliness with ladies on the street. Some irate husband or boyfriend was going to shoot him if he didn't change his ways.

"I want your badge, Ross. This isn't the first time you've offended one of the ladies in this town. You have a lot of potential, but you've got some growing up to do before you'll be worth anything as a deputy."

The younger man's face turned red. Royce expected him to take a swing, but instead he ripped the badge from his shirt and slammed it on the desk.

"If you so much as look at my wife wrong again, you'll regret it."

Ross clenched his fists and walked from the room.

****

Texanna and Garrett had just finished putting the horses out to graze when Jason and Sally rode up. Garrett ran to his uncle to help him put Sally's horse in the pasture.

"Good morning. Come in and have a cup of coffee."

Sally set a basket filled with apples on the table. "Coffee sounds great. I brought some apples, so we can make pies today."

Wouldn't Royce be surprised if he came home and found a fresh pie? Texanna grinned at the thought. "I'd like that."

When Jason came in, Sally got him a cup of coffee and he sat down at the table. "I expect you ladies will have a fine meal fixed for me and Royce when I come pick Sally up tonight."

Sally fixed him with a cocky stare. "And who said you were invited?"

"My brother, the lord of this here manor."

Texanna snorted. "Lord, my as...of course, you're both invited to dinner." She needed to watch her mouth and no need to get Jason in a debate about women's rights. "You've not forgotten Sally and I will be taking the guns out back for a session after my cooking lesson?"

"No, just remember Royce said no ammunition."

"Just how do you expect her to learn to load a gun then?"

"All right, load and that's all. No firing." He got up to go and took Sally's hand. "Walk me out."

Garrett got up to follow.

"Hey, sport. Stay inside with me." Texanna leaned over and whispered. "Jason might want to kiss Sally good-bye."

Garrett looked like he'd swallowed a worm. "Really?" At her nod, he added, "Yuck!"

By late afternoon, they had two apple pies cooling on the table. One Texanna made by herself. The crust wasn't as pretty or flaky as Sally's, but it tasted good, and Sally showed her how to use biscuit dough to make dumplings. She was proud of her new skills and anxious for Royce to taste her pie.

Texanna went upstairs to collect the Winchester. She dropped several cartridges in her apron pocket. They stood in the shade of the barn, and Texanna showed Sally how to hold the rifle when not in use, how to load and unload the firearm, and finally, how to aim.

"Whew, that's heavy." Sally lowered the gun, pointing it at the ground.

"Yes, it is. Remember, keep it pointed skyward whether it's loaded or not."

"Oh, yeah, sorry." She sighed. "Sure wish I could fire it to see what it feels like."

Texanna bit her lip, thinking. Royce wouldn't find out. Of course, Garrett was sure to tell him, and she wouldn't ask him to lie to his father. Oh hell, she could handle his anger. "Okay, I'll let you shoot two rounds."

Garrett looked indignant. "Ahem, Pa said not to. He's gonna be mighty mad."

Guilt rushed over her. Here she was being a bad role model for the boy, but Royce was unbending. They weren't going to hurt anything. He'd let her shoot out here, so what was the difference?

"We'll just fire two cartridges to let her feel the rifle's kick, and then I promise we'll put the gun away."

He wasn't mollified, just stuck his hands in his pockets and shuffled his feet.

Texanna made sure the horses and cow were out of the way. She collected a couple of cans from the back porch, and set them a short distance from where Royce had set them up before.

"Pa don't ever shoot that direction."

"How come? What's over there?"

"Don't know."

Texanna shielded her eyes with her hand and looked out across the field. A small hill rose about a mile away and made a good backdrop from both positions as far as she could see. Moving their target position just a tad from Royce's kept them from looking into the sun. "I think we'll be just fine here, Garrett."

****

Texanna expected Jason to come in the house with Royce, but he didn't. Royce stalked in, favored her with a glare, and turned to Sally. "Jason has your horse saddled. Do you need any help carrying your things?"

"Royce, they're staying—"

He whirled on her, face rigid with anger. She clamped her mouth shut.

"Sally?"

She glanced at Texanna with concern. "No, I don't have much to carry. Just this basket." She lifted it across her arm.

"Thank you, Sally. I appreciate your help today."

The younger woman hugged her. "I had a good time. I hope I see you again soon."

Royce muttered, "You can count on it." As soon as she was out the door, he turned to Garrett. "Son, go do your chores."

The boy shot Texanna a sympathetic look as he walked out the door. "I tried to tell her, Pa."

Hands on his hips, Royce glared at Texanna. "What the hell did I tell you about firing that rifle today?" She rolled her eyes. "Don't look at me like that, woman. You disobeyed my orders. I ought to blister your butt."

"Blister my...how dare you? You're not my boss. I don't take orders from you."

"You think not?" He removed his gun belt and hung it on the peg by the back door. Next came his hat and coat. "You'll learn when I give an order, I expect it to be obeyed."

"Well, get ready to be disappointed, Mister."

"Texanna, you're stubborn and think you know

it all. I'm here to tell you different. Your impulsiveness could get you or someone else killed."

She started backing away toward the stairs. "No need to run. I won't lift a hand to you. I've got a much better punishment for you and Sally."

She relaxed and a small smile curled her lips. "Look, I'm sorry we went against your directive, but we didn't hurt anything. It won't happen again."

"Didn't hurt anything, huh? Don't think Mr. Thompson's sow thinks so. As a matter of fact, Mr. Thompson is hopping mad, and the only way I could pacify him was to tell him you two gun-toting ladies would be out tomorrow to help him slaughter and dress his hog."

****

Royce cast side-ways glances at Texanna as they returned home from the Thompson's. His first reaction upon seeing her had been to laugh, but then she'd turned, and he'd seen her face. All humor died a quick death. Her damp hair was plastered to her pale face. Bloodstains marred her dress. She slumped in the saddle and looked ready to collapse any minute.

"Pa, you shouldda seen her. She'd work awhile and then run puke. Work, puke, work—"

"Okay, Son. I get the picture."

"Mrs. Thompson tried to get her to lie down but, no, she kept on aworkin' and pukin'."

Before they'd left, Texanna had apologized again to Ed Thompson, she wouldn't let Sally take the blame. Sally may have fired the rifle, but Texanna was the one who bore responsibility for the incident. Royce was proud of her for owning up to her mistake.

The minute they stopped inside the barn, Texanna started struggling with Strawberry's saddle. Royce stilled her hand. "I'll take care of her. You go on and get cleaned up. Don't worry about dinner, we'll eat something cold."

Texanna was too numb to speak. She nodded and started toward the creek. She heard him holler, "That water is cold." But she didn't care, she wanted out of her blood-stained dress and the stink washed off her body. Without undressing, she walked into the water and sat down. The water reached her neck and felt like heaven.

Garrett's voice echoed across the field. "Are you decent? Pa had me bring you some soap, towels, and a blanket."

She turned around. "I'm decent."

He gaped. "You're in the water with your clothes on?"

"Toss me the soap and leave the linens on the rock." She caught the lilac-scented bar. "Thank you, Garrett. I'll be in after awhile." She stripped and scrubbed her hair and body. At last she felt she'd survive.

The hot air quickly dried her body, so she wrapped the towel around her hair and folded the blanket around her body. Still wearing her tennis shoes, she squished her way back to the house. Royce had coffee boiling on the stove. He and Garrett sat at the table eating a ham sandwich and peaches from a can.

"I think I'll lie down for just a minute."

Two hours later Royce walked upstairs to the spare room to check on her. She'd dropped the quilt and towel across the chair and crawled under the sheet. The room was hot with the door closed. He opened the transom above it and raised both windows higher. Hopefully, there'd be enough of a breeze to keep her comfortable.

He wanted her in his bed, but neither wanted to confuse Garrett by seeing them sleeping together. Something needed to be settled between them soon.

****

Texanna woke the next morning feeling refreshed. The smell of coffee drew her downstairs. Royce turned when she entered the room, but didn't speak. They eyed each other for several moments. Finally, he asked. "Do I need to worry about my life?"

"Nah, I had it coming." She walked into his arms.

He buried his face in her neck. "Thank goodness. I'm sorry you got so sick yesterday. Feel okay now?"

"Yeah. I'm hungry, but it'll be a while before I can choke down a piece of sausage." She shuddered.

"Let's hurry and get ready for the picnic. We don't want to miss Jason in the horse race."

After breakfast, Royce fried two chickens while she made biscuits and another apple pie. With a recipe from the cookbook, she made potato salad, and then filled large jars with sweet tea.

As soon as the food basket was packed, she ran upstairs to change clothes. At the back of the chifforobe she located a yellow gingham dress. The sleeves were short, and though fitted at the bodice, it wasn't confining. Her tennis shoes weren't dry so she found a pair of Pearl's button-up shoes. She knew they required a hook but couldn't find it, so stomped around in them flopping around her ankles. They pinched like the devil but would have to do.

Just before she left the room, she remembered the locket. It wasn't on top of the dresser where she'd left it last time she'd worn it. Panic washed over her, making her gasp for breath. It had to be here somewhere, it had to. She yanked open drawers and tossed items on the bed in her frantic search. The blue dress, maybe it had caught on something inside. Searching inside the chifforobe, she located the blue dress, threw it across the bed, and checked every fold.

Resigned, horror clouding her brain, she sat

down on the bed and sobbed.

Chapter Sixteen

Unable to contain her misery, she called, "Royce, Royce!"

He bounded up the stairs and rushed through the door. "What's wrong? Are you hurt?" Hands on her shoulders, he looked her up and down.

"The locket, Pearl's locket is gone. I've looked everywhere and can't find it." How could she have lost it? That it was her trip back home wasn't as important anymore, but it was hers and held a great deal of sentimental value for her as well as Royce.

"Lord have mercy, woman. I thought you were hurt."

"You don't know how important the locket is to me. It's my tie to Pearl. It's also my ticket home, the key to time-travel."

His face hardened. "I thought there was something between us, Texanna—something permanent. Do you still intend to return to your time?"

She threw her arms around his neck, and his arms wrapped around her waist. "No, love, I've been battling with my conscience and have decided to stay. I love you and Garrett."

He groaned and pulled her closer. "Thank God. I want a life with you, Texanna, to have babies and grow old together."

"I want that too, but I worry about my father, what he'll think if I don't come back." It was terrible to have to choose between her father or Royce and Garrett. In her heart she believed her daddy would be happy for her if he knew, but he'd suffer not knowing her fate. Right now, she wanted the locket back. "I have to find the locket. I feel incomplete without it."

"When was the last time you wore it?"

She thought back. "Sunday at church. I specifically remember putting it on." She'd been so anxious to get out of that damn corset she'd forgotten all about the locket. It hadn't been around her neck when she'd changed clothes. "I must have lost it at church or at the restaurant." It could be lying in the churchyard, or maybe Maybell found it and was holding it, not knowing who it belonged to.

"We'll find it. It's easily identifiable with your initials and Garrett's picture."

Texanna nodded in misery. Losing the heirloom hung over her like a dark cloud.

Royce cupped her cheek. "Come on. Let's get those shoes buttoned and on the road. Don't let this spoil your day. The locket will turn up."

****

That evening, with Garrett sound asleep from the exciting July Fourth festivities, Texanna lay with her head on Royce's shoulder, one leg thrown across his thigh. He stroked her arm enjoying the softness of her skin. She twirled her fingers in the hair on his chest. Royce pushed up to his elbow to study her. His heart thumped. Damned if he wasn't nervous.

"I have something I want to show you." Her brow furrowed with questions. He tapped her nose. "Just a minute. I'll be right back."

He ran downstairs to the pile of clothes he'd dropped on the kitchen floor and fished in his pants pocket for the small box. Texanna was sitting up in bed, arms wrapped around her raised knees, when he returned to the bedroom. He sat at her feet and cleared his throat.

"I love you, Texanna. I want us to be married. I know it's awkward to ask Brother Riley to marry us, but..."

"We could tell him we want to renew our vows. It's a growing custom in the twenty-first century, and since Pearl was gone so long, and I don't remember my *prior* life, maybe he'll see our reasoning."

"That sounds perfect."

He opened the box and showed her the two gold bands inside, one delicate, one bolder, less fragile. "I want us to have new rings for a new beginning."

She reached out and stroked his face. "Oh, Royce, nothing would make me happier than to be your wife." He didn't realize he'd been holding his breath until it left him with a whoosh. He pulled Texanna to him and pressed her face to his chest.

"Sweetheart, you've made me a happy man." He kissed her forehead. "I'll talk to Brother Riley tomorrow and see if he can marry us after the services Sunday."

****

Texanna looked at the jars and jars of apricot jelly they'd put up that day. She'd never been so tired in her entire life. Well, maybe not as tired as when she and Royce had done the wash, or after the hog butchering. But, the physical work along with the stress of refereeing the two older women sapped her. Not only had they washed and scalded what seemed to be thousands of jars, but Aggie and Edna had also snipped at each other all day. Between the two, Texanna doubted the jam would be fit to eat. One said to do one thing, the other, something else.

At lunchtime she fell gratefully into a chair to eat the fried chicken she'd put in the larder yesterday. With it, they had deviled eggs and cold biscuits. She chewed slowly, lost in thought, only half listening as Aggie and Edna regaled each other with horror stories of the Civil War.

Edna snorted. “I still can’t believe those two Dyson boys fought for the Union.” She cast a glance sideways to see if Texanna heard her remark. Texanna froze under the older woman’s gaze, but pretended indifference. Royce and Matthew fought for the Union? At the knowledge, pride surged through her. She was all for being faithful to her southern roots, but when it came to the war, she supported the Union. If they knew her views, they’d call her an abolitionist, especially Edna. The woman didn’t mince words.

Aggie chided, “Men have to follow their conscience, old woman, even when it’s not a popular decision.”

“That’s easy for you to say, you didn’t lose your husband and son to the damn Yankees.”

“No, I lost mine to a liquored-up Johnny Reb too scared to hold his fire until Samuel found his position.” Aggie had tears in her eyes. “Dead is dead regardless of who pulled the trigger.”

Edna dropped her head and nodded. “You’re right, Aggie. As much as I respect Matthew and Royce, I feel the bitterness rising again sometimes.” She turned to Texanna. “What about you, girl, how’d it feel having your man fight against his southern brothers?”

Texanna could understand Edna’s bitterness. She hadn’t seen history’s future or had the advantage of the whole picture of the war as they’d been taught in high school. To delay having to answer, she took a long drink of water. “Seems to me, despite which side he fought on, he waged war on his countrymen.” She shrugged. “Anyway, Royce has never told me about his part in the war, and I don’t ask him.”

“But, you lived it girl, surely you have your opinions. You were just, what, twelve-years-old when the war broke out?"

Yes, Pearl had been twelve, but she'd never expressed her views to Texanna. Everything Texanna knew about the Civil War she'd learned in history books. Royce would have a fit if she told the women she'd not been born yet. What would they think of the movie *Gone With the Wind?* She had a good idea these two didn't know many women like Scarlett O'Hara.

Aggie noticed her reluctance. "Leave her alone. Can't you see she doesn't want to talk about it?"

Edna sniffed. "Well, excuse me, Aggie. Didn't mean to ruffle anyone's feathers." She smiled at Texanna patronizingly. "Truly, dear, I didn't mean to make you uncomfortable. In fact, as much as I resented Matthew and Royce fighting for the Union, I admired their courage and determination when they came home." She shook her head. "Law, I feared that rambunctious little Jason was dead along with his parents, but within a couple days of returning, his brothers found him and two days later, they were back in their family home."

"What about Jason?" Somehow she'd never heard anything about Royce's life before he married Pearl. Why was that?

"Why, a nasty carpetbagger shot his folks down in front of him, and the boy not more than thirteen-years-old at the time. Would've killed him too, but he ran off. Took his Pa's gun and lived in a cave like a wild animal for three or four months. His brothers knew right where to find him."

"But why would the man do that?"

Aggie looked shocked. "Surely you know how dishonest those men were. Not that we had many here, but one managed to get elected as tax collector and tried to swindle the Dysons out of their farm. Said they owed back taxes, which wasn't true. When they wouldn't budge, he shot them down in cold blood."

Texanna was stunned. She'd read about such dealings but never knew Royce's family had been affected. "How'd Royce and Matthew get the farm back?"

Edna appeared taken aback. "Why, Royce did what that fool who was sheriff should've done, he—"

Aggie shushed her. "That's for Royce to tell her, not us."

They got up from the table and carried their dishes to the sink. Texanna wanted to know more, but at Aggie's admonishment, Edna's mouth had shut like a vise.

"Darn it, at least tell me about Jason. Was he safe and well?" The poor kid all alone. It's a wonder he didn't starve.

"Are you kidding?" Aggie laughed, and Edna joined her. "That tadpole had the time of his life. Hunted for game, stole from folk's gardens, even snuck in his ma and pa's house and ran off with all kinds of foodstuff and cartridges for his pa's gun."

"Yeah, put old crook Peters in a real tailspin. Came riding into town bawling to the sheriff about thieves taking enough food to feed an army." Edna slapped her leg and chortled. "The kid was leaving food on doorsteps all over the county." She sobered. "Was a blessing to some. Kept them from starving."

Texanna laughed with the two women. No wonder Jason was such a risk-taker. He sounded like a regular Robin Hood. It's a miracle he didn't try to take more revenge on Peters. Her laughter died and she had to ask. "Did he ever try to shoot his folk's killer?"

Aggie nodded. "Oh, he fired a shot or two into the house, shots barely missing Peters. But, even at thirteen, if Jason had wanted to kill him, he would've. He knew his brothers would take care of it when they got home."

They spent the remainder of the afternoon filling the rest of the jars with hot apricot jam. The ladies chatted as they worked, having bonded talking about the war, but when she let it slip about the wedding on Sunday, an argument broke out over who would bake the wedding cake. After a heated discussion, Edna conceded to let Aggie bake the cake, and she would provide the punch and table decorations.

Thankfully, by the time Edna got in her buggy to leave, jars of cooled jelly were lined up on shelves in the larder.

Texanna walked out with Edna and cringed at Aggie's parting words. "Good riddance you old biddy." If Edna heard the rude remark, she pretended otherwise and chattered all the way to her buggy. Once there, she stopped and placed a hand on Texanna's arm.

"I want you to know, even though he fought for the Union, your husband is well thought of around here. He saved more than one family from that crook Peters, including mine."

On impulse, Texanna leaned over and kissed the leathered cheek. "Thank you for telling me."

Rather than go back inside and face Aggie, Texanna sat down in one of the rockers on the front porch, leaned back, and closed her eyes. Whew, she didn't know if she was up to the hard work of life in the nineteenth century. She wondered when frozen food was invented, and electric refrigerators? That's what she needed. If she never saw another apricot, it'd be too soon.

She sighed and, with the toe of her tennis shoe, put the rocker in motion. Yes, she was tired, but it was a weariness of achievement. Royce would enjoy the jam—if it was fit to eat. How had she come to this? Wanting to please a man? A grin stretched her face. Well, he certainly pleased her. God, she loved the man and couldn't imagine not having him in her life.

Her mood sobered. She'd learned a lot about Royce today. Why hadn't he told her he'd fought for the Union? Were his nightmares flashbacks from the war or because of what happened when he returned home? She'd heard him thrashing in his sleep several times and wanted to go to him. A feeling of tenderness washed over her. Next time she'd be sleeping beside him. Hopefully, he'd tell her about his bad dreams.

It was important to make sure Royce was safe. Without the locket, she couldn't travel back and forth in time trying to change history. Dire methods were necessary. She needed a plan to somehow prevent the bank robbery so there'd be no room for error. What had she read about the Bass gang and their whereabouts before the robbery?

****

"Folks, today is a special day for our church family as Royce Dyson has asked to renew his vows of love with his lovely Texanna before this congregation." Brother Riley beamed as he spoke from the pulpit. "Now, I've never heard of this *renewing vows,* but I think anytime two people want to pledge their love in God's house before his children, the Lord is mighty pleased."

Applause and chatter rippled through the room. The preacher raised his hand for quiet. "This morning's service will be short to allow time for the ceremony. Our church ladies have prepared a special reception for the couple immediately following."

Texanna heard his words from her position in the small room at the front of the church. She inhaled the sweet fragrance of the white roses and baby's breath in her bridal bouquet as Molly straightened the skirt of the ivory satin and lace gown Pearl wore on her wedding day. If only she had the locket.

"You look lovely, Texanna." Molly's eyes were full of tears. She took Texanna's hands. "You've made Royce so happy. I hope you're as delighted as he is."

"I am, Molly, happier than I can ever express."

Sally poked her head in the door. "They're ready." Molly hugged Texanna and rushed to the door. Garrett slipped in as she exited.

Texanna was terrified. After all, a girl didn't get married every day and especially in a previous century. But she was marrying Royce—he was a special man and these were unique circumstances. She loved him with a passion, one that would never die. To think she'd almost settled for something less in a marriage horrified her.

Royce's heart beat so hard he thought it would jump out of his chest and run down the aisle to Texanna. This beautiful woman was actually marrying him, and Pearl's son escorted her down the aisle. Garrett took Texanna's hand and placed it in his father's then moved to stand beside Jason. Royce's eyes locked with Texanna's. He kissed her hand, placed it on his arm, and drew her closely to his side.

"Dearly beloved, we're gathered here to join this man and this woman in holy matrimony." Royce repeated his vows without lifting his gaze from Texanna's. Her lips trembled as she spoke hers, but her voice was clear and unfaltering. "I now pronounce you husband and wife. Royce, you may kiss your bride."

He didn't need to be told twice. He raised Texanna's veil and smiled, his heart in his throat. "Hello, wife," he whispered against her lips. He'd meant the kiss to be short and sweet, but as their lips touched, it deepened. His lips plundered hers. At the sounds of laughter, whistles, and applause, they broke apart. Royce whooped with joy and looked down into his wife's radiant face. She blushed, but her giggles blended with his laughter.

Royce took Texanna's arm and rushed her down the aisle and outside to the small porch. Brother Riley was the first person to file from the church. "Congratulations, Royce, Texanna. It's a joy to share in your happiness today." As the pastor moved on, Edna Murphy hugged first Royce and then Texanna. She patted Texanna's cheek. "Lands, child, I believe you're prettier today than the first time you wore that dress."

They'd eaten, cut the wedding cake, and accepted everyone's good wishes. Royce was ready to have his wife to himself. He started maneuvering Texanna toward the buckboard. When they were almost to the wagon, he felt a tug on his jacket.

Garrett stood beside him. "Pa?"

Royce leaned down to his son's level. "What do you need, Son?"

"Is Texanna my ma now?"

Royce didn't doubt Texanna's affection for Garrett, but they'd never openly discussed her now being his son's mother. He'd slipped up. They should've talked about it before Garrett asked. "Would you like for her to be?"

Attitude solemn, Garrett nodded. Royce's heart twisted at the need on Garrett's face. "Why don't you ask her?"

Garrett moved to Texanna's side and waited for her to notice him as she laughed at something Jason had said. The boy squeezed closer until Texanna felt his presence and reached out to embrace him as she continued to listen to Jason. He tugged on her skirt, and she leaned down. Royce couldn't hear their conversation, but Texanna's face turned soft and loving, and she kissed Garrett's forehead and hugged him.

Someone clapped him on the shoulder, and Royce turned to see Matthew. “Molly’s anxious to get home to the twins, so we’re leaving.”

“Thanks for keeping Garrett for us.”

Matthew laughed. “He’ll be a big help with the babies, and we always enjoy having him.” His brother studied him for a minute then crushed him in a bear hug. “Congratulations, Royce. It’s wonderful to see you smiling again.”

Garrett squeezed his way back to Royce’s side, but spoke to his uncle. “I’m ready, Uncle Matthew, but I need to talk to Pa for a minute.”

Matthew patted Garrett’s back. “Okay, squirt. Meet us at the buggy.”

Garrett’s face was sober. “What’s bothering you, Son?”

“Nothing, Pa. Texanna told me she loves me, and if I wanted to, I should call her ‘Ma.’”

Royce sighed with relief. “She did? What’d you say?”

Garrett drew in the dirt with the toe of his boot. “I said I wanted her to be my Ma.”

“You did? I’m glad.” He studied the boy’s expression of indecision. “Aren’t you happy about that?”

He nodded. “Yes sir. But, she’s not my real ma, is she?”

The boy was sharp as a tack. Royce squatted to Garrett’s eye level. “No, Son, she’s not. Can you trust me for a couple of days, until you come back from the farm?” Garrett nodded and Royce pulled him into his arms. “Just remember we both love you very much. I’ll explain everything when you get home.”

Garrett smiled and threw his arms around Royce’s neck. “Okay, Pa. I love you too.”

“Run on to Uncle Matthew’s buggy now, and be good for your Aunt Molly.” Royce watched as Matthew lifted Garrett into the buggy, and then he made his way to Texanna's side. It was time to head home—past time, in his opinion.

As Matthew's buggy passed them, Garrett yelled. "Bye, Pa. Bye, Ma."

At the boy's words, Texanna covered her mouth with one hand and waved with the other. She flashed Royce a teary smile and laid her head on his chest.

"Let's go home." He lifted Texanna into their wagon and went around to climb inside. Royce flicked the reins to urge Josie into a trot. Texanna scooted closer on the seat and took his arm. His heart expanded with pride. "Are you sure you don't want to take a short trip while I'm off? Stay in a nice hotel?" He'd wanted to take her to San Antonio for a couple of days, but even though the locket was lost, she refused to get on the train. She wouldn't even consider taking the train to Dallas.

"I'm sure." She squeezed his arm. "But thank you for offering to take a trip. I'm sure we'll find plenty to do right here." She gave him a suggestive wink.

"Royce?"

"Hmm?"

"I'd like to have our rings engraved with something special."

So, she hadn't noticed the inscription inside hers yet. He'd pondered for hours over what to say. He hoped she'd be pleased. "I've already had yours inscribed."

She leaned back. "You have?" She slipped it off and squinted to read the message. "My Love, My Wife—A Second Chance in Time."

****

Royce had just finished checking on his two prisoners when Edna Murphy stomped into his office. "Good morning, Edna. What are you doing out and about so early?"

She snorted. "Don't you try to sweet talk me, Royce Dyson. What do you mean by firing that nice young deputy of yours?"

"You mean Ross?" Why would Edna care who he hired or fired?

She nodded and straightened her spine.

"I fired him because he was disrespectful to Texanna. And she wasn't the first woman he's insulted. He was turning out to be a good deputy, but I can't have men on the force who offend the good women of this town."

Edna plopped down in the chair across from his desk, a defeated look on her face.

"Why do you ask? Has he bothered you?"

She drew herself up as if insulted. "Of course not. He came by this morning looking for work. I hired him to fix my roof. It's been leaking some since this spring. I didn't know he'd been fired until I mentioned Ross to Pete a minute ago." She shook her head. "I don't understand him acting that way. He seems to be such a nice boy."

That's what Royce thought when he'd hired him. And to be honest, he still thought the kid had more good than bad in him. "He's had a hard life—told me his mother was a whor...ahem...a woman of ill repute, and the only thing she'd taught him was how to survive. He can't have learned many manners growing up like that."

She twisted the strings on her beaded reticule. "I guess I should fire him, but he seems to need the work."

"Don't be too hasty. He's not mean, just needs to learn to respect women. Working for you may be the best thing that ever happened to him. Maybe you can teach him some manners."

Edna stood, drew herself up to her full height, and strode to the door. "Thank you, Marshal. I'll keep you apprised of the situation."

Royce watched her go, a grin teasing his lips. If the kid didn't learn manners from Edna, he was a lost cause.

****

Texanna cleaned the breakfast dishes, made the beds, and dressed in a riding skirt and blouse. Wouldn't Pearl be tickled if she could see her now? The tomboyish neighbor girl being Little Miss Homemaker. Rather than put on her tennis shoes for all to see, she tugged on a pair of boots she'd bought at the general store. She'd just shrugged and looked confused when the storekeeper remarked on how much her feet had grown since the last pair of shoes she'd bought. Yeah, two sizes.

She made sure her .32-caliber model Colt was loaded, and slid it into her skirt pocket. It was small enough to not be burdensome, was single action so she didn't have to worry about it going off, and had just enough punch to cause some damage, if needed. The very idea she'd once believed all cowboys in the old West wore a gun and holster was embarrassing. Movies and television were to blame for that misconception.

She saddled Strawberry and walked Garrett over to Aggie's.

"I don't see why I can't go with you." Garrett drug his feet and kicked up dirt along the path.

"Because, I have some business to tend to and don't want to have to worry about you."

"I wouldn't be no trouble."

That was true, but she didn't want him along to witness her crime. She ruffled his hair. "Of course you wouldn't, but you know, women sometimes need to do some shopping on their own."

He looked at her with hope. "I could stay with Pa."

"Not today, young man. You can go with me another time."

"Oh, all right." His shoulders slumped. "But I gotta tell you, Aggie is going to make me work in the garden, and I'll get my clothes all dirty."

She couldn't restrain her laugh. "Don't you worry about the dirt. We've got enough water for your clothes and you."

He mumbled and looked at his feet. "Yeah, never seen anybody waste so much water."

They stopped at Aggie's open gate. She stood inside the screen door. "Do I hear this boy grumbling?" He ran up the steps, and she opened the screen to him.

"No, we're just discussing the conservation of water." She mounted Strawberry. "I'll be back by to pick him up in a couple of hours."

"No rush. He's welcome to stay until dinner time if you want."

It might not be a bad idea for him to stay until Royce was finished chewing her out. She wondered if they'd be able to hear him yelling at her clear across the field. Most likely they'd understand every word. "We'll see. Thanks, Aggie." She waved and kicked Strawberry into a trot.

The streets were busy in Waco and it wasn't even nine o'clock. People probably wanted to take care of business and get home before it got too hot. She avoided the marshal's office and tied her horse to a hitching post outside the druggist's. The telegraph office was two doors down, and she didn't want people to see Strawberry hitched out front. Not that anyone would take notice, but just to be safe.

The heels of her boots made a loud resonating sound on the wooden sidewalk, and she tried to step quieter. No need to bring extra notice to herself. Inside, the clerk bent over his desk writing on something. He grumbled, "Be with you in a minute." He finished his task and looked up. "Sorry, ma'am, didn't mean to keep you waiting."

"It's no problem. I'm not in a hurry."

He stood up and walked up to the counter that separated his desk from the rest of the room. "Need to send a telegram, do you?"

"Yes, I do." She felt like turning and running but had to see this through.

He handed her a sheet of paper and a stubby pencil. "Make it as few words as possible to save cost."

She nodded and wrote out her message. By now she knew it from memory. "What's that sheriff's name over in Limestone County?"

"Why that'd be Sheriff Avert. Why you askin'?" His brows furrowed above the round, wire-rimmed spectacles. "You needin' to get a message to him?"

"Uh, yes, I do. Telegrams are confidential, aren't they?"

He drew himself up to his full five-foot, four-inch height and fixed her with a stare. "Of course they are. We got rules about tellin' folk's business."

She nodded and moved the paper toward him. He picked it up and read it aloud. "On good authority, Bass gang, old line shack five miles south of Groesbeck. Dyson."

Chapter Seventeen

Texanna remained on pins and needles all afternoon. She expected Royce to ride up any minute, murder shooting from his eyes. Painting was the only thing to keep her mind off the war of words she knew would come. Garrett's portrait was ready for framing. She'd stretched a canvas to do a self-portrait and quickly put a wash over it in preparation to begin. Lightly she sketched in the outline of hair, face, and torso standing by the railing of the front porch. The white of the porch against the blue of her dress would be a good contrast.

The confrontation didn't arrive until the following day, when he came home for dinner. Texanna could tell by the set of Royce's shoulders as he rode into the yard he was royally pissed. From the kitchen window, she watched as he brushed down Samson and put him in the pasture. Garrett hopped along beside him as he worked, and they both washed up before they came inside.

"Supper's ready and on the table." They had leftover biscuits, cold ham, deviled eggs, and canned peaches. Texanna poured both Royce and Garrett milk and a glass of water for herself.

Always the gentleman, Royce held her chair for her to be seated but didn't touch or kiss her as he usually did. They held hands as he returned thanks and then silence closed in around them. Garrett, feeling the tension, for once was quiet and looked back and forth between them. Finally, he chirped,

"Sure is a good supper, ain't it, Pa?"

"Yes, it is, Son. Just perfect for a hot day." He shot a glance at Texanna. "And a trying one."

"Is...Ma in trouble again?" His little brow wrinkled with worry as he glanced at her with concern.

Royce cleared his throat. "You might say that." A muscle in his jaw twitched.

Texanna reached for Garrett's hand. "Don't you worry about me. This is between me and your Pa. We'll work it out. Finish your supper."

Eyes serious, he turned to his father. "You're not going to take a strap to her, are you, Pa?"

Royce choked on his food, coughed, and gasped for air. "Have...have...I ever taken a strap to you, Son?"

"No, sir, but I spect there's a first time for everything."

"I suspect your right. There may come a time when I have to use a strap on you, but your ma is not a child. I can't whoop her to make her mind me, and I'd never hurt her." He took a long drink of milk. Garrett visibly relaxed. "Now, finish your supper so you can get your chores done and get to bed."

"Yes, sir, Pa."

Royce finished his meal in silence. It infuriated him Texanna had the gall to act as if she'd done nothing wrong. She ate her meal without the slightest bit of nervousness. Dammit, she should be shaking in those rubber shoes.

He'd just locked up several prisoners for fighting in one of the saloons this afternoon when Sam Avert, the sheriff from Limestone County, came in. Filthy, covered with road dust, and looking worn to a frazzle, the big man dropped into a chair in his office. Royce poured him a cup of coffee.

"What brings you to Waco, Sam?" He poured himself a cup and rounded his desk to sit down.

"Why...on account of your telegram yesterday."

"Telegram? What the hell are you talking about? I didn't send you a message."

Sam searched in his pocket and came up with a crumbled bit of paper. "Well, somebody sure as heck did. Read this."

Royce took the paper and scanned it. Hell's bells! What was he going to do with his foolish, interfering wife? If he had a lick of sense he'd lock her up and throw away the key. He crushed the note in his fist. "I didn't send this, but I know who did, and I assure you they'll pay for mixing in my business."

"Is that right? Well, whatda ya know?" He scratched his chin.

"I hope you didn't spend too much time on a wild goose chase."

"Now, wouldn't exactly call it that. Sam and his boys were right where that telegram said, but they was watchin' for us and got away. Wounded one of my deputies pretty bad, but he'll live."

Royce was stunned. How could Texanna have known? He'd read that book and seen nothing about the Bass gang being in Limestone County. If she'd known this, why hadn't she told him instead of involving someone else?

"I'm sorry to hear that. Who was hurt?"

"That new kid you met last time you were in town—Tom Sayers. He's a strong young fella, won't have any trouble mending."

"You know if I'd sent the telegram, I'd have been on my way to help out."

"Yeah, thought about that after all was said and done. Jumped the gun on my part and got the boy hurt."

"It wasn't your fault, but I know who's to blame, and I assure you they'll suffer the consequences."

Royce drank his coffee on the front porch while

Texanna cleaned up the kitchen. He could hear Garrett fussing about having to take a bath. The boy acted like he hated the new tub, but after being wrestled into it, he laughed and splashed around like a catfish tying to get off the hook. It took Royce ten minutes to get all the water off the floor.

The screen door squeaked, and he glanced up to see Garrett standing barefoot and in his white night shirt. "Night, Pa."

"Goodnight, Son." He let the screen slam, turned, and ran up the stairs. The bed in his room shook and hit the wall as Garrett landed in it and yelled, "Night, Ma."

Texanna's, "Night, Garrett," carried on the breeze.

Royce sighed and stood. He might as well get this over with, and would just as soon face a rattlesnake as to go through this, but Texanna had to learn her place. He didn't know what it was like in the future, but here in 1880, women didn't interfere in a man's job or disobey when given a reasonable order. It must be total mayhem in her era.

Texanna wasn't as calm as she wanted Royce to believe. And she wouldn't put it past him to try to spank her. She'd heard how men used to punish their wives, but if he thought he'd smack her on the butt he had another thought coming. Just let him try.

Back ramrod straight, she walked with Royce to the barn. The location of their little talk was another bad sign. At least he wasn't taking her to the woodpile. Isn't that where whippings used to take place? The lantern he carried cast a light glow around them. Moths and other insects gravitated to the light, and she batted at them with her hand.

Inside the barn, he hung the lantern on a pole and motioned her to a bale of hay.

"Thanks, but I'll stand."

Murder written on his face, hands fisted, he barked. "I said sit down, dammit. Do you have to defy everything I say or tell you to do?"

She plopped down on the hay and folded her hands in her lap. "You are not my boss, Royce Dyson. I'm your wife, not your personal servant."

Face twisting, he bellowed like a mad bull and slammed his fist into one of the studs holding up the hayloft. It vibrated and hay and dust rained down on Texanna's head. She jumped up and moved from under the dust cloud. Coughing, she beat at her clothes and hair.

"You're my wife, by God, and you stood before Him and the people of this town and promised to love, honor, and obey me." He snorted. "You've done nothing but cause one problem after another, and this time you stepped over the line." His voice rose to a roar. "I ought to charge you with forging the town marshal's signature, and lock you up."

"I did no such thing."

"What—falsify your marriage vows or put Dyson on that damn telegram?"

She meant her marriage vows. Maybe she missed the one about obeying, but... "I didn't falsify your name. If you recall my name is Dyson now and I—"

"Don't give me that, woman. You knew the sheriff would assume I'd sent that telegram." He grabbed her shoulders and shook. Her head rattled around on her shoulders. "Do you realize your selfish behavior got a young deputy shot?"

Texanna felt the breath leave her body. *Oh God, no.* She hadn't meant for anyone to get hurt. She stifled her sob with her fist and shook her head.

"I'm sorry, I never intended—"

"I'm tired of hearing that. What were you thinking to achieve?"

"I...I'd hoped they'd...catch the gang, and...and they wouldn't be able to rob the bank." She turned her back to keep from seeing the disdain on Royce's face. "Did they catch them?"

"No, they were ambushed, and a young man almost lost his life. Your fault, Texanna. All your fault."

His words were like blows hitting her back. "I'm sorry, I'm sorry..."

"Well, I'm sorry too. I'm sorry you didn't trust me enough to tell me you knew the gang's whereabouts, sorry you have so little regard for what you know I'd disapprove of, and the stain you've placed on my name and reputation as Marshal of Waco, particularly with my fellow peace officers."

Texanna whirled and quaked before him not from fear, but from regret. She'd sent the telegram without thinking it completely through. Damn, damn, damn! She should have put an anonymous signature on the telegram. Hand outstretched to him, she pleaded. "Royce...oh, God. I didn't realize."

"Don't touch me right now. I've sworn not to hurt you, but you're tempting fate. I'd like to take a riding crop to your butt."

She'd never seen him so angry. "I'm sorry, Royce."

He raked his hands through his hair. "Yeah, well, I'm sorry too. I thought you could be the wife I needed, a strong woman to stand by me and build a life with, but at every turn you go against my wishes." He shook his head. "I'm not so sure anymore."

"You don't mean that. Please, I said I'm sorry. What can I do to make things right?" He couldn't be serious. He wanted to hurt her, punish her for what she'd done.

"I think you've done enough. For the next few days, you will not leave this place." She started to say something, but he reached out and grabbed the front of her dress, yanking her forward. His face an inch from hers, he growled, "Did you hear me?"

She nodded and choked on her sobs. He shoved her away from him. "Get in the house. I can't stand the sight of you right now."

Blinded by her tears, Texanna turned and ran. She tripped and fell face down in the dirt but scrambled to her feet and continued toward the house. Oh God, he'd had such hate and disgust on his face. She'd ruined everything, killed his love for her.

She stumbled inside, carried water up to the guest room, washed, and put on her gown. Curled up in a ball under the sheet, she bit back her sobs in fear of waking Garrett.

Royce watched the spunky woman he loved so much run from him in fear. His stomach twisted with hurt and regret, and when she fell in the dirt, it took all his resolve to remain rooted to the spot. He wanted to wrap her in his arms and kiss away her hurts, but he couldn't. She had to learn not to interfere in his business. She'd meant well—he knew that, but a man could have died. If she'd just told him about the hideout, he'd have organized a posse large enough to apprehend them. But no, she was trying to protect him, didn't have enough faith in his ability as a lawman. That hurt his pride and fueled his anger.

He took the lantern from the pole and walked slowly toward the house. The lamp wasn't lit in their bedroom, but the one sitting on the kitchen table still shone brightly. He put out the lantern, left it on the back porch, and carried the coal oil lamp upstairs with him. At the top of the stairs, he paused and stared at the closed spare bedroom door. So that's how she planned to handle the situation—pout and avoid him. That was fine. She'd learn it wouldn't gain her any sympathy from him.

Tired to the bone, he sat down in the chair to remove his boots and then stood to shuck out of his clothes. Without turning back the covers, he lay down on the bed and stared at the ceiling.

He'd exaggerated the impact of the telegram. His job wasn't in jeopardy, but his pride damn sure was. No way would he let her out of his life. They belonged together, and if she tried to leave, he'd love her senseless or lock her up and hide the key. He'd let her suffer and think about what she'd done tonight. Tomorrow, they'd talk again and come to some agreement.

****

The sun was up when Texanna woke. Stretching, she blinked and looked at her surroundings. The guest room? Then she remembered the events of last night—Royce's harsh words and her utter shame. Would he send her packing today? Is that why he'd not woken her to cook breakfast? Maybe he just couldn't stand to look at her anymore. She dressed, made the beds, and went downstairs to find a note on the kitchen table telling her Garrett was at Aggie's. That's it, no 'have a nice day," or anything? He didn't even sign his name.

She went outside to see Strawberry, but the pasture and barn were empty. Even Josie was gone. Dread weighed on her heart. Was he trying to keep her here, or was he sending a silent message? Well, he'd forgotten she could run, and it wouldn't take her long to jog into town. But she wouldn't. She'd do what he said.

On the walk over to Aggie's, she pondered Royce's words from last night. He was wrong. She had all the faith in the world in him, knew he could take care of himself, her, and Garrett. Why then didn't she tell him about the hideout instead of wiring the sheriff of Limestone County? God only knows why she didn't. She had a lot to make up for—if he'd let her. She could be an obedient wife. It might go against the grain, but she'd give it a good shot. Lord, she loved the man and couldn't live without him.

Garrett eyed her with caution all day. If he asked again, "Are you okay, Ma?" one more time she'd scream. By late afternoon, she searched for a way to keep the boy from following her around like a puppy. He needed cheering up, distracting.

"Do you have a checker game, Garrett?"

"Pa does. It's in the parlor in that little table by the window. Gots cards too."

"Really? Do you know how to play poker?"

"Nah, Pa won't teach me. Never has time."

When Royce rode up that evening, she and Garrett were on the front porch with a competitive game of twenty-one going. The boy was either good or lucky and had a large pile of matchsticks on his side of the table. Garrett yelled, "Pa, Pa, we're playing poker, and I'm winnin'."

Royce drew Samson up at the porch and grinned down at the boy. "Is that right?" His eyes drifted to Texanna.

She stood and smoothed the front of her dress. "Supper will be ready in a minute. I'm afraid we forgot the time."

"No hurry." He reached for Garrett. "Come here, squirt. Help me put Samson away." Garrett stood on the rail, and Royce lifted him in front of him on the saddle. He glanced at Texanna as she picked up the cards and matches. "We'll wash up before coming in."

She nodded and turned to go inside. His heart lurched at her lack of spunk and dejected manner. He turned Samson, and they headed for the barn.

"Well sport, what'd you two do today?"

"Ma moped around the house most of the day, but then all of a sudden she asked me about checkers. But we ended up playing poker instead. I like that game, Pa."

"You do? Looks like you're pretty good at it too."

"I am. Ma says I'm a regular card sharp."

Heaven forbid, thought Royce. "You understand you only play cards with family. I don't want you out gambling with friends. It's a bad habit and can lead to all sorts of problems."

"Like what?"

"Why do you think we have so many fights down at the saloons? Because people get to arguing about a game or someone cheats. Then somebody draws a gun or a knife, and a man gets hurt or killed."

"Okay, Pa. Only with family. You reckon Uncle Jason would play with me sometime?"

"I imagine. But be careful. He cheats." Royce gigged him in the side, and Garrett squealed with laughter.

Royce watched as Texanna tried to smile during dinner, struggled to act normal for Garrett's sake, but she wouldn't look at him and jumped when he touched her. He grabbed her hand and squeezed, and saw the gleam of a tear in her eye.

He helped her with the dishes while Garrett took the scraps out to the chickens. When he came back in swinging the tin pail, Royce rinsed it and sat it on the back porch.

"Here, I want you to take this over to Aggie." He handed over several bills of money. "Don't stay long because it'll be dark soon."

Garrett stuffed the money in his pocket and looked at him with concern etching his brow. "You and Ma aren't going to argue again are you?"

"No Son, we're not. I love your ma, and adults do fuss on occasion." He chucked him under the chin. "But they make up too. So make lots of noise when you come back. We might be kissing."

He grinned, and then muttered, "Yuck! I'll holler before I come in. Sure don't want to see no kissin'." Royce didn't miss the look of relief on the boy's face.

In the kitchen, Royce swooped Texanna into his arms and carried her to a rocker on the front porch. With her in his lap, he rocked them both as they sat quietly, her head nestled on his shoulder.

"I love you, woman. But I won't tolerate anymore of your interference. If you don't trust me..."

"I do trust you, Royce—with mine and Garrett's lives, the lives of our future children. It was a stupid thing for me to do. I wasn't thinking straight."

"You could've told me, and I'd have taken care of locating the gang."

"I know. Please tell me I'm forgiven."

"You're forgiven, love." His voice was gruff. "I know my words were harsh last night...you know I'd never let you leave or put you away from me. Ever. We belong together." Hell, he'd take a strap to her before he'd let that happen. He squeezed her close, his hands smoothing over her back and hips. "Kiss me, sweetheart."

The kiss was sweet and tender. With his lips, he tried to sooth the hurt he'd inflicted and reassure her of his love. Thank God she wasn't the type of woman to go around pouting and holding a grudge. When they drew apart, he held her and rocked, the rhythm music to his soul.

"Royce?" Her breath teased his cheek.

"Hmm?"

"When are you going to trust me enough to tell me what happened in the war to give you such nightmares?"

He stiffened at her words, but turned his face into her palm when she touched his cheek and kissed it.

"I know you and Matthew fought for the Union, and I respect that, but as your wife, I think I should know the rest."

He took her hand, laid it over his heart, and covered it with his. His words were so soft. He barely heard them himself. "I know. I will, but not tonight." He kissed her softly. "All right?"

She dropped her forehead to his cheek. "Okay, but I'm going to hold you to it."

Out of the fading light they heard Garrett returning from Aggie's. He was whistling loudly. At the back door, he hollered, "Hey Pa, Ma, I'm home," before stomping into the kitchen.

Texanna leaned back. "What on earth?"

Royce whooped with laughter and called back. "We're out front, Son."

Chapter Eighteen

The next afternoon, Texanna stood at the sink looking out the window when Royce rode into the yard with Strawberry and Josie on a lead rope. She dropped the dishtowel and joined him in the barn. He'd put Josie in her stall, and now Garrett stood on a wooden box brushing her down. Strawberry nickered a greeting and nibbled at her hair as Texanna stroked her mane and hugged her neck. "I missed you, girl." She watched Royce, busy unsaddling Sampson, grin at her enjoyment of the animal. She asked pointedly, "You sure you trust me with transportation on the property?"

At his deep chuckle, she tossed her hair and went to the storage shelf to find another brush. "Honey, I didn't believe the lack of a horse would keep you here. If I was really worried, I'd have assigned an armed guard to you. Or hide your rubber shoes."

"You wouldn't dare!"

Grinning like a jackass, he asked. "What? Take your sh—"

"Oh, you brute. You know what I'm talking about—an armed guard."

"Whatever it takes, sweetheart, whatever it takes." He dropped Samson's saddle across a rail and walked toward her. Before she noticed the gleam in his eye, he caught her around the waist and tossed her on the hay in an empty stall. He landed beside her, threw his leg across hers as he drew her into his arms, and nuzzled her neck.

"Mmmm, I've been thinking about this all day."

Texanna turned and curled her arms around his neck. Their mouths met in a sweet kiss of longing. She sighed with contentment as he stroked her back.

He pushed to his feet and pulled her up, dusting the straw out of her hair and off her clothes. "Let's get these horses bedded down. I'm starved." He winked. "In more ways than one."

Garrett peeked over the top of Josie. "Pa, looks like she's got new shoes."

"Yes, Son, she does. All three horses got new shoes while in town. Big Tom at the Blacksmith's Shop shoed them himself." Royce put Samson in his stall and gave him a bag of oats.

Texanna eyed him suspiciously. She picked up Strawberry's front hoof and looked at the new horseshoe.

"Wished I could of watched him." Garrett was in awe of the giant of a man.

"Maybe next time."

Texanna snorted. "Did they really need new shoes, or were they just an excuse to keep me home?"

He filled a bag of oats for each of the mares. "Why both, of course."

****

This was the last time Texanna would bring Garrett into town with her. July was almost over, and she didn't want to take any chances on him being around when the Bass gang entered town. He would stay with Aggie where he'd be safe. She looked at Pearl's son atop Josie and felt her heart twist with love. How it must have hurt to be unable to return to him.

They stopped at the hardware store before going to see Royce. It didn't take long to buy more framing material, canvas, and some paint. She'd finished Garrett's portrait and needed additional colors for her self-portrait. While the clerk wrapped their purchases, Garrett went out onto the sidewalk to wait.

When she stepped outside, she noticed him several stores down bent over scratching a mangy-looking dog. Heavy treads drew her attention and she looked in their direction. A burly cowboy covered in road dust and Lord knows what else, strode up the sidewalk. Over six-feet-tall and probably three-hundred-pounds, he sneered as people dodged out of his way. It was that awful man Bull Tate. Before she could call Garrett, the man backhanded him. "Get away from my dog, brat." The boy flew through the air and landed in the dirt street.

Texanna choked on her scream and rushed to Garrett's side. She gasped as terror squeezed her lungs. She ran her hands over him to check for broken bones. "Do you hurt anywhere?" He appeared unharmed, but the breath had been knocked from him.

Garrett sobbed but shook his head.

She hugged him. "It's all right, Garrett, you're okay."

The clerk joined her on the street. "We've sent for the marshal, ma'am. Bull Tate is worthless. I wish Royce would shoot the varmint and put us all out of our misery."

Texanna looked down the street. The man was a half a block away and hadn't even looked back to see if he'd done any damage. Her jaw clenched, and her hands trembled as fury ripped through her. She turned to the clerk. Her voice shook as she spoke. "Please carry him inside. I'll be back in a minute."

She stood. Her instincts told her to wait for Royce but rage and hatred said, *"Kick that man's ass."* She was on the man before she realized she'd taken off at a run. Lifting her feet, she flew through the air and landed between his shoulder blades. He hit the ground hard. She dropped and rolled before springing to her feet.

"You sorry son-of-a-bitch. How dare you treat a child like that?" Frenzy kept her from remaining calm, and crying, she shrieked. "Get up, you...you...worthless sack of s...shit."

Before the words left Texanna's mouth, he'd rolled to his feet and spit dirt from his mouth. "You bitch. I'm going to enjoy messing up that pretty face of yours."

"Come on, big man. It's a shame you don't have the balls to attack men your own size. You're such a pussy you have to beat up women and children."

Texanna kicked her skirt out of her way. The damn thing slowed her down. Bull reddened and with a roar advanced. She managed to deliver two swing kicks, one to each side of his soccer ball-sized head. With each hit, his dirty hair flew out from his face. The big man shook his head and wiped blood from his mouth. He looked from his bloody hand back to her and grinned before coming at her again. Texanna swung her leg and connected with Bull's dirty mug when his fist shot out and caught her jaw sending her flying backwards to land in the dirt on her ass. She rolled and tried to get up, but sparks danced in her head. Then darkness rose up and enveloped her.

****

Royce was tired. He'd caught Jake Tate trying to steal pies out of the kitchen at Maybell's. Pies ended up all over the floor along with a bunch of dishes. After wrestling Jake to the ground, he'd had to literally drag the three-hundred-pound man's worthless hide the two blocks to his office. Royce wished he'd shot him in the foot and let someone else haul him over to Doc's. He left Jake lying in the floor of the jail cell. As soon as he'd locked the door, the fat man pulled himself up and with a grin, stretched out on the cot.

Royce had just sat down when Tommy Thompson charged through the door. His lips were trembling and tears ran down his face. Royce rushed to the boy's side. "What's wrong, son?"

"Come quick...Garrett and his ma...hurt...Bull Tate hit 'um over by the hardware store."

Fear lodged in Royce's heart. *Garrett, Texanna? No!* Ice water hit his veins. He gripped Tommy's shoulder. "Stay here. If Pete comes in, send him over."

Royce grabbed his shotgun and ran three blocks up the street and over to Franklin Avenue. A large crowd blocked his way but moved at his order. He could hear the sound of fists on flesh. Sweat poured from his body as terror and fury threatened to cloud his judgment.

Texanna lay in a heap on the ground. A woman kneeling at her side quickly reassured him. "She's all right, Marshal, just knocked out cold." Royce was torn between checking Texanna for himself and taking on Bull Tate. The woman gestured. "Hans needs your help right now."

Royce nodded and turned to the two men fighting in the middle of the street. Hans must've come to Texanna's aid and was taking a beating. Royce stepped between the two men and handed the shotgun to Hans.

Mouth bloodied, Hans grinned. "Thought you'd never get here, Marshal."

"Well, now, Marshal, this fight is between me and Hans. He butted into my business."

Royce turned toward Bull. The rage on his face must have registered with the idiot because the fool took a step back and held up his hand.

"No need for me and you to scrap." Bull grinned. He probably thought he was engaging, but Royce was beyond being pacified. Bull weighed as much as his fat brother Jake, but he was all muscle. He'd always thought Bull the smarter of the two, but today's behavior killed that belief.

"Is that right? I think you're mistaken. Even a fool knows we don't take kindly to men hitting women in this town."

Bull's eyes flicked to Texanna. "Now, Marshal, she started it. Bloodied my mouth, she did."

Royce felt a stirring of pride. It quickly evaporated as the thought of the danger she'd put herself in. "Good for her. I think you deserve more than that for knocking her son around." He started toward Bull.

"Now, don't take on so. I didn't hurt the boy none." He pointed to where Texanna lay. "She's just a woman and looks like she's gonna be just fine."

"That's where you're wrong. That woman is my wife and the boy is my son." His fist connected with Bull's jaw, and the bulky man fell on his butt, surprise registered on his face.

Bull looked around at the people watching. Royce knew the man didn't see one sign of sympathy. He was a troublemaker they could do without in the town. With a roar, Bull pushed up from the ground and attacked. Royce stepped aside and caught him between the shoulders with his locked fists. Bull went down again but didn't stay. He stood and circled, his fists the size of hams. Royce knew Bull could beat him in a fair fight.

But today wasn't fair, his fury changed the odds. Bull rushed in and caught Royce on the jaw sending him to the dirt. Royce jumped to his feet, shook his head, and charged landing three blows before Bull could react. Bull reached out and grabbed Royce's shirt, taking him down with him. They rolled in the dirt and Royce landed on top. He pummeled the big man's face taking pleasure in each blow.

Hands grabbed Royce from behind, pulling him

away, but he fought them off and continued his attack. Suddenly he was yanked to his feet.

"Stop it, Royce. That's enough." Pete had him by one arm. Enraged, Royce tried to jerk free, but Hans grabbed his other arm and held like a vise. He shook them off and stood gasping for air, trembling with the force of his need to commit murder.

Royce stared at the man on the ground. Bull wasn't worth dirtying his hands. He then nodded to Pete. "Throw him into a cell well away from his brother."

He turned searching for Texanna. She rushed into his arms. Oh God, she'd scared the shit out of him. His hands traveled over her body.

She whispered in his ear. "I'm fine, Royce, fine."

He pulled back and examined the swelling on her jaw. His own was rigid. "What the hell were you thinking, woman?"

"I wasn't. I'm sorry, Royce. He hurt Garrett, and I just..." She shrugged.

Royce could understand her emotion but wasn't relieved. "You can't take on men like that, Texanna. You've got to send for me. I'll take care of it."

Texanna's body trembled, and she buried her face in his chest and sobbed. "He knocked Garrett aside as if he were a piece of dirt on the sidewalk. I wanted to kill him. It took all my willpower to resist drawing my gun."

Royce stiffened. "You can't just go around shooting people. I don't want to have to lock you up for murder."

"I wouldn't have killed him. But I'd sure as hell have hit him somewhere that would hurt for a long time."

Royce sighed. "Come on, let's check on Garrett. I want Doc to take a look at both of you."

In the end, Doc looked at all three of them. Garrett was fine. Texanna needed to ice her jaw and limit her talking for a few days until the soreness subsided. Royce knew that would be a challenge. Doc also cleaned up the cuts and scrapes on his face and hands, then pronounced him fit for duty.

They walked out of Doc's office. The humid early August heat hit them taking Texanna's breath. "Garrett and I better get home. It's almost lunch time."

Royce stroked her arm. "Why don't we eat lunch at Maybell's today? It's too hot for you to cook, and I'm afraid you're going to have a headache from that blow."

Texanna didn't tell him she had one already. He looked like he hurt too. Garrett appeared unscathed.

They found a table, and when Maybell came to take their order, Texanna asked for a place to freshen up. The older woman led her upstairs to a room and found linens for her to wash with. The cool water felt good on her dirt-covered face.

She patted Texanna's shoulder. "So sorry about your locket, dear. We didn't find it."

"Thank you, Maybell. I'm not going to give up hope." Royce and Jason had scoured the churchyard but didn't come across it. He'd offered a reward, and the poster was plastered around town.

When she returned to the table, Royce handed her a folded dishtowel filled with ice. She held it against her jaw.

"You're quite a celebrity around here."

Texanna glanced around the room to see people staring at her, smiles on their face. Some nodded. She didn't deserve their admiration. She'd messed up again.

"Yep, you bloodied old Bull's nose." Garrett's grin was proud.

Texanna didn't return the boy's grin. "You know, Garrett, it wasn't a smart thing for me to do. Bull could have hurt me bad. I should've waited for your pa, but I let anger get the best of me." Her actions weren't a good example. Then she remembered her language.

Face hot, she stammered. "I used some pretty bad language. I'm sure I shocked many of the town's people." The men more so than the women. The women probably wanted to utter a few cuss words on occasion and understood her rage. She looked at Royce. "I'm sorry. I hope it won't cause you any embarrassment."

Garrett nodded. "Yeah, Tommy's brother Nathan said you called old Bull some really foul names. Reckon you could teach 'um to me?"

Royce ducked his head and pinched the bridge of his nose. He was enjoying her discomfort and trying not to laugh.

She straightened in the chair. "I most certainly will not. And I don't ever want to hear you using foul language. Do you understand me?"

He sighed and dropped his shoulders. "Yes, ma'am."

By the time she and Garrett reached home, her headache was raging. After they tended the horses, she took one of the powders Doc had given her and laid down. Garrett promised he'd stay in the house and work on his drawings or play with his tin soldiers while she rested. Within minutes, she was asleep.

When she woke, Garrett was curled beside her on the bed, out like a light. Contentment filled her. She had a husband and a child, and before too long she hoped to have a baby to add to their family. A boy for Garrett to play with would be nice, but she longed for a little girl—a cutie she'd name Rosie.

Shame enveloped her at her earlier behavior. With children depending on her, she needed to curb her recklessness. Her life and health weren't the only things at stake now. She eased from the bed to keep from waking Garrett and went downstairs. At the kitchen table, she wrote the day's events in the journal she'd started the day she and Royce married.

Chapter Nineteen

Making a frame was harder without modern tools, but Texanna managed. By the middle of the afternoon, it was finished, and she let Garrett stain it while she built an eleven-by-fourteen inch mount and stretched canvas over it. What she wouldn't give for a staple gun.

She worked on her self-portrait for a while. It needed to dry before she added the finishing touches. Her next project was a portrait of Molly, Matthew, and the twins. She put a wash of oils and turpentine over the entire canvas and then started blending colors for the background.

Garrett came in through the kitchen, letting the screen door slam with a whap. "I'm finished staining. Can we put the portrait in it now?"

"We have to make sure it's completely dry first."

"Feels dry to me."

"I'll check it in a minute."

"I can't wait for Pa to see it. He's gonna be surprised!"

Texanna grinned. Yes, indeed, he was.

As soon as Royce got home, Garrett bounced around him as he tried to unsaddle and groom Samson. The kid had so much energy he was about to bust.

"What's wrong with you, sport?"

"Nothing, Pa," the boy said with a grin.

Inside the house, Texanna waited for them in the kitchen. Royce took her in his arms for a kiss. Garrett burst out. "Pa, can't that wait? Times a wastin'."

Texanna giggled and stepped away from him. "Okay, go ahead and show him."

Garrett pulled Royce by the hand into the parlor. His son stood before the fireplace and looked up at the portrait hanging above it and cast glances his way to check his reaction.

Royce could only stare at the artwork before him. Texanna was more talented than Pearl. Pearl had been a good artist, but Texanna was spectacular. His son's face was so alive he waited to hear the portrait speak. Garrett looked out from the canvas with a teasing smile on his face, his blue eyes lit with humor. Texanna had added another figure—him. Royce stood, his mouth tilted in a grin, eyes bright with laughter, with his arm draped loosely across the boy's shoulders as he bent to speak in his son's ear.

It was quiet for several minutes. Texanna and Garrett were waiting for his response, but he couldn't seem to find his voice.

"Ma said we needed a reason to give you a gift, so we invented Father's Day." Garrett slipped his arm around his father's waist. Royce instinctively hugged his son's shoulders. "Do you like your gift, Pa?"

Royce took several deep breaths to calm his thundering heart. "I love it, Son. Thank you." He turned to Texanna and reached out for her. She walked into his arms. He breathed in her sweet scent, and the feel of her soft body against his made the ache in his chest deepen. "Thank you, love, thank you both."

"You're welcome." Texanna squeezed him and stepped away. He let her go with reluctance. "Come on, Garrett. Give your pa a chance to study it alone."

Their chatter faded as he continued to study the portrait. Texanna saw so much. His love for Garrett flowed from the canvas, as did his son's happiness. That she saw him so clearly humbled and flattered him. He had one regret. He wished she'd added herself to the portrait.

****

Texanna stepped back and considered the picture. It needed a few more reddish highlights added to her hair and some shadows to the blue dress Royce bought for her. Since her hair was shorter than customary for nineteenth century styles, she'd painted it up on top of her head with tendrils curling around her face. Tomorrow she'd add the finishing touches to her complexion, and the portrait would be done.

Royce stuck his head in the door. "Can I talk to you for a minute?" She knew he was dying to see what she worked on, but respected her secrecy.

"Sure, I'll be out in just a minute. Let me clean my brushes."

The sun was setting when she stepped out onto the porch. She sat down in the rocker beside him.

He reached for her hand and cleared his throat. "I don't want you coming into town for a while. Bull Tate has two more brothers, and there's likely to be trouble when they come to bail Jake and Bull out of jail."

"I need to come to town," she said. "I don't plan to bring Garrett with me anymore, but I have to be there when the Bass gang arrives."

"Dammit, you do not. Don't you trust me enough to be able to protect myself and this town?"

"Of course I do, but for some reason it's necessary for me to be in town to prevent you from being hurt." She held her stomach and shivered. "I feel it here in my gut."

He stood and walked over to lean against the porch post and look out at the field. "You're being unreasonable. I won't be able to function knowing you're in danger. How can I protect myself and the town when I'm worried about you getting hurt?"

Texanna thought about what he'd said. His reasoning was sound, and she didn't want to endanger him, but knew she had to be there to cover his back. She knew it as well as she knew her name. It wouldn't be pleasant to lie to him, but she would if necessary.

She'd be so glad when they were beyond August eighth. There were so many things she wanted to do, but the impending bank robbery hung over their heads. She still didn't have a clue who the killer might be. Ross had reason to hold a grudge, but Bull Tate and his brother Jake did also. How many other men out there had reason to want Royce dead?

Texanna stood and walked to the edge of the porch. "Royce, have you had previous run-ins with Bull Tate and his brothers?"

Royce turned and pulled her back against his chest. Arms around her waist, his breath rustled her hair. "I sent one of the brothers to prison a few years ago. He was caught rustling cattle and should be released in another year or two."

His arms were crossed under her breasts. "What about Ross? Any reason he'd want to kill you?"

"Not that I know of. Ross is new in town and doesn't have any relatives nearby." He leaned down and kissed her ear. "I'll do some checking tomorrow."

Royce turned her to face him and settled his chin on her head. "There are lots of men out there whom I've sent to prison or killed brothers or fathers, but that doesn't mean they're out for revenge. Most folks know when their loved ones are no good and don't hold the law to blame for putting them away."

Yeah, but then there are those who can't see their loved ones as being anything but perfect. Some people have sick ideas of who is at fault and are quick to blame anyone but the guilty person. They were the ones that were dangerous.

Royce cupped her cheek. "I need your promise, Texanna. I don't want you in town."

She turned her face into his palm and kissed it. "Okay. You won't see me in town. I promise." The lie was necessary to ease his mind—and her own. She couldn't live in the nineteenth or any century without him.

His eyes narrowed. "Now why doesn't that ease my mind?"

****

August eighth, the day Texanna dreaded, had finally arrived. Worry and fear closed over her heart like a vice. Royce had finished breakfast, and Texanna watched as he strapped on his gun belt.

She dried her hands and walked into his arms. He held her close and stroked her back. Her arms slid around his neck and pulled his head down for her kiss. His mouth was hot. As his tongue twined with hers, desire shot through her nerve endings, making her groan and press closer to his heat. Would she ever get enough of this man's loving?

His large hands spanned her waist, kneading her flesh before he lifted her and set her on the table forcing her legs apart with his thighs. His arousal pressed against her and her sex clenched and became moist with wanting him. With a groan, he broke the kiss and pressed his lips to her forehead.

She ran her hands down his muscled buttocks. They tightened in response to her touch. She squeezed and pulled him closer. Trying to keep her apprehension out of her voice, she teased. "Are you sure you have to go in today? If you stay home, I'll make it worth your while."

A chuckle rumbled from his chest. "Shame on you, woman."

He stepped back and she slid to the floor. "I

won't be home for lunch the next couple of days."

"Why—"

"Maybell will send a plate over." He caught her chin and tilted her face up to his. "Remember, you promised me you'd stay at home."

"Royce...I—"

He tapped her nose with his finger. "Bull and Jake Tate were released on bail yesterday. They're dangerous. It would grieve me to do it, but I'll lock you in a cell if I have to."

She wanted to argue but kept her mouth shut.

He dropped a lingering kiss on her lips. Voice hoarse, he whispered. "I love you more than life. Help me here."

Texanna chewed her inner lip and nodded. "I love you, Royce."

An hour before noon, Texanna sent Garrett over to Aggie's for the afternoon and saddled Strawberry. She wanted to do as Royce had asked but couldn't. Guilt gnawed at her for going against his wishes again, but she knew, without a doubt, it was vital, crucial, for her to be on the scene when the robbery occurred. Why, she didn't know. But she couldn't defy her instincts. She prayed Royce would be safe, and he'd forgive her for interfering one more time.

Today she'd worn her jeans, one of Royce's shirts, and an old duster jacket she'd found in the chifforobe. She'd piled her hair on top of her head, put on an old work hat, and stuffed any stray locks under the band. For good measure, she spit on her hands, rubbed them in the dirt, and then smeared it over her face and neck. Dressed as she was, she didn't think anyone would recognize her. Strawberry was a different story. She'd have to hide her somewhere while she skulked about town.

Texanna tied her horse to a tree in a grove just outside of Waco and, with the Winchester balanced on her shoulder, walked the rest of the way into town. Avoiding the stores where she might be recognized, she continued to walk up and down the sidewalk within easy viewing distance of the bank. Shortly before noon she noticed Royce, Pete, and several other deputies stationed at various points around the block. She tried to remain in the shade under the overhang of the storefronts so she wouldn't be seen.

It was time to get inside the bank. Her plan was to somehow get upstairs and set up a position from the second floor window. From there she'd be able to see directly down on the street and the side street. She'd just started across Austin Avenue to the bank when four riders came down the street. They stopped a block away, tethered their horses, and split up.

Texanna imitated the walk of a cowboy thrown from his horse one too many times. From under her hat she noticed Royce glance her way and then toward the scattering four riders. She sighed with relief, and mimicking a gimp leg, hitched herself up the steps and into the bank.

At the teller's window, she kept her head low and spoke through her nose as if she had a speech impediment. "Kin you gibe me the papers to deposit my dollars?"

Herschel, if she remembered his name correctly, eyed her suspiciously and slid a form and a pencil across to her.

She gave him a twisted grin and snorted a couple of times. "Be kay ifin I sits on them thar steps?"

He nodded. "Yes, Ma...sir...ahem, uh, I mean yes, that'll be fine."

Texanna wanted to laugh but bobbed her head and moved to sit on the stairs. She laid the Winchester on the step above. From there she had a good view of the front door and could crawl up to the second floor without being noticed. One of the riders made the block and was about to enter through a side entrance. She quietly grabbed the rifle and hustled up the stairs.

The man walked up to the teller and dropped a sack of coins on the counter. "I'd like to leave this for deposit."

"Do you have an account with us, Mister?"

"No, but I'd like to open one."

The teller cut his eyes toward where Texanna had been sitting on the steps, looked back at the customer, and then shoved paper and pencil toward him. "Please stand here, and I'll take it when you're finished." He turned and glanced to the second story landing.

Texanna's stomach clinched with nerves. The man was Jim Bass. His picture had been in the history book of Pearl's. She removed her hat so Herschel could see her face and held her finger over her lips. It shook so much she was afraid he'd think she was waving. She forced it to stay steady and pointed to the man at the counter and then to the one standing on the outer steps with his back to them. Before she could mouth, "wait," Herschel had sounded the alarm.

The man at the counter quickly drew his gun, aimed at the teller, and covered his mouth with a bandanna. "Hold it right there, fella." Herschel stopped, hands in the air. "Now, turn around."

Texanna drew a bead on Bass with the Winchester. She was shaking so hard, the words came out in a stutter. "Drop...the gun, Mister."

The robber swung the gun her direction and without thinking, she shot him in the arm. The gun dropped from his hand and slid across the floor. The robber at the door fired, forcing her to hit the floor. Before his bullet hit the wall above her head, the outlaw was down from an outside bullet.

On her knees, she crawled into the upper floor office facing the front of the bank. She positioned herself at the open window and kept her eyes on anyone at Royce's back. His men were placed along both sides of Fourth Street across Austin Avenue from the bank. Shots came from each side of Fourth Street. It paralleled the bank, so she couldn't see how many robbers there were. With all the shots, it had to be more than four.

Royce was positioned behind a water trough in front of the barbershop directly across from the bank. Pete was a yard back and partially hidden behind a stack of wooden storage boxes. Jason was across the side street, lying flat in the bed of a buckboard.

Texanna heard cries of pain and realized two of the robbers on the street beside the bank had been shot. She'd started to relax some when she noticed a gun rise from behind the buckboard where Jason hid. The man rose until she saw it was Ross. Her heart stopped. Ross was the murderer. The young man looked toward Royce, and Texanna stood and screamed. "Royce, behind you!" The words were no sooner out of her mouth when Bull Tate stepped from the alley behind the McLelland Hotel and aimed his pistol at her. Gunfire exploded. Pain ripped through her shoulder, knocking her backwards. Her legs crumbled beneath her, and the world went black.

Royce had heard Texanna scream, but he couldn't see her. He'd swung at her warning and seen Bull step from the alley and fire spurt from his gun, but he wasn't hit. Evidently Ross had seen him at the same time, and they both had opened fire on the big man. The gun smoke was settling as Pete and Jason checked the bodies.

He turned to Ross. "What are you doing here?"

Ross shrugged. "I saw the trouble and thought

I'd give you a hand."

"Thanks. I appreciate it." Royce looked around him and toward the bank. "Did you hear a woman yell?"

"Yeah, I did. She said, 'Royce, behind you." That's when I turned and saw Bull."

Oh, God. Texanna had been here. Royce hadn't dreamed her voice. Where the hell was she now? He ran toward the bank and stopped at the sight of Herschel's prisoner. "How'd you catch him?"

Herschel nodded toward the second story. "Someone shot his gun arm before he could shoot me."

Fear curled in Royce's belly. He bellowed. "Texanna! Where the hell are you?" Alarm and dread sent him racing inside and up the stairs. Jason was close behind him. "Dammit, Texanna, answer me!" Panic quivered in every cell of his body. On the second floor, all the doors were closed except one. With long angry strides, he charged into the room and stopped. Texanna lay on her back in the floor. The left shoulder of the duster she wore was covered with blood and it pooled onto the floor, forming a puddle beneath her. Royce fell to his knees and drew her into his arms. A howl of pain and rage rose from his chest. "No, God, please noooo."

Royce held Texanna in his arms, rocking back and forth, sobs shaking his body.

Jason's eyes never left Royce and mirrored the terror Royce felt. He yelled down the stairs, "Get Doc. Make it fast."

Jason knelt and pulled a clean handkerchief from his pocket. "Here, Royce. Hold this on the wound to stop the bleeding." Royce nodded and held the cloth in place. "Doc will be here in just a minute."

Just as he finished talking, Doc walked through the door. He kneeled beside Royce. "You know I've got to check the wound." Royce nodded and gently leaned Texanna back across his arm. Doc tore Texanna's blouse and gently probed the wound. "I'm sorry, son, but she's going to need surgery."

Royce's face was gray. Jason reached for Texanna. "You look like you're about to fall over any minute. Here, let me carry her to Doc's office for you."

"She's my wife. I'll carry her," Royce growled.

"Can I do anything to help?"

Royce looked back at the window. His voice broke. "Get the Winchester."

Half the town stood in the street and watched quietly as Royce carried Texanna to Doc's office. Women wept and wrung their hands, and men shook their heads in dismay. Jason stopped beside Pete. "Would you ride out to Matthew's and tell him he's needed?"

"Sure thing. On the way back I'll stop and take care of the evening chores at Royce's."

Jason clasped Pete's shoulder. "Thank you. Please, while you're out there stop at Aggie's and check on Garrett."

"I'll do it."

****

Danielle stood on the landing as Judge Stokes, her father, came through the front door. Tonight, his shoulders sagged with fatigue and when he removed his hat, she saw lines of worry etched his face. She lifted the hem of her green and black striped gown and walked down the stairs. "Here, Papa, let me assist you." She helped him ease out of his jacket and hung it on the rung beside his hat.

"Thank you, dear." He turned and kissed her cheek. "You look lovely this evening. Another new gown?"

Yes, it was but she didn't want to talk about clothes. "Is it true, Papa? Is the marshal's wife near death?"

"Yes, dear, I'm sorry to say she is. Such a tragedy. That a woman in this town could be gunned down in a robbery attempt is beyond considering. Of course, if she'd been at home where she belonged, it wouldn't have happened. But then, gossip about town said the marshal would have been killed if she'd been at home."

"Well, from what I heard, she got what she deserved. The very idea, dressing up like a man."

His jaw dropped. "I didn't raise you to have such unchristian thoughts, young woman. Your remark was callous."

Tears pooled in her eyes, she worried her bottom lip. "I can't help it...Royce was supposed to marry me." Her hand played with the locket around her neck. "Especially this time. You know he was about to court me..."

His eyes left her face and landed on the necklace she fingered. "Lord forgive me for spoiling you so. You've grown into a spiteful, insensible woman. I'm ashamed of how poor a job I've done raising you after your mother's death."

"How can you say that about me?" The old man was a fool. She was only protecting what was rightfully hers.

"Give me the locket, Danielle."

"What...why?" She backed away from him.

"You know why. It's not yours. It belongs to Texanna Dyson."

Her laugh turned into a horrible shrill chortle but she didn't care. "That bitch won't need it anymore. She's dying and I'm glad." She clutched the locket. "The whore ruined my life and she owes—"

His hand caught her on the cheek sending her flying into the wall. Her head bounced, and she slid to the floor. It was the first time he'd ever raised a hand to her. Maybe she'd gone too far this time.

He shook his head. "Dear God, I fear it's too late to save your evil soul."

****

Royce sat in a chair by the bed where Texanna lay, still asleep from the gas Doc had given her for the surgery. His white shirt was covered with Texanna's dried blood. It sickened him, and, with a yank, he sent buttons flying around the room. Standing, he tore the shirt off and stuffed it in the trash can beside the door. He sat back down, stroked Texanna's hand and kissed the palm, noticing its unnatural coolness due to her blood loss. Matthew sat on the other side of the bed watching him, always there to help him if needed. Royce shook with the need to weep and howl like the wounded animal he was. Why did God give such love and joy and then take it?

His eyes were dry and hurt as if they were being sucked from their sockets. He was about to get up and find water to soothe them when Doc came back in the room and handed him a wet cloth.

"Lay this over your eyes. It'll help a little."

"Thanks." Royce slid down in the chair, laid his head back, and covered his eyes with the damp rag.

Doc pulled a chair up beside him and sat down. "I'm going to be straight with you, Royce. She's bad. The bullet hit the bone near the joint and damaged a lot of tissue. If she lives, she may not have full use of her arm. She's lost a lot of blood, but if fever doesn't set in, she may be able to overcome that. We should know something by tomorrow morning."

At Doc's first words, Royce froze, not ready for the rest he knew were coming. He couldn't look at the man, just squeezed his eyes tight behind the cool linen to stem the fresh flow of tears. *Oh, God, no. Please don't take her from me. Haven't I suffered enough?* He sat forward and dropped his head into his hands. The wet rag fell unnoticed to the floor.

Doc cleared his throat. “I’m sorry, son. I wish I could do more.”

Chapter Twenty

Matthew moved his chair around the bed. His brother's big hand moved over Royce's back, kneading the muscles. "Don't give up, brother. Miracles do happen."

Royce nodded. Tears clogged his throat. If he spoke, he'd lose all control. He had to be strong for Texanna and for Garrett. Oh God, Garrett. What would he tell the boy if Texanna didn't make it? His body shook as he struggled to hold his agony inside.

He lifted his head and turned to Matthew. His voice was hoarse and foreign to his ears. "Where's Garrett?"

"He's at Aggie's. I'll pick him up and take him home with me in the morning."

"If...if she's not better in the morning, I want Garrett here." His voice cracked. "To say...goodbye."

Matthew's eyes were filled with worry. He nodded. "We'll have him here." Royce stood and embraced the man who'd been with him through every tragedy and celebration of his life. They clung to each other for a moment then Matthew squeezed his neck and stepped back. "I'll be outside with Doc if you need me."

Doc brought warm wash water. Dressed in a clean shirt, Royce pulled off his boots, cautiously climbed onto the bed, and lay facing Texanna. He curled his arm over the top of her head, being careful not to jostle her injured arm, and breathed in the scent of her hair. His other hand touched her waist and stroked her ribcage. "Please, honey, don't leave me. I need you so."

Texanna's mouth was dry, and a deep throbbing echoed in her left shoulder. She felt Royce's presence next to her, smiled, and moved to turn toward him. Searing pain tore through her shoulder, and she cried out. "Hurt...Royce...hurt."

"Be still, love. You've been shot." He kissed her forehead. "Let me get Doc. He'll give you something for the pain." She heard his stocking feet pad across the wood floor.

The pain built, and she tossed her head from side to side. "Oh God! Please make it stop."

He kissed her, and she tasted his tears on her lips. "Doc's coming. Breathe slow and deep." He brushed the hair back from her forehead. "I love you so much, Texanna."

"Royce...happiest month of my life." She curled her good hand in his hair and drew his lips back to hers. "My husband, my wonderful husband."

The door opened and Doc, Matthew, and Jason came into the room. She tried to smile for them, but the pain was splitting her wide open. She started at the sight of the large syringe Doc carried. Dang, it looked like something you'd use to oil a car. She closed her eyes and waited for the painful stick. As the medicine entered her bloodstream, the room began to spin and fade.

"Love you Royce. Love you forever. Garrett. Want to see Garrett."

Royce sat or lay beside her all night long. She woke again twice, and Doc gave her another shot. While awake, she continued to ask for Garrett. Royce knew she believed she wouldn't make it and wanted to say goodbye to the boy.

Four years ago, when Pearl disappeared, Royce thought he'd die with grief. Now, watching Texanna suffer and knowing she wouldn't make it, he knew what death felt like. His heart was a stone in his chest. Its weight was hard to carry and threatened to choke him.

Matthew brought him breakfast before leaving for home. Royce tried to eat, but the food wouldn't go down. Coffee was the only thing he could tolerate.

Royce stroked Texanna's hand. Her skin was soft and warm—too warm. Early this morning she'd developed a fever. They'd sponged her every hour, but it continued to rise.

Later that morning, Matthew and Jason came in with Garrett. Garrett rushed to his father's side, and his eyes pleaded with him to deny what Matthew had told him. Royce gathered him close and let the boy's tears mingle with his own.

"Why, Pa, why?" Royce held him until he could regain his control and speak.

"You remember when Texanna told you her neighbor Pearl, your real mother, sent her here for a purpose?" Garrett nodded. "She came to save me from getting killed in that bank robbery yesterday. Bull Tate found a way to hurt me worse than if he'd killed me. He shot Texanna."

They looked at the bed to see Texanna watching them. She tried to smile and winced but held out her hand to Garrett. Garrett grasped it, and she pulled him closer. "I love you, Garrett." Her lips trembled, and she shuddered. "You're the son...I've always wanted."

He laid his head on her stomach and sobbed. "Don't leave me, please don't leave me."

She laid her hand on his hair. Every word was an effort as she spoke. "I want to stay...watch you grow to be a man, but...I can't." She cupped his cheek. "I need...promise me." Texanna's eyes found Royce's as she stroked Garrett's hair. "Listen to your father."

Royce put his hand on Garrett's back and rubbed gently. "Texanna came to us to deliver a message from your ma, because the history books say you died robbing a train when you were eighteen-years-old."

Garrett straightened. "I wouldn't never rob a train." His expression was indignant and drew a chuckle from the adults in the room.

"Maybe not, Son. But sometimes when we've lost people we love, we forget our upbringing and do stupid things."

Garrett looked back at Texanna and squeezed her hand. "I promise, I won't do nothing stupid."

She brought his hand to her lips, kissed it and then laid it against her cheek. "I love you so much...as does everyone...here. When you hurt...or feel lost, find them..." Her hand knotted in the sheet and she gasped. "They...will help...you."

He nodded, sobs wracking his body. "I love you, Ma."

Texanna's body started shaking as tears rolled down her cheeks. Her pain-filled eyes found Royce's.

"Doc," Royce bellowed.

Jason scooped up Garrett and rushed him from the room. Matthew followed leaving Royce alone with his wife. Doc gave Texanna another injection and quietly left.

"Kiss me, Royce."

His lips touched hers and clung. She smiled and closed her eyes. Dropping his head to the bed, he caressed her leg with his hand. He didn't know if his stroking soothed her, but touching her brought him a small degree of comfort. She curled her fingers in his hair. Voice slurred and raspy, she said, "Nightmare...tell..."bout...it."

And he did, slowly at first telling how he'd gotten into the secret service, the lives he felt responsible for, and finally how he'd killed Peters for murdering his folks and making Jason live like an animal for months. When the gates opened, the words came through in a torrent. He held nothing back from her. Guilt ate at his soul for all the lives lost due to his spying.

Her palm cupped his cheek. "Think...lives saved. War would've dragged, more men...both sides...died."

Her words of comfort soothed him when others had been unable to do so. He was grateful she didn't condemn him for his part in the war, but what about his act of revenge? Yes, Peters had falsified records of several people in the area and taken their homes. The man lied, cheated, and stole from innocent folks. He'd murdered four men and one woman, but Royce shot the man twice in the chest and felt no remorse.

"Peters...rotten skunk...die...defended...family."

He raised his head to look at her, watching to see if it was Texanna talking or the drug. Tears pooled in her eyes, and they glistened in the low light of the room. An invisible fist loosened around his heart at her lack of censure. "I feared you'd be repulsed knowing what I've done."

She shook her head and then groaned, "Ooh wee, room's spinning." Her voice shot up in pitch. "Stop world, let me off." Her outburst ended as quickly as it began. "Proud you...always." With a grin, she added. "My...macho warrior...love...forever, Royce." Her hand faltering, she tried to touch his face. He grasped it and brought it to his lips. "Be...happy." And then she was quiet.

A knock sounded at the door. Royce dried his eyes and turned to see Judge Stokes.

"Can I come in a minute, Royce? I wouldn't bother you if it weren't important."

Royce couldn't imagine what business the judge had that could be more important than the fact that his wife was dying, but...he nodded.

The judge pulled a chair close to his and sat down. He took a handkerchief from his coat pocket and unfolded it to reveal Texanna's locket. Royce took it and closed his fist around it.

"I'm sorry for all the misery your wife has suffered due to the loss of the heirloom. Danielle's had it all this time." Lines of pain etched his face. "I'm afraid I've failed at raising my daughter." He stood and gripped Royce's shoulder. "I pray your wife gets better, son. Let me know if I can do anything."

Royce could only nod and watch as the older man left the room. The locket grew warm against his skin. He opened his fist and studied the stone his father had placed in his care for safekeeping. Turquoise wasn't a stone natural to this area. It had to have come from far away and if his father was correct, it was ancient.

His mind made up, Royce kissed Texanna's still lips. He gently wrapped her in the bed sheets, lifted and carried her from the room.

****

On the morning of August 15, 1880, the day was clear with a few white puffs of clouds scattered across the sky. A light breeze rustled the leaves of the big oak trees lining the Brazos River. Royce walked across scorched grass back to the cemetery to Texanna's grave. Everyone was headed to his house for the wake to give him time alone. Wildflowers and some of the garden varieties covered the dirt mound. Most common were the roses so many ladies grew in their yards.

Royce removed his hat and stared down at his wife's resting place. A sense of peace filled him as if Texanna had reached out and squeezed his hand. He would never forget her—her smile and laughter, her teasing. Their short time together had been packed with more joy than some couples shared in a lifetime. He'd been twice blessed. From now on his life would be filled with raising Garrett and helping Matthew and Molly with their children. One day, Jason and Sally would have a family, and he'd have more nieces and nephews to dote upon. Never again would he marry for love. Later in life he might marry for companionship, but he didn't ever want to hurt as he had on losing Texanna.

Bull Tate hadn't died from his gunshot wounds. His brother, Jake, confessed Bull was out to get even with Royce for sending their younger brother to prison. The boy had been in a knife fight in the penitentiary, and died as a result of infection. Bull blamed Royce. Their fight in the street cinched it. The big man was out for blood. Now Bull would go on trial for Texanna's death.

Settling his hat back on his head, Royce walked toward the tree where he'd tied Samson. The big horse munched the green grass under the big oak but raised his head when he approached. "You ready to head home, boy?" The last few days, he'd sensed Royce's mood and acted especially attentive. With a whinny of welcome, he butted Royce in the chest. "Love me, do you?" Royce chuckled as the stallion nibbled on his ear knocking his hat askew. He righted it and stroked his friend's neck. "I love you too, fella."

On the day of the robbery, Pete found Strawberry in a grove of trees just outside of town. He'd continued on to fetch Matthew and on the way back, he'd collected the mare and took her home. Strawberry still looked for Texanna. Every time the back door closed, she ran to the fence in anticipation. She'd been disappointed so many times she was off her feed. Who knew animals could grieve as humans did?

"We better get home, boy. The house is probably crawling with people waiting to extend their condolences, and there's enough food to feed an army."

The house was full. Aggie and Edna made peace for the day and were busy seeing to it everyone was fed. In their shared grief, it looked as though they might even become friends. He looked around at those who'd come to pay their respects. Their attempts to take care of him and Garrett were a testament to how lucky he and the boy were. They were loved and had folks around them who'd do whatever they could to ease their pain. What a shame they couldn't return Texanna to them.

Royce looked toward the fireplace and the two portraits above it. His eyes dropped to his son as he stood, his eyes trained on the painting of Texanna. Royce found it uncovered on the easel yesterday, the paint dry, when he'd returned home. Evidently, Texanna finished it before going into town. Tired and weary hearted, he'd gone to the barn to get the tools needed to make a frame. Having watched Texanna, Garrett was full of advice on the proper technique. Together, they'd built the frame and stained it to match the portrait of the two of them. The two pieces of art fit together perfectly. It was if they'd been designed to hang side-by-side.

Ross came through the front door, looked around the room, and strode to stand before Royce. "I'm very sorry for your loss, Royce. She was a beautiful woman." He studied his feet. When he spoke again, his voice was hoarse. "I truly regret my crude behavior that day in your office. I hope you can forgive me. I just wish it wasn't too late to beg her pardon, and for her to know I'm really sorry."

Royce clasped the younger man's shoulder. "I do forgive you, Ross. We've all been young and stupid at some time or another. And I think Texanna would have been proud to accept your apology."

Eyes full of torment, Ross nodded and turned to leave.

"Ross?"

"Sir?"

"Come by the office Monday morning, and we'll

see if we can't somehow salvage your job."

Ross's eyes gleamed with hope. "I'll be there. Thank you."

****

Texanna woke to see Dr. Richard James mulling over her chart. He'd been very kind and attentive. He called her his mystery patient. Burning with fever, she'd been found at the train depot wrapped in linen sheets, an old carpetbag at her feet, and inside, along with some nineteenth-century clothes, was a note with her name which read, Texanna Baines Keith Dyson.

Because of her gunshot wound, the police had become involved; they were particularly interested in the bullet removed from her shoulder as it came from an old Colt that could only be found in museums. She wouldn't be surprised if the Texas Rangers or FBI were called to investigate.

She needed surgery, but it was important to reduce the amount of infection before Dr. James operated. He'd ordered a powerful antibiotic by IV, and, in the couple of hours she'd been receiving fluids, she felt a little better. She was so groggy and the medicine added to her confusion. One minute she knew where she was—the next she didn't.

"Miss Dyson, can you open your eyes for me?" He patted her cheek gently. "Come on, let me see those beautiful blue eyes."

Her eyes rolled behind closed lids and finally opened. "Royce?" She licked her dry cracked lips. "Thirsty."

The doctor held the straw to her mouth. "Here you go, take a couple of sips."

She did and sighed with pleasure. "It's cold."

He smiled. "Yes, the nurse just brought fresh ice water. I want you to drink as much as possible."

She nodded and then looked around the room. When her eyes lit on the IV tube and monitor, she panicked. "Royce. Where's my husband?" She tried to push up and screamed with pain.

Dr. James hit the call button. The nurse's station immediately answered. "Miss Dyson needs her pain medication."

With his hand on her chest, he gently held her against the bed. She was gasping with the pain, and tears trickled down her cheeks.

"It's Mrs. Dyson, not Miss." She watched the nurse inject the medicine into the IV catheter hub, dispose of the syringe, and leave the room.

The doctor chuckled. "I stand corrected. Darn. And here I thought I'd found my future wife, but I see you're already taken."

Ah, his remark had brought a twitch to her lips. "So, Mrs. Dyson, how can we reach your husband?"

Her lips quivered. "You can't. He's the Marshal of Waco in 1880." She whimpered. "He brought me forward to 2008 so I could be treated with modern medicine. I'd have died if I stayed. He didn't give me a choice."

He squeezed her hand. She couldn't tell if he believed or not. Even men of science knew some things were unexplainable. Maybe he was one. "Your husband must love you very much."

The same nurse popped her head in the door. "Doctor, her parents are here." Her father pushed his way past the nurse, her mom on his coattail. "Texanna, baby," he gasped as he rushed to the bed. "Who did this to you?"

"Daddy!" Sobs racked her body as she tried to explain.

Her mother hurried to her other side. "Don't try to talk right now, honey. Just rest. We're here, and no one else will hurt you." Her mother stroked her hair. Her movements were awkward. This was an unfamiliar side to the woman who'd raised her. She wasn't used to giving comfort, but there was no denying the pain and panic etched on her face.

Dr. James spoke, "She just received pain medication. As soon as she's asleep, I'd like to talk with you. I'll be at the nurse's station."

Three days later, Texanna's bone infection had lessened, and she was cleared for surgery. Her heart was heavy as she rolled through the double doors. Today Dr. James would scrape away any damaged bone tissue, and if grafting were needed, coral would be used to repair the small chip in her clavicle.

She didn't fear the operation. Her fear revolved around having to remain in this time. Royce needed the locket to return to Garrett, so she was stuck here forever—without him. In truth, Royce was dead now. If she died in surgery, she'd be able to join him in heaven. But as much as she loved him and Garrett, she felt a pull from somewhere to stay alive. Maybe God was speaking to her. She didn't know. Unable to do anything else, she would respond to that pull and do her best to get well

When she woke in recovery, Dr. James clasped her hand. "It went well, Texanna. Though there was damage to the deltoid, after some therapy, I think your arm will be as good as new. The chip to the clavicle was minimal, no need for a transplant. In all, the damage wasn't as bad as I'd first thought."

"Thank you, Dr. James." Personable as well as an excellent doctor, he could easily become a good friend. The fact he didn't pooh-pooh her story of traveling back in time endeared him to her, but he was also good company. He patted her hand. "You're welcome. Now, your folks are anxious to see you."

They stayed until the pain medicine took over, and she drifted off to sleep again. Her last thought was her mother had changed—she'd never seen her so upset.

The second time Texanna woke, she was back in her room. The only light came from a wall lamp behind her head and from the slightly cracked door. She lay still and watched the slow drip of the fluids in her IV tube. She moved her head and heard the creak of a chair, the rustle of clothes, and smelled the tangy scent of aftershave. A handsome man walked out of the shadows and moved to her side.

"Hello, Texanna."

Texanna gasped at the sound of his deep voice and the blueness of his eyes. Probably in his thirties, he was tall with dark hair and wore khakis and a white shirt. Pinned to his chest was a circular badge with a star suspended inside—a Texas Ranger's Star.

Her heart beat so hard she feared she was experiencing a heart attack. Her voice came out a squeak. "Royce?"

Chapter Twenty-One

His smile, so like Royce's, twisted her heart. "No, ma'am. I'm told I favor him, but I'm Garth Dyson, your stepson Garrett's great-great-grandson."

Texanna started shaking. "Oh, my God. Garrett's great-great-grandson?" She covered her mouth to still the trembling of her lips. Now she knew Pearl's son lived to adulthood, fathered children.

"That's right, ma'am." He reached out and patted her good shoulder. "No tears now. Everything will be all right."

Tears flooded her eyes and she sniffled. "I can't get back to Royce and Garrett. What am I going to do? I don't think I can live without them."

Garth looked disconcerted. "Please don't cry. You're going to hurt your arm, and the nurse will kick us out of here. Hold on a minute. I've got someone with me who can make you feel better."

He turned and held out his hand to someone sitting in a chair in the shadows. An older woman, probably in her sixties, drew closer to the bed and smiled down at her.

"This is my grandmother Lucia Dyson McFee. She's Garrett's youngest and only surviving grandchild."

That would make Lucia Texanna's great-grandchild. This was unreal. Panicking, her eyes flew around the room for a clue that would help her make sense of this situation.

Lucia touched her hand. "Don't fret, Texanna.

You've been through a lot." Her eyes were Garrett's, as was her smile. Texanna tried to stifle her sobs, but at the compassion on the woman's face, she wept with abandon.

Lucia brushed the hair from her forehead, and whispered words of comfort. "Shhhh, child. It's going to be all right, you're not crazy. You left a journal with all the details of your time-travel. Everything has been kept safe for just this day. We've known for years you were going to show up and need our help, we just didn't know exactly when." She chuckled. "As a matter of fact, we thought it would be last year. The ink got wet and smeared so we couldn't read the exact year. Garth and I will get you back to your Royce." She turned to the young man. "Won't we, Son?"

Garth put his arm around the older woman's shoulders. "Yes, Grammy, we will." He reached down and squeezed Texanna's hand. "We'll get everything sorted out. Leave it to us."

Lips trembling, she nodded. "Thank you. I didn't think I'd see Royce again, or Garrett."

Garth laughed. "You'll do more than see him. You're going to have three children within the next ten years."

Lucia swatted at her grandson. "Shame on you, that's personal business." But she laughed and winked at Texanna.

The San Antonio police visited her the next day and pounded her with questions. They'd contacted Waco to see if they knew of a Texanna Keith Dyson and how she had come to be shot in their area between August eighth and ninth. They had no record of such an incident, so the Texas Rangers were called to investigate.

Garth's home base with the Rangers was in Waco, so when the call came in, he was immediately dispatched to San Antonio. Little did they know he'd already visited Texanna. Not content with the information he'd obtained, his superiors visited her several times asking more questions. She always gave the same answer—she'd been in Waco but had no recall of what happened to her. Because the trail was one-hundred-twenty-eight years old, they found nothing.

She worried about Garth's job and if he'd have to falsify records or something worse.

He reassured her. "As soon as you travel back to 1880, the entire case file will evaporate, and no one will remember you showing up here. If not, the case will be buried in mountains of other unsolved cases."

****

Royce strode from his office buckling on his gun belt as he walked. "Pete, I'm headed down to where Tehuacana Creek meets the Brazos. Heard that's where the two Meade brothers are holed up with those cattle they stole from over in Navarro County." He stuffed extra shotgun shells and cartridges for his Colt and Winchester in a saddlebag and headed for the door.

Pete stood. "You ain't going by yourself, are you?" He rushed around the desk. "Let me get Jason to come in early, and I'll go with you."

Royce turned back. "No need for that. Don't expect those two to be much trouble. They're not smart enough to try to escape and not quite dumb enough to fire on me."

"You ought not to be going out by yourself at a time like this."

At his words, Royce studied his deputy, discomfort evident by the frown on his face. "What are you saying, Pete? Do you think I'm incapable of doing my job?" He could feel the heat rising on his neck and struggled to tamp down his anger.

Pete choked out the words. "Ah, hell, Boss. You're still grievin' and don't need to be puttin' yourself in danger."

Royce slammed his hat down on his head. "I'll be fine, Pete. If I'm not back in two days, send someone out looking for me." His expression brooked no argument.

"Yes, sir, Marshal."

He stomped out of the office slamming the door behind him. The men had been coddling him for a month now. Enough was enough. He had to get on with life, and if they didn't think he could do his job, they damn well better see about getting him replaced.

He picked up food and supplies at the store then set out southeast of town. The heat of summer was over, yet the air wasn't crisp like fall in other parts of the world. The leaves were red and golden, but temperatures still rose to the eighties during the day. He urged Samson into a trot and let him run for a few minutes. The animal's powerful muscles bunched beneath him, and they flew over the ground covering the short distance to where he turned off the road for the banks of the Brazos.

Big boulders, rock cliffs, as well as an abundance of scrub brush and trees surrounded Tehuacana Creek. It was used years ago by the Waco, pronounced Wă-co, Indians, a band of the Wichita tribe, as a watering hole for their ponies, and was the perfect place to hide cattle. Herd them against a cliff, string rope across the front, and you had an ideal makeshift corral that kept the animals inside.

Several miles from the creek, he left the bank of the Brazos and swung around to approach from the opposite direction. The wind blew from the south, and he could smell wood smoke and manure along with frying fish. The occasional sound of voices carried on the wind. It didn't appear they were expecting him.

Royce dismounted and let Samson's reins trail in the dust. As he unsheathed his rifle, he whispered in the horse's ear. "Stay here, boy. Come if I call."

Bent over low to the ground, he crept through the brush to get a closer look. They'd set up camp in a small ravine, probably a ten-foot-drop from where he hid. Sure enough, there was the makeshift corral and ten or twelve head of cattle. Joe Bob and Billy Bob Meade sat around the campfire. Joe Bob turned fish in a skillet while his brother drank from a whiskey bottle.

Royce stood and brought his rifle to his shoulder. "Hey, boys," he hollered. They jumped and scrambled for the guns leaned against a rock. Royce opened fire and knocked their rifles to the ground, busting the wooden stock of one. "Stop right there. It's Marshal Royce Dyson. Don't make me put a bullet in one of you."

Both froze and threw their hands in the air. "Don't shoot, Royce, we'll go peaceable like."

"Glad to hear it. Now—" A shot rang out and his left shoulder blade burst with searing pain. *Someone shot me in the back* was his last coherent thought as he pitched forward.

He woke and tried to open his eyes, but quickly shut them against the glare and painful throb. He hurt, oh God, his shoulder was on fire...and his head... Damnation! Someone had shot him in the back. He remembered the force of the bullet and being propelled down the incline. Taking a deep breath to still the nausea, he made to reach his pistol to discover his hands were bound in front of him.

Voices sounded close by, and he cracked his eyes, trying to see in their direction. Squinting against the bright light, he made out the two Meade brothers with a gangly kid backed up against a tree. He was probably eighteen but looked more like fifteen.

"Look what you done, you stupid pissant. You know what they do to men who shoot marshals in this state? They hang 'um, that's what." He heard the sound of flesh hitting flesh. "Don't think we'll share the blame, either. You done this on your own."

"How's I supposed to know he was the law, Joe Bob? He was snooping around our business. What else could I 'av done?"

"Tell him to drop the gun, you idiot. Get a rope, Billy."

Royce tried to roll to his side to see what they were doing. A scream of pain burst from his mouth and everything went black. When he woke again, the Meade brothers were bending over him. They'd removed his bedroll from Samson, and he lay face down on it. His shirt had been ripped away, and Joe Bob held the half-empty bottle of whiskey. "Bullet went all the way through. We cleaned it as best we could. Hate to do this, but maybe the alcohol will keep the wound from turning putrid 'til your brothers get here." He started pouring, and Royce blessed the darkness that overtook him again.

Throughout the night, water was forced between his lips. He'd been rolled to his back propped against his saddle. Samson whinnied, and Royce felt his nibbles as the horse tried to rouse him. Around dawn, Joe Bob squatted and cut his bonds. "I'm mighty sorry about this, Royce." He nodded toward a tree. "Got that stupid kid tied up so he can't run off the minute we leave. Leavin' your Colt lying right here by your hand in case you need it."

Royce felt around and found the pistol. His hand closed around the grip. Voice hoarse, he managed to croak, "Obliged for what you've done, but...I'll be coming after you."

"Know it, wouldn't expect nothing else from you, but least ways we'll get a head start."

The day passed in a blur as he wove in and out of consciousness. He drank from the canteen lying on his chest and spilled water over his face in the process. He could hear thrashing sounds coming from the tree where they'd tied his prisoner but couldn't remain awake long enough to care if he got loose or not.

It was dark, and a cry split the night. He thought the sound had come from him, but then heard the angry snorting of Samson and the stamping of his hooves. The moon shone through the trees and glanced off the water—just enough light for him to see the kid scooting like a crab back to his tree. The screams continued, and he realized Samson was pursuing the boy and stomping him. Panicked, he felt for his gun, relieved when his hand closed over it.

He whistled. "Samson, whoa boy. Come here." The horse continued to snort and shake his mane but finally came over and dropped his head to nuzzle his hand. "Good boy, Samson. Settle down, now."

Moans and wails came from the tree. "I just wanted to leave, wasn't going to hurt you none." Royce heard movement and a scream. "Shit! I think he broke my leg. I don't wanna die out here."

"Oh, shut up. You're not going to die."

"Whadda you know? You're gonna die too." His wails turned to sobs.

"My brothers will be here by noon tomorrow, if not sooner. After Doc sets your leg, you'll have a comfortable bed in a jail cell until you go on trial for shooting a Texas marshal."

"Will...will they hang me?"

"Hard to say. Now stay put or sneak off. Either way, I don't care, just stay away from me, or Samson will aim for your head next time."

The effort required to talk sapped him. He closed his eyes and didn't wake until Matthew lifted him from the ground to put him in the buckboard. Screams of pain vibrated from his chest.

"Hold on, little brother. You'll be home soon, and Doc will fix you up."

Royce was burning up and thirsty. Matthew brought the canteen to his lips and let him have small swallows. Cradled in his brother's arms, the jolts from the ruts in the road were softened, but the pain was too much to bear. As he drifted in and out of consciousness, he heard sketches of their conversation. "Fever...doesn't look good...infection..."

****

Royce felt himself lifted and raised heavenward. He flowed as if on a cloud that held him suspended above the room. There was no more pain, just peace. He laughed out loud at the sheer absurdity of the situation. For the first time in several months, his heart and soul were content.

Was he on his way to heaven? If so, the journey was as wonderful as the Bible had promised. Where was the bright light everyone talked about seeing?

A man's heart-wrenching sobs drew his gaze to the scene below. His body lay in the bed he'd slept in as a child and on into manhood. He chuckled at the memory of his younger brother Jason climbing in beside him in the middle of the night. The kid was scared, and Royce didn't have the heart to kick him out. He just pretended he didn't notice he had company.

The sobs grew in intensity. They came from a man in the chair beside his bed. *Jason, oh Jason! Don't cry little brother.* He tried to reach out and touch his shoulder, tell him it was all right, but the force holding him kept him in place.

Jason's hands dropped from his face. Hands fisted, he beat them against his thighs. He leaned toward the bed, grabbed his arm, and shook. Voice hoarse, he growled. "Damn you, Royce, you've given up. I never took you for a quitter. Fight dammit!"

The door opened and Jason covered his grief before he turned. *Garrett, his son, and all he had in the world to live for.* Shoulders slumped and face stricken, his son crept into the room. "Is my pa dead?" His lip quivered. Jason pulled him close and sat him on his knee.

"No, tadpole, he's not, but..." Jason cleared his throat. "I don't want to lie to you...it doesn't look good." Garrett threw his arms around his uncle's neck and cried against his shoulder. Jason rocked and patted his back unable to find the words to give him comfort.

When Garrett's crying slowed, he slipped to the floor and sobbed, "I wanna...hug...hug my daddy. I won't hurt him...I promise."

"Then that's what you should do." Jason stood with Garrett in his arms and laid him on top of Royce, his head near his heart. Garrett cried and patted his arms. His little body shook with grief. Jason rubbed his back. "It's okay, Garrett. You just lay here and cry as long as you want. Nobody would understand any better than your pa. He loves you so much." Jason stepped outside the room and partially closed the door.

Royce's heart twisted with pain. *God, please! My son needs me.* His body soared, and the world went black.

Muted sounds broke through the darkness and rose in intensity—someone was crying. It was a child, his child, Garrett. "Help, help me, Pa." Panicked, he looked around trying to discern where the cries were coming from. His eyes lit on the pond. He could just see Garrett's head as he struggled in the water, cries of fright gurgling from the water. Royce broke into a run, but his legs felt like lead and he sagged with fatigue as he struggled to reach his son. *I'm coming, Garrett. Hang on, Son, I'll get you.*

Pain hit him in the chest. He fell to his knees and clawed at the earth trying to get up. *Help me, Lord...my boy...save my boy.* He pulled himself to the pond's edge, and like an alligator, dug into the water, crawling across the mud bottom. At last his hands grasped clothing and he hung on, pushed his way back to the bank and fell over with Garrett clutched to his upper body. He squeezed his son against his heart, trying to force water from his lungs. His chest hurt, it hurt so bad he couldn't breathe. Sobs wracked his body as he clutched at the boy, willing him to take air into his lungs. *God, no...Not my boy. Pleaseeee!* A horrible wail broke the darkness, echoed across the water, startling the birds sending them aloft.

Great sobs wracked Royce's body as he clutched at his son's lifeless form and moaned, "No, noooo."

Loving pats touched his face. Garrett's voice broke through the haze in his mind. "Wake up, Pa, I'm okay. You was havin' a bad dream."

Royce forced his eyes open, blinked to clear his vision, and looked down at the boy in his arms. A cry rose from deep within his chest. *Thank you, God! A dream, just a bad dream.* He cupped Garrett's head and stroked his hair. Horror at how close he'd come to leaving his son fatherless, struck him like a blow to the chest. If he gave up, it was just as good as leaving his child on his own in that pond. Shame washed over him, and he hugged Garrett tighter. His throat constricted with emotion. He had so much to live for right here in his arms. "Don't leave me, Son."

"I won't, Pa. I'll be right here." He sniffed. "Promise you won't leave me."

Smile on his lips, Royce closed his eyes and whispered. "I promise."

****

Royce sat in a rocker on his front porch, a cup of

coffee in his hand. The October night air was cool and fresh, natures sounds comforting. Garrett was upstairs in bed, tired after a long day of making sure his daddy didn't overdo. His son's protectiveness brought a smile to his lips. He was a lucky man to have such a wonderful child, family, and friends. Only one thing could make him happier—to have Texanna with him, but that wasn't meant to be.

Today was his first day home. Aggie would be coming over every morning the remainder of the week to cook for him and Garrett. Doc said he had to eat three good meals a day and start moving around slowly to regain his strength. He was as weak as a baby. Just getting upstairs wore him out. Tomorrow he'd start working his arm some, stretching the muscles. His shoulder hurt like hell, but he'd been lucky the bullet had passed clean through without hitting bone or a major blood vessel.

The morning after he'd been found, Pete set out after the Meade boys. He caught them a week later in San Antonio headed for Mexico. They didn't put up a fight when he arrested them. Most likely they'd serve a couple of years for stealing cattle. The kid who'd shot him hadn't gone to trial yet. Royce didn't want to see him go to prison. Hopefully, he and the judge could work out a fitting punishment where he might be reformed. Put him to work on one of the ranches far from town where he'd get plenty of food, work, and discipline.

He pushed up out of the rocker and tossed the dregs of his coffee over the porch rail. For a minute, he stood there looking up at the moon and stars, thinking about Texanna. She was living in her time. He was living in his. Regardless of the years between them, did the moon, the stars, and sky remain the same? He believed they were constant, just like his love for Texanna.

Chapter Twenty-Two

Texanna's parents wanted her to stay with them, but she wanted to be in Pearl's house. Settled in bed, her mother approached and pulled up a chair. "Texanna, I think it's time you told us where you've been and how you got shot."

Her father came in with a tea tray. He sat it on the bed, poured them each a cup, and handed her a teacake. "I agree with your mother. Lord knows, we haven't agreed on much these past twenty years, but we do this."

She nodded. "You're right. You deserve to know what my plans are."

When she finished her story, her mother sobbed as her father paced the floor raking his hands through his hair. "How can you expect us to believe such an outrageous story?" he asked.

Texanna picked up the journal and handed it to them. "Read the first five pages of this, and it'll help you understand."

Their heads bent together over the book, they read the entry she'd placed there shortly after she and Royce married. In that first account, she'd included Pearl's story and both her trips from 2008 to 1880. Though she'd been tempted, Texanna hadn't read past the entry of the bank robbery. She didn't want to know what would happen in her life with Royce.

Madeline Keith wiped her eyes. "It's a beautiful story, dear, but surely..." Her voice broke, and she couldn't continue.

"Mama, it's true. Every word of it." She looked between her stricken parents. "I know it's hard, it's outlandish, unbelievable...but as soon as I'm well, I'm returning to Royce and Garrett."

Her father's face was pale. For the first time, he looked old and fragile. Scared, she reached for his hand. "Daddy, are you all right? Don't have a heart attack and die on me. Please, please understand."

He tried to smile, but his chin trembled, and he ducked his head. Clearing his throat, he said, "I always knew I'd lose you someday, but this isn't quite how I pictured it."

"Daddy, I love him. I'd given up hope of ever finding a man to give my heart to. God sent me back to be with him, I don't doubt that for a moment. I don't want to go through life without him." She placed her hand over her lower abdomen. "And my baby needs her father."

****

Her months of therapy were slow, but the time went by in a blur. Some days Texanna wondered if she'd dreamed the entire time-travel experience. But, in December, when she knelt to place flowers on Pearl's grave and read her name, Pearl Baines Dyson Thompson, she knew it had been real and every minute precious.

Her parents came by that evening. It was cold, even for December, so Pauline built a fire, and they sat around the old room sipping hot cocoa.

"Pauline, sit down with us. I need to talk to all three of you." It didn't escape her notice that her mother reached for Daddy's hand. He took it with his left and placed his right arm around her shoulders. Texanna smiled at the new closeness evident between the two. "I'm leaving tomorrow."

Voice gruff, her father asked. "How will we know you made it back to him, that you're happy?" Her mother was sobbing, her face buried against his shirt. Pauline sat ramrod straight, but lines of worry crossed her face.

"I don't know, Daddy, but I'll find a way." She twisted her wedding ring, and then held her hand out to them. "Search the history books, look for Dyson descendants. The proof will be there, I promise."

****

The next morning, Texanna dressed in the lovely blue taffeta party dress Lucia brought her.

"Won't I look odd on the train in an evening dress?"

Lucia shrugged. "Maybe, but according to our historical records, this is what you were wearing when you reappeared. Don't have a clue why or where the dress came from, but you'll be attending Jason and Sally's wedding reception."

Texanna fingered the fabric. It was old, and though threadbare in places, in relatively good condition considering its age. "It's beautiful." The bodice was off the shoulder with long sleeves and a fitted waist. The skirt was long and full.

"Over it, you'll wear this black wool cape as the weather will be cold. Your train is delayed, so you won't arrive until after sunset."

Texanna asked many questions, but all Garth and Lucia could tell her was what she'd be wearing, approximately what time her train would arrive, and the date, December 18, 1880.

"Trust your instincts, child. All will be well."

That was easy for her to say. She wasn't the one traveling back in time. But Texanna knew worry wouldn't change a thing.

Texanna twisted the gold band on her finger. She wondered if Royce had picked his ring up at the jewelers. Would he like the inscription she'd had engraved inside? For the ninety-ninth time, she wondered what it would be like when they were reunited. Heaven, it would be like heaven. Unexpectedly, anxiety made her gasp, and she had difficulty breathing. What if he'd found someone else while she was gone? She shook herself trying to ward off her fear. He had the locket. Had he lost hope, or did he believe she would somehow locate it and return to him? Was he waiting for her? It had been almost four months. *Oh, God. Please help me to have faith.*

At the station, Texanna hugged Garth and Lucia good-bye.

Lucia, with tears in her eyes, laid Pearl's locket in Texanna's hand. She held it tightly in her fist.

"Take care, child. Live and love hard. The locket will come back to us, and we'll see the next generation takes care of it."

"Thank you, Lucia. I love you."

The older woman's eyes twinkled with mischief as she winked. "I love you, too, Grammy."

****

Texanna's heart beat a mile a minute. She was finally going home—back to Royce and Garrett. Dressed in her 1880's finery she felt like a fool, but she'd have boarded the train buck naked if necessary to get back to Royce. The dress fit her like a glove but wasn't too confining, and she didn't have on a corset. Black high-top shoes peeped out from under her dress. She'd used a buttonhook to fasten them so they were tight. They pinched a little but weren't bad. At least they were warm.

Her carpetbag sat on the seat beside her. Inside were the sheets she'd been wrapped in when Royce brought her forward to the present. Royce had also added her jeans, tank top, and her tennis shoes. Her underwear was glaringly absent. The thought of Royce purposely keeping the pink bra and panties pleased her. She reached up to make sure the locket was securely in place around her neck. Royce had finally admitted he loved her skimpy 'unmentionables' as he called them. As a surprise, she'd bought and was wearing a pale blue set. If he thought the pink set was sexy, she couldn't wait to see what he thought about her thong.

Grinning like a Cheshire cat, she closed her eyes and concentrated on her mission. Her nerves were stretched taut. She was so tired of waiting that she was ready to get out and start pushing the train down the tracks. *Let's get a move on, folks. Please, Lord. Let this work. Take me home.*

The speakers shrieked. "Sorry for the delay, folks. We're ready to leave San Antonio. Shouldn't be more than two hours late arriving in Waco." Texanna felt the train give as it started moving and they slowly picked up speed. Two hours late. But Lucia told her to expect the delay. Her heart beat faster and she gulped in air. She was on her way.

****

Royce smoothed the vest of his dark suit down his abdomen—the suit he'd worn when he and Texanna married. It fit looser today than it had then. Like Strawberry, he'd been off his feed, and it showed in the fit of his clothes. Actually, the gunshot wound had left him weak as a kitten. He'd lost weight, and regaining it and his strength was taking time. Time was something he had aplenty.

He looked at his reflection in the full-length mirror in the corner. The suit didn't look bad. In a month, it'd probably fit just right again. His appetite had returned to normal. Everyday he felt stronger, using his shoulder was less painful.

His heart wasn't beating ninety to nothing this evening, as it had been on his wedding day in July. But today was an entirely different situation. He'd put on a smile and pretend he was having the time of his life. He was happy for Jason and Sally.

He opened the drawer of the chifforobe and

fingered Texanna's pink unmentionables. They were so sheer his hand was visible through them. He lifted them to his face. They were soft against his cheek and carried the scent of the lavender sachet she'd sprinkled in the drawer. He sighed and put them back. No need to torture himself. She was gone, and he had no reassurance she'd find her way back.

The locket lay on a lacy handkerchief. Sunlight winked off the polished gold. With his thumb, he rubbed the turquoise stone until it warmed. He'd wanted to leave it with Texanna, but needed it to return to Garrett. It had entered his mind to take Garrett with him and live with Texanna in the future. But the picture she'd painted of the future stopped him. It didn't sound like a place he'd want to raise a child. No, they belonged here.

Though Texanna told him how the locket supposedly worked, he couldn't bear putting her on the train alone or without seeing her to her final destination. That fateful day, he feared she'd disappear without him, so he'd held her close and wrapped the locket around each of their wrists. Evidently it worked. He'd propped his booted feet on the wall of the train car so when the light burst and the train lurched, Texanna had been jostled as little as possible. The sights he'd seen, he'd never forget, nor the agony of watching Texanna being ushered away in an odd conveyance with flashing lights.

Garrett's boots sounded in the hall outside his door. "Pa, I'm ready. Let's hurry. I want to see the twins."

"Coming, Son." Royce dropped the locket back onto the lacy cloth and closed the drawer, unaware how the turquoise grew even hotter making the gold glow warmly. He slipped into his jacket. At the front door, he retrieved his dress hat, and they started for the buckboard out front.

Garrett was finally beginning to move past his grief. Texanna had only been with them a little over a month, but she'd forged a place in their hearts. School had started and that helped. He was busier, and his young, pretty teacher spent extra time with him and a few of the other kids. He brought books home in the evening, and he and Royce sat at the table and worked on his letters. The boy had a good mind, and learning came easy for him. Royce was proud.

Royce and Garrett arrived at the church in plenty of time. Royce half listened to the chatter on the lawn as he unhitched Josie and hobbled her so she could enjoy the grass and stay in the shade. He'd leave her here and walk to the town hall for the dance. It wasn't far, so there was no need to hitch Josie to the wagon again. He leaned against the wagon and tried to relax while he waited. No need to enter the church any sooner than necessary. Garrett ran ahead to visit the babies.

Royce had to admit, they were a treat to see. Both were happy and loving. Doc had been worried Nathan might not be normal due to his lack of oxygen at birth. But the boy kept up with his sister and was ahead in some areas. He was even-tempered while Pearl was impatient with a terrible temper. She could shout the house down. Matthew's happiness and contentment pleased Royce. But sometimes, it was all too much to bear, and he had to distance himself from the happy family. Molly was quick to understand and helped him find an escape route if he needed one.

The church was full. It was time for the ceremony to start, so Royce joined his brothers at the altar. Garrett sat with Molly to help keep the twins quiet. The boy would love to have brothers and sisters, and Royce hoped someday he'd have them. He just wished their mother would be Texanna. But it wasn't meant to be, so he might as well put the notion from his mind and get on with life.

The organist started the wedding march, and the bride started down the aisle on her father's arm. She was beautiful with her gold blond hair and blue eyes. Her happy smile beneath the veil both warmed and twisted his heart. Her father placed her hand in the groom's, and they turned to face the preacher.

Brother Riley beamed down at them and cleared his throat several times. "Dearly beloved, we are gathered here today in the sight of God and these witnesses to join this young couple in the vows of holy matrimony."

The vows of commitment fell heavy on Royce's heart. Why God had given him so much and then taken it away leaving him empty and broken, Royce didn't know.

"Do you take this woman...for better, for worse...in sickness and in health...for as long as you both shall live?"

Royce felt a roaring in his head making him slightly dizzy. He closed his eyes and let his mind wander back to another day—a day in July. On that day, his heart had been whole and near bursting with happiness. Royce shoved the image aside. Today was Jason's day. Royce's had been several yesterdays ago.

When the ceremony ended, Jason kissed Sally. The crowd stood and rushed forward to congratulate the couple. Royce stepped up. "Move over, Jason. It's my turn." Royce grinned at Jason's rigid jaw as he took Sally in his arms. He pretended to aim for Sally's mouth, deflected at the last minute, and kissed her cheek. With a chuckle, Royce whispered in Sally's ear. "I don't have to tell you to keep Jason on his toes. I know you will. Texanna said you were the perfect wife for him."

Sally's blue eyes turned tender, and she hugged

him. "She was some lady. I miss her."

Royce nodded and stepped back.

Jason, big grin on his face, grabbed Royce around the neck. "Get away from my wife, old man."

Royce hugged his younger brother. "I'm happy for you, runt." Matthew stepped up and took Royce's place.

Royce needed to get outside. He made his way to the church lawn and sucked in deep gulps of air. *Put it behind you, Royce. Move forward, not back.*

Royce started as a hand touched his arm. Sally's widowed sister from Austin looked up at him. He wasn't sure but thought her name was Ruby.

"It's lovely out tonight." As she spoke, she looked up at the sky.

He cleared his throat. "Yes, it is. I'm surprised it's not colder." Her arms were bare, and her skin had a pearly glow. If he touched her, she'd be smooth as silk. Her gown dipped low in the front exposing a good portion of her breasts. They were lovely, but he preferred women to be a little more modest when it came to showing their charms.

"Don't you need a wrap?" Royce knew she wouldn't be shocked if he touched her. Over the past month she'd been in Waco, he'd seen her at church and at Sally's folks, and she'd made it clear she would welcome his advances.

"I have one in Papa's buggy. Will you walk me there to fetch it?" Royce took her arm, and they strolled toward the buggies.

He reached into the back seat and picked up a blue velvet cape. "Is this yours?"

"Yes, it is." She turned her back to him and dropped her head forward exposing the skin of her neck and back where her gown dipped low. The exposed skin was tempting. He wanted to lean forward and place a kiss on her nape. The thought chilled him, and he quickly covered her with her cape.

She turned back around. “Thank you.”

He extended an arm. “May I walk you to City Hall for the dance?”

“I’d like that.” She placed her hand on his arm.

Chapter Twenty-Three

Texanna almost shouted with joy when the light burst behind her closed eyes. It had happened. She'd traveled back. She wanted to open her eyes and see the train's changed interior, but fear kept them tightly closed. Gingerly, she touched the seat and sighed with relief to find it hard and uncomfortable. Her rear-end told her it was, but she'd had to double check. She opened one eye and saw the lit kerosene lamps on each side of the door that led to the next car and breathed, "Thank you, God."

Her hand went to her breast to clasp the locket. It was gone. Panicked, she searched her clothes hoping to find it in the folds. When that failed, she stood and searched the seat, and then the floor. *No! Oh God, please don't do this to me.* She sat back down, closed her eyes, and took deep breaths to calm herself. *She had to be in the right time, please God.* Tears dropped from beneath her eyelids, and she gulped back her despair. *Have faith, Texanna. Just compose yourself and have faith.*

The noise of the train speeding along the tracks kept time with the gallop of her heart. Her mind wouldn't stop jumping from one thought to another. *Forget the locket. Think about something else—Royce.* How would he react when he saw her? It'd been over four months. What had he told folks when she'd disappeared again? Was her reappearance going to be a problem? That was too bad if it was. They'd come up with something to tell them.

When the train stopped, she stepped off the

coach and stared at her surroundings. It looked the same as when she'd left. Heart pounding with anticipation, she breathed in the cool fresh air. Yes, there was the smell of manure and coal from the train, but the scent was comforting.

It was dusk, and few people were out on the streets. Dim lights flickered from a couple of businesses. Laughter and the tinkle of the piano from the saloon across the street echoed on the air. The streetlights didn't give off much illumination, especially compared to the bright ones of the twenty-first century. She picked up her carpetbag and started toward the community center. It was getting too late to be on the streets alone, and she had to know if she'd arrived on time. Without the locket, she wasn't sure.

The lights in City Hall were dimly lit. She'd never been inside but knew the building was used for community functions such as weddings, receptions, and dances. Her shoe heels echoed on the wood plank floor as she entered. But for the beautiful table set with a tall cake, punch bowl, and other snacks, the room was empty. Atop the cake stood the delicate figure formed of confectioner's sugar of a bride and groom. Napkins lined the one end of the table. She sighed with relief at the banner reading 'Congratulations Sally and Jason' tacked on the back wall.

Texanna was nervous and didn't know how she should go about presenting herself. She'd considered standing outside to wait for Royce but discarded that idea. Maybe she could stay incognito for a while until an opportunity arose. She hung her cape on the cloak rack and found a chair in the far corner of the room. It was so dark, and, with the deep blue of her dress, she'd be hard to spot.

As guests arrived, Texanna watched with pleasure as they filled the room with happy chatter.

When Royce entered, she stopped breathing and gaped. She stifled the moan that bubbled in her throat with her fist. Her husband, her love...he'd lost weight, and his face looked gaunt. Had he been ill, worse yet, wounded? Fear rushed through her veins like ice water. *Oh Royce, my love...* She stood to move toward him and then noticed the handsome woman on his arm. Stunned, she plopped back down into the chair.

The woman's blond hair was piled high on her head, and pearl earrings hung from her ears. When Royce took her cloak and hung it on the rack, Texanna could see her low-cut dress showed the skin of her back and a fair amount of breast above the neckline. The woman clung to Royce and squeezed close to whisper in his ear. Her action brought her breasts in contact with Royce's arm and gave him a good view of her cleavage. His eyes dropped to the abundance of flesh. Jealousy clawed at Texanna, and it took all her strength to keep herself seated.

Jason and Sally entered on a flurry of laughter and chit-chat. Sally, lovely in Pearl's wedding gown, was flushed with happiness. Texanna's heart sang for the joy she saw in both Jason and Sally's faces. She tried to concentrate on the happy couple, but her attention kept returning to Royce and the blonde together in the receiving line. Texanna noticed his face was drawn, but when he smiled down at the woman, the lines vanished.

Matthew moved to the middle of the room. "Folks, raise your punch cups. I'd like to make a toast to my baby brother and his beautiful bride." The young couple moved to his side, their faces aglow. "Sally, Jason. Live and love as if every moment is your last. Don't let the sun go down on your anger, and love each other enough to forgive. We hope your lives will be blessed with many special moments and lots of healthy children."

Royce raised his cup. “Here, here!” Through the tears in her eyes, Texanna could see the sheen in Royce’s. A look passed between the three brothers, and they moved together to slap around on each other in a manly hug. Texanna had to bite her fist to keep from sobbing.

A cord sounded as one of the violinist drew his bow across the strings. It broke the tension. At the end of the room, a musical group was set up ready to play. The bride and groom moved onto the floor as the band started playing a waltz. Like Royce, Jason was a good dancer, and he twirled Sally around the room. They had eyes only for each other and didn’t notice when their guests joined them on the floor.

Royce hadn’t once glanced her way. Why should he? He had the blonde’s breasts to keep his eyes occupied. Texanna’s face heated with anger. She wanted to walk toward the pair, grab the woman’s exaggerated neckline, and yank it up to her eyeballs. But that would serve no purpose and only make her appearance more shocking.

Texanna’s heart turned over when she saw Garrett push his way through the guests to get a piece of cake. She choked back a sob. He’d grown taller in the past few months. He looked up to make sure he wasn’t watched, and when he did, his eyes locked with hers. He froze, looked around, and then back at her. Mouth open, he drew in air to yell, but she covered her lips with a finger and shook her head. His mouth snapped shut, but he still hadn’t moved. She held out her hand and, like a sleepwalker, he started toward her.

Thanks goodness the dance floor was crowded. Due to swirling guests, she could no longer see Garrett but within a short moment he stood before her.

Tears choked him. “Ma?”

Texanna nodded and opened her arms. He flew

into them, and her soft sobs joined his. "Shhh now, don't cry. We've got to be quiet. Sit beside me so we can talk."

"But you're dead. We buried you."

"Garrett, I don't know the whole story, but I think your pa used the locket to take me back home. He didn't want me to die and knew I could be healed in my own time. Since he had the locket, he never expected me to get back and thought it best for everyone to think I was dead." She clutched his hand. "That's all I really know. Can you trust us to tell you everything later? I don't have a clue how to let your pa know I'm here."

With a big grin on his face, he blurted out. "I'll tell him." He turned to race off, but she caught him by his jacket.

"No Garrett, wait a minute. And keep your voice down. I don't want to make a scene and spoil Sally and Jason's wedding." *But I sure would like to spoil the blonde's fun.* "Who is the woman your father's been dancing with? The blonde? Has he been seeing her?"

Garrett shrugged. "We see her at church every Sunday and at Sally's folks. She's Sally's older sister. Her husband died a year ago, and she moved back here from Austin."

"Does your Pa like her?"

Garrett's brow furrowed. "You mean like a sweetheart, to kiss and stuff?" He turned to watch his father on the dance floor. "I don't think so. He hasn't kissed her like he used to you."

Texanna felt better but wasn't completely reassured. It was time to get out of here. She'd wait for Royce by the buckboard.

"Garrett, you see that black cape on the first hook."

"Yes, ma'am."

"Will you get it for me, and I'll meet you at the

door? Then you can take me to the buckboard. I'll wait for your pa there."

They'd made it outside when the door opened again, and Royce called out to his son. Texanna slipped into the darkness under the tree.

"Garrett, where are you going?" The blonde joined Royce on the porch and closed the door behind them.

"I want to go check on Josie, Pa. She might be lonely."

Who'd taught this kid how to lie? She'd have a talk with him tomorrow about lies turning around and biting you on the butt.

The blonde's sugary voice reached their ears. "Let the boy go, darling. You know how impatient children get at events like this."

Darling? Texanna wanted to snatch the woman bald. She started forward when Royce answered. "All right, Son. Don't be gone long. We'll head home soon."

Garrett had no choice but to keep walking leaving Texanna in her hiding spot.

"Let's stay outside for a minute, Royce. It's so stuffy in there." Royce took her arm and they walked down the steps.

Why, that hussy is dying to get Royce under the darkness of this tree. Texanna stayed still and tried not to breathe. They stopped on the other side of the tree trunk. The tree was a tall pecan, and it had very few leaves left, but with the shadow of the building, it still afforded enough darkness to hide her.

"Royce, I'm cold."

"Is that right? Here, let me give you my jacket."

She stopped him. "That's not necessary. You don't want to let your wounded shoulder get cold. Just let me slide my hands under your jacket, and you put your arms around me."

Royce Dyson, if you touch her you're going to

sorely regret it. Texanna was about to explode with fury. Blondie was coming on to him, and he wasn't doing a thing to stop her. Then the realization hit her. Wounded shoulder? Oh dear, had he been shot? Was his shoulder permanently damaged, could he use it? Well hell, from her vantage point, it looked like he could. There, not fifteen feet away from his wife, her husband stood with his arms wrapped around another woman. Blondie titled her head back and Royce's dropped down and...he...he kissed her.

"You pervert!" Texanna's hiss echoed louder than she'd intended.

Royce froze. His head came up like a deer sniffing danger. He shoved the woman toward the building and said something under his breath.

Texanna turned and ran.

"Stop right there, woman. If you know what's good for you...dammit, I said stop."

Texanna ran as if her life depended on it. Then she started giggling. By the time she reached the buckboard, it was all she could do to keep from howling with laughter.

****

Royce was enjoying Ruby's company, but she was a bit clingy for his taste. He might have been interested in her, but it wouldn't go any farther if she didn't loosen her grip on his arm. Dancing with her was fun. He didn't doubt she'd be an interesting sexual partner, but, as to a good mother for Garrett, he had his reservations. Why was he even thinking about her? If he wanted sexual release, he'd visit Josephine's. Getting involved with a widow wasn't smart. Her goal would be to get him to the altar.

He looked up to see Garrett with a woman. Just before she'd covered her hair with the cloak, he'd caught a glimpse of red hair. It couldn't be. Many women had hair the color of Texanna's, but the mere possibility made his heart thunder. The black cloak completely covered the woman except for a small part of her skirt, which was blue taffeta. It was a color that would have been beautiful on Texanna. She slipped through the door, and Garrett followed her.

"Excuse me, Ruby. I need to check on Garrett." He tried to remove her hand from his arm, but she clung to him.

"I'll go with you. It's hot in here."

He nodded, and they walked toward the door. When they got outside, Garrett was alone. Royce looked up and down the street but didn't see a woman. Maybe he was mistaken.

Ruby wanted to stay outside so they moved off the porch onto the lawn. Before he knew what was happening, she had her arms inside his jacket and around his waist, and she was kissing him. He'd be lying if he denied enjoying it. His body was starved for the feel of a woman's, but for some reason holding and kissing her just didn't feel right.

Royce'd been about to break the kiss when he heard the hissed whisper. He knew only one other person who'd used that term. Texanna. But it couldn't be her. Who was out here hiding behind trees? He remained still and lifted his nose to the wind. The scent of strawberries reached him, and his heart twisted with longing.

The woman turned and started running. He shouted some orders but damn if she didn't ignore them. Whoever she was, she'd catch hell when he caught her. He gave chase, but she was fast as lightning. The thought made his heart drop to his stomach. No, it wasn't possible. He had the locket. She had no way back to him.

Hand fisted, his wedding band cut into his palm, bringing him to a halt. The jeweler brought it by his office one afternoon the week he'd 'buried' Texanna. After reading the words, he'd gotten drunk for the first time in four years. *My heart will always find yours. Love, Texanna 1880.* He shook off the words and his hope. It wasn't possible.

Gun drawn, he approached the buckboards and buggies around the church. "Garrett, come here. Come here right now."

"Pa, I'm all right. Nothing's wrong."

"You heard me young man. Woman, whoever you are, you better stay far away from my boy, and walk out with your hands up."

Garrett appeared at his side. "Pa, it's really okay. She's not here to hurt anyone. She didn't want to make a scene and spoil Jason and Sally's wedding."

"Yeah, but you pissed me off when you had the gall to stand and kiss that blonde hussy right in front of me. You're lucky I didn't snatch every hair out of her head."

Royce grew dizzy and thought he'd faint. He holstered his gun. It wasn't possible. It wasn't.

Garrett grasped his hand. "It's true, Pa. It's her. She came back to us."

The lady stepped from behind the buckboard and walked toward him. Moonlight caught the glint of her hair and the shine in her eyes.

"Royce, I couldn't stay away. You're my life, the blood in my veins, my destiny. I love you. How could I not return?"

He couldn't speak. It was Texanna, his wife, his love. She was thinner, her hair longer and curled on top of her head. How could she be here? The locket was in the drawer of his chest. She'd have needed it to get back to him. He drew closer and marveled at how beautiful she was as moonlight shone on her hair, and creamy breasts exposed by the neckline of her dress. Her hands were clasped at her waist. His ring adorned her wedding finger, and the scent of strawberries reached his nostrils.

"My God. It really is you." In two long strides, he had her in his arms, crushed against his body, breathing in her scent. Lips against her hair, he whispered. "Oh, Texanna. Please don't disappear on me. My old heart can only take so much."

She trembled in his embrace. "I'll never leave you again. I promise. I have it on good authority we're going to have three children and live to a ripe old age. You'll have loads of grandkids to keep you young in your old age."

"But how did you do it? I have—"

"I'll explain everything soon. It's God's plan for us and the most miraculous story you'll ever hear."

Royce heard the sound of running feet coming towards them and turned to see Jason and Matthew.

"Royce, what's going on over there? Ruby ran in all upset. Said you were chasing someone." At the mention of Ruby, he felt Texanna stiffen.

"Jason, you better tell your sister-in-law, Ruby, to keep her hands off Royce."

Both men stopped in their tracks. Neither Matthew nor Jason said anything, but they looked at each other then continued forward. Royce turned around, bringing Texanna with him, his hands around her waist. They stopped and stared.

"What's going on here?" asked Matthew. "That can't be Texanna, I know it can't."

Jason stepped forward, lifted and tilted her face toward the moonlight so he could see her better. "Well, I'll be damned. It is, Matthew. It's Texanna."

Amid shouts and whoops, Texanna was dragged from his arms and hugged and kissed by his brothers.

Royce knew he was grinning like a jackass, but he couldn't help it. He grabbed Matthew and Jason's collars and pulled them away from Texanna. "Back off you guys, I've not even had a chance to kiss my wife yet."

Garrett piped up. "We'll turn our backs, Pa. But don't take too long."

Royce's laugh was cut off when Texanna's lips found his and gave him a scorching kiss that left him hard and aching. Both brothers looked at him and chuckled. Neither one had an ounce of sympathy.

"Hey, squirt." Matthew tousled Garret's hair. "You want to go home with me, Molly, and the twins tonight? We'll drop you back with your pa and ma tomorrow at church."

Royce was ready to agree when Texanna pulled Garrett to her side. "Thanks, Matthew. But I think we all need to be together as a family tonight. I want Garrett with us."

Royce's heart filled with pride and love. His brothers looked from his wife to him, and their smiles echoed his feelings. Jason took out his handkerchief and blew his nose while Matthew coughed to cover his emotion. Royce's vision blurred as he cradled Texanna close.

Matthew looked from Royce to Texanna. "Will we see you guys at church tomorrow?"

"I can guarantee you won't see me and Sally," said Jason.

Royce laughed. "I doubt you'll see us either, but stop by in the morning, Matthew. I'd like to put off telling everyone Texanna is alive, but...Lord, don't you know it's going to cause a stir."

"Well, be getting your story straight. We'll see you in the morning and carry the news to town."

"And be sure and send Ruby Royce's regrets."

"Dammit, Texanna—"

"Pa was kissing Ruby tonight outside the party. It pissed Texanna off."

"Garrett, don't—"

Jason laughed so hard he could hardly talk. "Don't worry, Texanna. I think one look in your eyes and the way you wear that gun, and her passion for

Royce will disappear."

Matthew scratched his chin. "You could come on in to the party and tell her yourself."

"That's not funny, Matthew." Royce didn't want to think about the two women meeting.

The grin on Jason's face got broader. "Yeah Royce, come in for a while. Might as well let people see Texanna and get the shock over with. Then maybe folks won't be quite as gossipy at church tomorrow."

His suggestion wasn't bad, though he knew people would be gossiping about Texanna's reappearance for at least six months or until something else outrageous took its place. He looked at Texanna. "Are you up to facing them right now?"

"After what we've been through, I think this should be a piece of cake."

Jason added. "Yeah, Royce, she needs to have a bite of our cake and see Sally on our wedding day. Not to mention Molly and the twins."

"Okay, let's do it." He took Texanna's arm. "By the time folks start asking questions, I'll have answers for them. Relax."

She stopped walking. "Royce, I'm so happy nothing could make me uptight tonight."

Her face was turned up to his, eyes bright and sparkling. Without looking away, he said. "We'll be inside in a minute."

Matthew put his arm around Garrett. "Come on, squirt. Let's get inside and get a good seat for the fireworks."

Royce leaned down and kissed his wife. He poured four months of love and longing into the kiss, and when he lifted his head, they were both crying. "God, I've missed you."

He lifted her off her feet and twirled her around in the air shouting. "Thank you, God! Thank you. Thank you."

When they walked in the room, Matthew, Jason, and their wives were lined up across from the door pretending to be deep in conversation. Garrett stood in the middle of them. As they entered, Molly and Sally, faces lit with joy, started toward them, but the men held them back.

Royce took Texanna's cape and hung it up. Then he took her in his arms and swung her into the waltz being played. Of the roomful of guests, Ruby was the first to notice Royce had found another dance partner. The expression on her face wasn't pretty. Royce struggled to keep a grin off his face. One by one, couples stopped dancing and moved to the sidelines to watch and whisper. The whispers became a buzz, and when Edna Murphy and Brother Riley noticed the pair, the buzz became a roar.

The music stopped and Royce led Texanna to her sisters-in-law. With squeals and tears, they embraced, talked, and cried, then hugged again.

Royce pulled Texanna from the emotional women and, with his right arm tight around her shoulders, turned to face the crowd. "Folks, it looks like I have some explaining to do."

Brother Riley spoke up, "That's an understatement, son."

"You all know I got on the train to San Antonio with Texanna in my arms." Nods and words of agreement sounded around the room. Yeah, many had been at the depot to see them off that day.

"When we arrived and got to the hospital, Texanna was unconscious. They put her on a stretcher and rolled her into a surgical room." Royce cleared his throat. "They wouldn't let me go with her. I fought to stay with her, but they escorted me to a room to wait and told me the doctors would come speak to me when they knew something."

Edna Murphy, dressed in a gray bombazine dress decorated with purple soutache, mopped at her tears with her handkerchief. Pete stood at her side and patted her shoulder awkwardly as murmurs of sympathy echoed around the room.

“Two hours later, I couldn’t wait any longer and charged into the room where they’d taken Texanna. It was empty. I started yelling.”

Brother Riley shook his head sadly. “You poor boy.”

“Finally a doctor showed up and pulled me into a room. He said, ‘I’m sorry, sir, but your wife is dead.’”‘

Women’s sobs could be heard around the room. He didn’t intend the story to be so dramatic, but seemed regardless what he said, the ladies’ hearts would be touched. He cleared his throat. “Sometime later, a mortician arrived with a casket. They said Texanna’s body was placed in it, and I didn’t have the heart to look. The casket was taken to the depot.” Actually, on the return trip he’d used his badge to order the train to stop in Temple for a short layover. He’d arranged to have a coffin filled with rocks loaded on the train.

He looked down at Texanna and hugged her waist. “Somehow they’d gotten her confused with someone else, a woman who’d come in off the street. They didn’t have her name or anything to identify her. She was feverish and out of her head for several months, then once Texanna started getting well, it took her a long while to recover. As soon as she did, she boarded a train home.” Royce had no idea what her recovery had been like in the future, but he looked forward to finding out. He bet Doc would like to hear the details too. The fact she was indeed alive and here with him was a miracle.

Edna’s head jerked up in alarm, and she bustled toward them. “Lord have mercy, Marshal. Who did we bury out there in the cemetery?”

Chapter Twenty-Four

Texanna slipped from the bed, lifted and dropped the gown over her head. The floor was cold against her bare feet as she walked down the hall to Garrett's room and quietly pushed open the door. In the moonlight, she could see her son snuggled under the heavy quilts. Since they'd gotten home, the weather had turned colder. She leaned down and kissed him. Tears of joy pricked her eyes. He was so beautiful, as was his great-great-grandson Garth. She couldn't wait to tell Royce all she'd learned and about their descendents she'd met. But they had plenty of time.

Around Easter, they'd have a baby to put in the room next door. In time, they'd need to add on to the house. The knowledge Royce's child grew in her belly filled her with wonder and joy. Its presence helped sustain her during the long months of her recovery. She touched her slightly rounded belly, aching to feel life moving inside her. Sometimes she felt tiny flutters, but she longed for a firm kick.

She felt Royce's arm go around her waist. "He's beautiful, isn't he?"

"Yes, indeed he is. And just like his father, his heart is as beautiful as his body." She turned in his arms and snuggled close. Her fingers traced the scar where the bullet had exited his body. "I can't believe you were shot and lay waiting two days for help. If I'd known, I'd been beside myself with fear and worry."

He kissed the top of her head. "I'm glad you

didn't know then. Everything turned out fine. I knew Jason and Matthew would come looking for me, and Samson was there to scare off any predators."

"I'm glad you were able to keep the boy who shot you out of prison, though if I'd been here at the time I'd probably have voted to hang him."

Royce chuckled. "It's over. Put it from your mind."

"Oh Royce, I'm the luckiest woman on earth."

"No, sweetheart, we're the luckiest three people on earth." He lifted her in his arms and carried her back to their bed. With his big hands, he rubbed her feet and legs to warm them, then crawled in beside her and pulled her close. "And since you said your diary revealed there are supposed to be six of us in this family, I think we need to be working on those additions."

"You don't want to work yourself to death."

He chuckled against her neck. "If I do, I'll die a happy man."

"Actually, no need to worry about the growth of our family." She carried his hand to her belly. "Meet your daughter, Rosie."

Epilogue

Houston, Texas, December 2008

Andrew Keith sat in the library of a prestigious home in an old section of Houston. It once belonged to Rosie's son, Joseph Crocker, but now belonged to Rosie's granddaughter, Julianne Evans, and her husband Nathan.

"Can I get you some more coffee?"

He looked up at the middle-aged woman who was his daughter's great-grandchild.

"No, but thank you. I can't tell you how much I appreciate you allowing me to go through these things."

Slim, her dark hair attractively streaked with gray, Julianne bent to lift the tray that held the remains of the refreshments she'd provided. "Well, it's an honor to share them. Grammy would be pleased someone was interested in her keepsakes. Take all the time you want." With the heels of her dressy slides clicking against the marble tile, she left the room.

He'd read the pages of Texanna's journal after her arrival in 1880 Waco. She described Royce's joy at her return and his delight about the baby. Andrew smiled at the passage, but it all seemed so unreal—time-travel, fate, and God's grand plan.

An old photo album lay in the bottom of the small trunk. He carefully removed it and placed it on his knees. Fingers trembling, he opened the leather-bound book and gasped. In black and white, Texanna smiled out at him. There was no denying it was his daughter. The saucy smile was the one she'd given him as a child when he'd tried to correct her.

She was seated in a chair under an oak tree, Royce in one drawn up close to hers, his right arm across the back of her chair. His hand held the locket as if he'd just draped it across her knee as he smiled at the camera. Andrew looked closely to see if the wedding ring Texanna wore resembled the one she had on her finger when she left. It was too small to see. Then he noticed her other hand. She'd lifted the skirt of her long dress just enough for the toe of her tennis shoe to peek out.

A guffaw ripped from his throat. Leave it to his girl to leave no room for doubt. Laughter and relief lifted the heaviness from his heart and shoulders, and for the first time in over a week, he felt everything would be all right. He continued through the album and studied the faces of his grandchildren and great-grandchildren. Moisture filled his eyes. Oh, how he'd have loved them.

At the very back, he found an old newspaper article. It was dated June of 1955. He scanned the article. In the 1940's Joseph Crocker, Texanna's grandson, developed an important procedure needed for Salk to perfect his polio vaccine. At the bottom of the page, Texanna had written.

Hi Daddy. See, it was all God's plan.

The books used for reference are as follows:

A Pictorial History of Waco, revised edition, Roger N. Conger, 1964, Texian Press.

The Writer's Guide to Everyday Life in the Wild West from 1840-1900, Candy Moulton, 1999, Writer's Digest Books.

Everyday Life in the 1880's, A Guide for Writers, Students & Historians, Marc McCutcheon, 1993, Writer's Digest Books.

A History of Costume, Carl Kohler, 1963, Dover Publications.

The History of Colt Firearms, Dean K. Boorman, 2000, Salamander Books Ltd.

Online references are as follows:

The Handbook of Texas Online.

Waco Convention & Visitors Bureau, History of Waco, Texas, USA.

"Standing Stones, Stone Circles and Ley Lines, Unique Research into the Mystery of the Ley Line System," David Ro. Cowan.

"Pregnancy and Childbirth for the Historical Author," Elena Greene.

"Winchester Rifle," Wikipedia, www.answers.com/topic/ winchester-rifle.

"73 Winchester Rifle By Cimarron Firearms Co.," www.cimarron-firearms.com/win73R.htm.

A word about the author...

Linda LaRoque is a retired teacher who loves West Texas, its flora and fauna, and its people. Her stories paint pictures of life, love, and learning set against the raw landscape of ranches and rural communities in Texas. Linda is a member of RWA, her local chapter of HOTRWA where she serves as president, NTRWA and Davis Mountain Trail Writers. She makes her home in Central Texas. Watch for Linda's second book in The Turquoise Legacy, *Flames on the Sky*, coming soon from The Wild Rose Press.

Visit Linda at www.lindalaroque.com

www.ingramcontent.com/pod-product-compliance
Lightning Source LLC
LaVergne TN
LVHW020536100826
845148LV00010B/1487

* 9 7 8 1 6 0 1 5 4 4 9 0 2 *